Snow E
Wedding

De-ann Black

Cover artwork All-about-Flower, gst & paprika/Shutterstock.com

Published 2019

Snow Bells Wedding

ISBN: 9781096668435

Also by De-ann Black (Romance, Action/Thrillers & Children's books). See her Amazon Author page or website for further details about her books, screenplays, illustrations, art and fabric designs.

www.De-annBlack.com

Romance:

Snow Bells Christmas
Summer Sewing Bee
The Chocolatier's Cottage
Christmas Cake Chateau
The Beemaster's Cottage
The Sewing Bee By The Sea
The Flower Hunter's Cottage
The Christmas Knitting Bee
The Sewing Bee & Afternoon Tea
The Tea Shop
The Vintage Sewing & Knitting Bee
Shed In The City
The Bakery By The Seaside
Champagne Chic Lemonade Money
The Christmas Chocolatier
The Christmas Tea Shop & Bakery
The Vintage Tea Dress Shop In Summer
The Fairytale Tea Dress Shop In Edinburgh
The Bitch-Proof Suit
The Cure For Love
The Tea Dress Shop At Christmas

Action/Thrillers:

Electric Shadows. The Strife Of Riley. Shadows Of Murder.

Children's books:

Faeriefied. Secondhand Spooks. Poison-Wynd. Wormhole Wynd. Science Fashion. School For Aliens.

Colouring books:

Summer Garden. Spring Garden. Autumn Garden. Sea Dream. Festive Christmas. Christmas Garden. Flower Bee. Wild Garden. Faerie Garden Spring. Flower Hunter. Stargazer Space. Bee Garden. Scottish Garden Seasons.

Contents

Chapter One

The small town of Snow Bells Haven had celebrated Christmas in fine style, but after catching its breath in the new year, it was gearing up for springtime.

The morning felt bright and airy, perfect for a wedding weekend. Two of the local townsfolk, Ana and Caleb, were getting married and the whole community was preparing to celebrate.

Lucie gazed out the window of the bus as it drove into the town. Everything from the pure white snowdrops with their lovely green foliage to the lilac and yellow crocus added a dash of freshness to the scenery. It had been dark when she'd set out from New York in the early hours of the morning to head up north, and she'd slept most of the way, only blinking awake when the driver announced they were due to arrive. Sunlight shone through the trees that were covered in white and pink blossom, and most of the houses looked like they belonged in a picture book.

She caught sight of her reflection in the window and swept the wayward strands of her golden brown hair back from her pale but pretty features. Her hazel–green eyes didn't show signs of tiredness. Instead, they were filled with curiosity and excitement at finally having arrived in Snow Bells Haven.

The bus slowed down and pulled up outside the town's lodge. It was the main place to stay for those visiting the town, and Lucie was booked in for a long weekend to attend her friend's wedding.

Lucie grabbed her large duffel bag, shrugged her cozy wool coat over the cream sweater and jeans she was wearing and stepped off the bus. She breathed in the clear, country air and felt glad she'd accepted the invitation. A break away from the city was just what she needed, especially after working through most of the holiday season at the cake shop and bakery in a busy part of the city. As a young, single woman, in her early thirties, she'd agreed to shoulder the extra hours during Christmas and New Year to allow other staff time off to celebrate with their families. So when Ana's invitation popped through, she'd decided, yes, she would take a long weekend trip up north to Snow Bells Haven.

Walking up to the lodge, she looked around at the nearby stores. Spring sunshine highlighted all the pretty shops along the main street in the heart of the town, and she couldn't wait to go browsing and grab breakfast in one of the quaint little cafes or diners.

Continuing on to the front entrance of the lodge, she felt a surge of excitement. She barely remembered the last time she'd taken a proper vacation. Even though this was a short break, she felt the pressure of work slide from her shoulders and a sense of adventure brewing.

The lodge was quite substantial, and was built in a traditional design that fitted into the town's architecture. Outside the entrance daffodils, tulips, Easter lilies and other spring flowers blossomed in the window boxes and hanging baskets. The floral scent wafted towards her in the clear air as she approached.

Carrying her bag inside the lodge, hoping she'd remembered to pack everything she needed, she booked in at the reception.

It was a family–owned and run lodge with lots of wood paneling and had a homely, welcoming atmosphere. It had a fair amount of rooms on two levels, a dining room for guests that had a view from the front of the lodge, and a function room for parties and other celebratory occasions at the back that extended out into the rear garden. Clusters of snowdrops and crocus peeped through the well–cut grass on the lawn, and provided the ideal setting for wedding photographs against a background of cherry trees in full blossom.

Wedding decorations adorned the lodge's interior and it was obvious that Ana's special day had taken over most of it this weekend. Even the vase of daffodils on the reception desk was tied with bridal ribbons.

A woman in her fifties, and smartly dressed, smiled as Lucie approached the desk and handed over the little slip she'd printed out when she'd made the online booking.

'Welcome to our lodge. I'm Penny.'

Lucie recognized the name. Penny and her husband owned the lodge.

'Are you a bridesmaid or one of the wedding party guests?' Penny said, checking Lucie's name on the guest list.

'One of the wedding guests.'

'Ah, yes. You're booked into a single room for a long weekend.'

'That's right.'

'If you decide to extend your stay, let me know, and I'm sure we can accommodate you. People often become quite smitten with Snow Bells Haven and don't want to leave.'

Lucie signed the register. 'I can see why. It's beautiful here.'

Penny nodded in total agreement. 'Would you like to settle into your room, take a rest from traveling, or have someone bring you breakfast?'

'I slept most of the way on the bus from New York, and I can't wait to take a look around the town. I'll grab breakfast there.'

Penny handed Lucie her room key. 'I can recommend the diner, which you probably know is where Ana works, or used to. Now that she's getting married, she's going to be concentrating full–time on her sewing.'

Lucie nodded. 'I'll pop into the diner for breakfast.'

'Try their blueberry pancakes with maple syrup and vanilla cream with—'

'Nooo, that's not a great combination,' a man said, cutting in on their conversation and crushing the woman in a bear hug.

Lucie stepped back, startled. The man was very tall, fit in an outdoors sort of way, strikingly handsome and happy to intrude. Only when he kissed the woman on the cheek and called her ''Aunt Penny'' did she realize the connection between them.

'This is my nephew, Kyle,' said Penny by way of introduction while he kept an arm around her shoulders and squeezed her close to him. She gazed up at him. 'He's here for the wedding.'

Lucie smiled tightly and tried to fathom what was behind the intriguing look his blue eyes were giving her. His hair was dark blond and as unruly as his attitude, and yet...there was something about him that fired up her senses. She wouldn't usually have argued with a total stranger, but she happened to agree with Penny regarding the pancakes and spoke up before she realized how forthright she sounded.

'Blueberry pancakes, maple syrup and vanilla cream sounds quite fine to me.'

Penny picked up on the underlying fieriness in Lucie's tone before Kyle did. She tried to smooth things over, even though she outright agreed with Lucie. 'Kyle is so picky when it comes to cuisine. He's a chef.'

Lucie would've let the issue drop if it hadn't been for the self congratulatory smirk on Kyle's lips. So she had another run at him. 'A patisserie chef or an overall chef?'

From his great height he looked down at her and frowned. He sounded irritatingly facetious. 'Are we having our first fight?'

Our first and our last, buddy, Lucie thought to herself, giving him a brush–off look and a smile to Penny as she walked away.

Penny hurried to catch up with her. 'Let me show you to your room.'

Kyle leaned against the reception desk looking like he wasn't used to having his attitude thrown back at him.

Lucie sensed his eyes watching her as she headed along the lobby, with Penny now leading the way.

Wise guy, Lucie thought, then left the feeling behind her. She certainly wasn't going to let a man like him take the shine of this beautiful morning.

Penny unlocked the room door and pushed it open wide. Lucie stepped inside and put her bag down. She smiled as she gazed around the room. It was clean and cozy with the scent of fresh linen, and a patchwork quilt on the comfy bed that she was tempted to throw herself on in sheer joy that she was actually here. Situated on the ground floor, it had a view of the garden.

'This is perfect. Thank you, Penny.'

Penny smiled and kept her voice down. 'Sorry about Kyle. He can be a bit of a handful at times, but deep down...'

'He's nothing but loveable trouble,' Lucie finished for her.

Penny laughed and then the two of them exchanged a knowing look.

'He really is a sweet guy,' Penny confided.

Lucie nodded. 'I'm sure he is.'

'We didn't think he'd be here in time for the wedding. He works in New York, but we keep hoping he'll come back home for good and settle down.'

There was nothing about Kyle that gave Lucie the impression that he was the settling down type, but she kept her thoughts to herself. Penny obviously thought the world of her nephew.

Penny left Lucie to settle in and freshen up.

She put on a pale lemon sweater that somehow felt right for the mood of the bright, sunny day, and headed out into the town's main street. Thankfully she didn't have to pass by Kyle. The chef who'd frowned at her was nowhere in the vicinity.

Bridal banners adorned some of the street lamps along with springtime decorations. Yes, she thought, gazing up at the floral garlands, this town knew how to celebrate the seasons and special occasions.

A cheerful looking man in his fifties ambled towards her dressed as an Easter bunny and handed her a leaflet listing the local events that weekend.

Lucie smiled at him as she accepted it.

'Hope you can come along and join in some of the fun we're having,' he said.

She skim read the events and nodded. 'I'm attending Ana's party in the lodge tonight.'

'Wonderful. I'm Nate. My wife Nancy and I own the grocery store.' He thumbed behind him to the store that was sandwiched between the diner and Greg's cafe.

'I'm Lucie.'

'Nancy's going to the party. I'll tell her to look out for you, Lucie.' He smiled, waved and ambled on.

Lucie looked over at the diner. It was extra busy. People were stopping by to drop off last minute gifts for Ana and deciding to stay for coffee and pancakes. The aroma wafting from the diner was tempting, but it was simply too busy — but there was Greg's cafe nearby. Lucie loved the look of the cafe's front window. It was so spring–like and inviting with its pretty drapes tied back with yellow ribbons, but first she wanted to take a walk along the street, stretch her legs from all those hours sitting on the bus, and enjoy the early morning air.

Greg peered out the front window of his cafe that gave a prime view of the main street. He could see the other stores opening up for the day. But more than anything, he sensed the excitement brewing. He was as excited as anyone, though it was starting to feel like mild panic. He was worried he'd overextended on his promises. Ana was a dear friend and he'd promised to help with the bridal catering and bake her the most amazing wedding cake, which he thought he'd achieved because Ana was enthralled with his sugarcraft on the three–tier masterpiece. But silver decorations were still to be added and the entire cake had to be transported safely and assembled at the reception venue — the local community hall. The responsibility was crushing him.

He wished he hadn't promised to bake a hundred cupcakes adorned with silver bells and sprinkles, along with numerous other tasty bakes. Three hours sleep seemed sufficient so he could be up extra early to start baking, and that would've been fine except for the butterflies in his stomach every time he thought about the love of his life arriving for the wedding. Even the mention of his ex–girlfriend's name sent him into a tailspin.

Brie had been everything to him, but since they'd broken up years ago, he hadn't spoken to her. She was the one that got away. Or as she would no doubt phrase it — the one he'd let go, or didn't fight hard enough for when she'd left town to make a new life for herself in New York. Everything was always his fault.

He sighed and tried to gather himself and concentrate. There was a lot to do today, including finishing the chocolate cupcakes for his regular customers. He took another deep breath and straightened the drapes on the cafe window. He'd tied them back with yellow ribbons, and added a basket of little Easter eggs to the display. He'd sewn new yellow and white gingham covers for the tables, and planned to finish the quilted table runners when he had time. He was the only male member of the local quilting bee, and lately he hadn't even found time to attend the weekly bee at the community hall.

In the back of his mind he blamed the news that Ana had invited friends from her past to be bridesmaids, including Brie. When Ana told him, he felt like someone had plugged his brain into the nearest electrical socket and slammed a few thousand volts through him. He never thought he'd see her again. Not that he didn't want to, but it seemed futile to fry his heart again for nothing. Brie didn't give a hoot about him. He needed to get over her. But no matter how many times he told himself that, it didn't change how he felt about her. He'd been smitten with her for years. And now she was coming back to be a bridesmaid.

He was Ana's right hand man for the catering, the cakes and the whole caboodle. There was no way he could avoid meeting his ex. He'd no idea what his reaction would be when he saw her face–to–face, but the image in his mind wasn't pretty — a cross between a jackrabbit and a total fool, and this was when he was feeling optimistic.

A wave of emotion charged through him and he tried to focus on swirling buttercream frosting on to a tray of cupcakes. His hands were shaking but the sprinkles would disguise any wobbles.

Scooping butter into a bowl, he started to make more frosting. Adding icing sugar, vanilla extract and champagne, he whipped the contents like a man possessed. He knew Brie would look gorgeous in her satin dress. He'd been the one to help Ana select the exact shade of lilac from the fabrics at the local dress shop. They'd settled for heliotrope — strong but not overwhelming and perfect for the spring theme of the wedding. With Brie's blonde hair and blue eyes, she'd look amazing. Ana had shown him a recent online picture of Brie and she was more beautiful than ever.

The dress shop was owned by Virginia, and Ana now intended working as a dressmaker full–time. Several ladies from the town were part of Virginia's sewing team and they'd all worked hard to help Ana sew her fairytale wedding dress that was fit for a princess. Ana was an expert at beadwork, and when she'd given Greg a peek at the dress, he thought the crystal and pearl beads she'd sewn on the white satin sparkled like sunbeams.

The beadwork theme was extended to the bridesmaid's satin dresses. Yes, Greg thought to himself. Brie would look lovely, and he mentally prepared to have his heart crushed.

'You okay there, Greg?' said Dwayne.

'Yeah, you're looking a bit harassed,' Herb added.

Greg glanced at the two guys working for him in the cafe. 'I'm fine,' he lied.

The guys enjoyed dressing in theme for whatever they were celebrating. At Christmas they were elves. Now they were Easter bunnies. Dwayne was a tall, smooth, pale gray bunny, while Herb's outfit was fluffy blue.

Greg decided he couldn't deal with the entire furry rabbit suit this morning. He was sweating it just trying to whip up a large bowl of vanilla buttercream frosting. A pair of bunny ears was all he could handle. They'd been tucked away in a box from the previous year and one of the ears needed straightened and pressed. He hadn't even had time to iron the pristine white shirt he planned to wear with his suit to the wedding. So one of his ears remained bent and floppy.

'You look fine,' Dwayne had told him.

Every time Greg bent down he had to be careful not to stick the ears into the buttercream. He wished he hadn't bothered, but the guys were making an effort, even though they loved to dress up, so he couldn't let the side down.

Wishes were on his mind a lot. He wished he'd hadn't offered to bake a hundred vanilla champagne cupcakes for the bride's pre–wedding reception, otherwise known as the *girls only* party night Ana was holding that evening in the local lodge. Thankfully, Dwayne and Herb were helping him with the chocolate cupcakes.

'Is it one measure of cocoa, two measures of sugar and four measures of flour?' asked Dwayne. 'Or is it two measures of sugar, four measures of flour and one measure of cocoa?'

Greg pointed to the recipe pinned up on the wall behind Dwayne.

And he especially wished he'd listened to his friend Sylvie when he'd asked her whether or not he needed to visit the barber. She'd told him his hair was just the right length and style. He should've listened, but oh no, he'd popped into the barber's shop and emerged with quite a fine hair cut. The only thing was that it always took four to five days before his hair settled down and looked like it belonged to him. Right now he wasn't wearing it well. His hair looked like it belonged to someone else and hadn't settled into his style yet. Typical when he wanted to look his best for the wedding. Correction — to look good when he met Brie at the wedding which he inevitably would. Apparently, due to her busy work schedule, she wasn't arriving from New York until late on Friday evening and would be skipping the girls only party. This he was thankful for. It was a girls only event except for Greg and his two Easter bunny helpers. At least he didn't have to meet Brie until he was looking dapper in his suit at the wedding on Saturday afternoon. He could breathe a little.

The stress showed on his face as he carefully carried a tray of vanilla champagne cupcakes out to his station wagon. There were trays of cupcakes all over the cafe, and as these were to due to be delivered to the lodge later, he was racking and stacking them in his car.

Unfortunately, the last woman he expected to see walking past him was Brie.

His heart wrenched. She looked as beautiful, and aloof, as ever. No wonder his heart had never truly healed.

Gorgeous blue eyes stared at him, appraising him as if she'd scanned him like a barcode. Her voice was clear in the fresh morning air.

'Greg! You look...quirky.'

He opened his mouth to respond, but between total mortification that she'd seen him dressed with wonky bunny ears, and the shock of seeing her again, his voice faltered. Words were forming in his mind, but before he had a chance to say them, she'd iced him with a fake smile and walked on.

After years of wondering about meeting her again, and now given the chance because of the wedding, he'd pictured looking his manly best. Greg was a good looking guy with dark brown hair, not usually so short, brown eyes, not usually so wide with horror at his circumstances, and a fit build, usually due to being busy from morning until night. He was lean and strong. But this morning he felt like mush. Weak, disappointed. After all these years, the first time she sees him, he looks like a dork. Worse — quirky.

Dwayne and Herb dashed out of the cafe and grabbed Greg, one on either side, seeing the wind and hope knocked out of him. They ushered him back into the cafe. Even a cup of extra strong coffee failed to revive his senses.

Dwayne fanned him with a napkin. 'What did Brie say to you?'

Herb frowned and looked like he was ready to defend Greg. 'Was she mean to you, buddy?'

'I look like a bunny rabbit,' was all Greg could gasp.

'Yeah, but what did Brie say to you?' Dwayne asked again.

'She said I looked...quirky.'

Dwayne seemed relieved. 'Quirky's okay.'

'Yeah,' Herb assured him. 'Women like quirky guys. That's a good sign.'

Desperate to clutch to any shred of hope to restore his confidence, Greg looked at Herb. 'You think?'

Herb nodded. 'Definitely, bud.'

'What did you say to her?' said Dwayne.

'Nothing.' He sighed so hard, and even his other ear flopped as he sat slumped next to the display cabinet that showed the wedding cake he'd made.

Dwayne and Herb exchanged a glance.

'Good for you, Greg,' said Dwayne, punching the air. 'Show her she doesn't mean anything special to you, even though she broke your heart and you've never gotten over her.'

'Yeah, she was always snooty,' said Herb. 'No offence, but she was stuck up if you ask me. Maybe she thinks you didn't even recognize her after all these years.'

For some reason this thought perked Greg up. 'That's right. I can pretend I didn't recognize her. She was just another person walking along the main street in Snow Bells Haven as far as I was concerned.'

'You'll get your chance to impress her at the wedding tomorrow when you're looking sharp in your suit,' Herb assured him.

'A shame about your hair—'

Herb nudged Dwayne to shut up. 'We'll help you slick it with hair gel. No worries, buddy.' Herb patted Greg on the shoulder, then ran to save the cupcakes from exploding in the oven as the timer pinged for the second time.

Herb pulled the tray out just in time. The chocolate cupcakes were done to perfection.

Dwayne was about to ask about the cocoa, chocolate and sugar ratio again, but Greg still looked deflated, so he checked the recipe instead.

Greg whipped up another bowl of frosting and thought about Brie — and how to impress her next time they met.

Chapter Two

A rumbling tummy brought Lucie back to Greg's cafe. She'd been gazing in the store windows all along the main street, admiring everything from the flower shop and Luke's art store to Jessica's quilt shop. Ana had told Lucie about the quilt shop being a hub of creativity, and that Jessica was one of the women who helped run the local quilting bee. Lucie enjoyed sewing, but her quilting skills were minimal and nothing near the level of some of the quilts on display in Jessica's shop window. She'd stood for a few moments under the canopy admiring the beautiful patchwork quilt sewn from various cotton fabric prints with snowdrops, tulips, Easter lilies, crocus and other spring flowers. The shop hadn't yet opened and Lucie had peered through the window at the piles of quilts on sale along with bundles of fabric. The shelves were stacked with rolls of fabric including some that had been used to sew the patchwork quilt.

Lucie sighed and wished there was a store like this nearby where she lived — and a local quilting bee where women helped each other to make these amazing quilts. Then again, with all the hours she worked at the bakery from the crack of dawn until the end of the day, she barely had time for her own home baking never mind starting to quilt.

She glanced back along the main street. There were so many lovely little shops including an ice cream parlor selling chocolate Easter egg cones. One of these was definitely on her agenda for later.

She'd only seen half of the stores in the main street, but now she needed a cup of coffee and a cooked breakfast. She hadn't had anything to eat since a hastily made bowl of soup zapped in the microwave in her apartment before grabbing her weekend bag and dashing to catch the bus for her trip to Snow Bells Haven.

Peering through the cafe window she saw two large Easter bunnies working behind the counter and a man with floppy bunny ears looking downcast while beating frosting in a bowl. The tables were all set with gingham covers and she hoped they were open for business.

'Hey, Greg,' Dwayne hissed at him. 'There's a pretty lady looking in at us.'

Greg looked up from his fervent mixing and saw her gazing in. She was certainly very pretty. He'd never seen her before, and he'd have remembered a woman like her. Putting the bowl down, he wiped icing sugar from his hands and tried to straighten his ears. With one ear now perked up and the other still floppy, he opened the front door.

'Can I help you?' he said.

Lucie smiled brightly. 'I was wondering if you were open for breakfast?'

'Sure. We're open, come on in.' Greg stepped aside and held the door open.

Lucie walked in and looked around. The cafe smelled delicious, a combination of fresh baked cakes, vanilla and coffee. Trays were filled with cupcakes. But although the cafe was clean and the tables were vacant, she had the impression of mild chaos bubbling under the surface, despite the warm welcome from Greg and his bunnies.

'Take a seat.' Greg gestured towards a table at the window. 'I'll get you a menu. We're not doing any specials today, but everything else is available.'

Lucie shrugged her coat off and hung it on the back of her chair.

Greg smiled down at her as he handed her the menu. Her first impression was that he was a good looking guy with a great smile, but the warmth in his brown eyes disguised a hint of sadness. Something had happened. She couldn't figure out what it was. But she'd had days when she'd worked in the bakery shop and there had been chaos behind the scenes that staff hid from the customers. She knew that vibe only too well.

But...she didn't think it was appropriate to ask, and now she felt guilty giving them extra work fixing breakfast for her. The urge to get up and cook it herself was quite strong, and if she'd known them better she'd have offered to pitch in. Those two guys dressed as Easter bunnies were just too cute, but the taller of the two seemed confused as he measured out cocoa, flour and sugar.

Instead of meddling, something she was renowned for, she accepted the menu and read through the options. She'd at least select something easy. No fancy soufflé omelet with melted cheese topping even though it sounded delicious.

Greg was trying not to hover, giving her polite space to settle, and yet...that floppy bunny ear said a lot about him. Half perky and half flattened. He seemed like a nice guy, and the badge on his shirt said *Greg* so he was clearly the owner. Then she saw the bottle of champagne and recognized the aroma. That was vanilla champagne frosting he was whipping up. And that wedding cake on display in a glass cabinet in the corner was definitely for Ana's wedding. She recognized the theme. The pressure of baking extra cakes for the wedding party was surely the reason why these guys looked stressed.

Catering for a wedding could send most people into a frenzy with a hundred things to do and two hundred things that can inevitably go wrong. She looked over at the display cabinet. But whoever had created that wedding cake had got it right. The sugarcraft flowers on each tier were perfection.

'I'll have coffee and a slice of apple pie.' Lucie pointed to the pie in the cake counter as she handed the menu back to Greg.

He gave her a look and sighed.

'What?' she said.

'You don't really want that.'

How did he know?

'You look like you could use a cooked breakfast,' he said. 'You're new in town? Am I right?'

'Erm, yes, but I—'

'When did you arrive?' He voice was firm and yet caring.

She felt compelled to explain. 'I arrived this morning. I'm booked in at the lodge. They offered me breakfast, but I thought I'd eat out and take a look around the town. I'm here for Ana's wedding.'

His brown eyes flickered at the mention of the wedding. 'So what's with the coffee and apple pie?'

'I just...I...'

He was gazing down at her and she told him the truth.

'I thought you guys were stressed to the max and I didn't want to order anything fancy.'

Her honesty took him aback. 'Well, that's very thoughtful of you, Miss...?'

'Lucie.'

He nodded as she told him her name. 'But as we're all being straightforward here, I have to insist on cooking you a proper breakfast.' He smiled at her. 'Scrambled eggs, crispy bacon, grilled tomato...something like that sound better?'

Lucie grinned at him. 'That sounds great, Greg.'

'Coming right up.' And off he went to prepare her breakfast while the Easter bunnies continued to work on the cupcakes.

'That's quite a cupcake order you've got going there,' Lucie commented. 'I assume it's for the wedding party.'

'Yep.' Greg nodded while cooking the eggs, grilling the tomatoes and frying the bacon as the coffee percolated.

'Is that champagne vanilla frosting?' she asked.

He blinked. 'Sure is.' He frowned and studied her. 'How do you know something like that? Are you into baking?'

'Yes. I work at a cake shop and bakery in New York. One day I'd like to own my own place, or work for someone who appreciates new ideas.'

'I'm all ears for new ideas,' said Greg.

Lucie laughed, and suddenly the stressful atmosphere lifted.

'Where will I put this tray of cupcakes?' Dwayne asked Greg.

'I'll put them in the car. Sit them on the counter for a moment while I finish Lucie's breakfast.'

Greg served up her food fast and with a flourish. He'd even added a garnish of chives.

Having served Lucie, Greg lifted the tray of cupcakes and carried them out to the car.

Taking advantage of the situation, Dwayne ran over to Lucie. 'Thanks for being nice, Lucie.' Then he confided. 'Greg was really down and he's stressed out about the wedding catering.'

With the bunny being so open, she decided to pry. 'Why was he feeling down?'

'His ex–girlfriend, Brie, is in town for the wedding. She's one of the bridesmaids.'

Herb hurried over. 'Greg bumped into her this morning when he was taking cupcakes to the car.'

'What happened?' she asked.

'She skewered his heart and flattened his hopes like a pancake,' said Dwayne.

Herb confided. 'He hated her seeing him dressed as half a bunny rabbit. He hadn't seen her in years and planned to make a great impression all dressed up in his suit at the wedding.'

Dwayne nodded. 'Instead she said he looked...quirky.'

Lucie frowned. 'Quirky's okay.'

‘That’s what we told him, but he’s a guy.’ Herb shrugged his fluffy shoulders. ‘Guys like Greg and us prefer to be thought of as strong, capable, handsome and manly.’

By now both Dwayne and Herb were looking at her unaware of the cuteness factor they both had.

Dwayne had even drawn whiskers on his face and given himself a white–tipped nose.

Lucie smiled to herself.

The bunnies scarpered as Greg headed back into the cafe and made themselves busy with the cupcakes.

Lucie ate her breakfast, savoring the tasty bacon accompanied by a scoop of raspberry jelly.

Greg glanced at her to check she was enjoying her breakfast.

‘This jelly is perfect with the bacon and eggs,’ she said.

Greg smiled. ‘Glad you like it.’

‘Greg makes it himself,’ said Dwayne. ‘Picks his own fruit from his garden.’

Lucie looked impressed.

‘Greg has a farm and grows his own pumpkins,’ Herb elaborated.

‘Pumpkins? Wow!’ Lucie was genuinely impressed.

Greg gave her a sheepish grin. ‘It’s not a big farm or anything like that. I’ve got a house in Snow Bells Haven with some land that I use for growing stuff.’

Lucie sighed and sounded envious. ‘I’ve always thought it would be nice to do things like that...grow fresh herbs and fruit.’

‘Why don’t you?’ Greg asked her.

‘I don’t have that type of lifestyle. I share an apartment in the city with one of the girls from the bakery. There’s no garden, not even a balcony for growing flowers,’ she explained. ‘She’s getting married soon, and I’ve volunteered to move out. The apartment is more suitable for a couple.’

‘So you’ll be moving soon, huh?’ said Greg.

Lucie nodded. ‘I was even thinking about working in another bakery.’

‘Where they appreciate new ideas?’ added Greg.

‘Yes, all the decisions in the bakery I’m working in right now are made higher up. It’s okay, but sometimes I’d like more leeway to be creative, try new cake recipes. I’ve been considering moving to Long Island and working in a cake shop there.’

'Still planning on being a city girl?' said Greg.

Lucie shrugged. 'Never lived anywhere else.'

Dwayne stopped measuring out the cocoa. 'You could move to Snow Bells Haven. Find somewhere with a garden to grow your herbs.'

'Oh, I don't know...' she said wistfully. 'I've never thought of living in a small town.'

'This is a big small town,' said Herb. 'We pack a lot of everything into...well, everything.'

Lucie gazed out the window. 'It certainly looks pretty for springtime.'

'You should see the town at Christmas,' said Greg. And that was the first moment he looked more relaxed, as if he'd suddenly forgotten about being quirky.

The bunnies nodded and Dwayne told her, 'We were dressed as elves.'

'Ana mentioned to me about the Christmas decorations and celebrations in Snow Bells,' said Lucie.

'Is this your first time in town?' asked Greg.

'It is. I suppose you're wondering how I know Ana?'

All three of them nodded.

'I bought one of her dresses online, and a purse with exquisite beadwork. Ana's beadwork is amazing. Anyway, I emailed to thank her specially, and we ended up becoming friends online. And I met her a couple of times when she came to New York with Caleb.'

'So you don't know Brie?' Greg asked tentatively. The stressful expression fell again across his features.

'No. I don't know anyone here except Ana and Caleb,' she told him.

'And us,' Dwayne corrected her.

Lucie smiled. 'Yes, and you guys.'

Lucie finished her breakfast while Greg, Dwayne and Herb made cupcakes galore.

She put her napkin down, sipped her coffee and watched Greg load another tray of cupcakes into his car.

The bunnies came scurrying over to confide in her again.

'We're assuming from the things you've said that you're single, no boyfriend, no ties?' Herb asked her.

'That's right, but I'm not here looking for romance,' she told them nicely.

'I'm married,' Dwayne said, 'and Herb's got a date for the wedding.'

Lucie blinked.

Herb leaned down. 'We were thinking that you could be Greg's date for the wedding.'

Lucie shook her head. 'I'm not sure–'

'Greg's a cool guy,' said Herb. 'He's not usually this stressed out. We're the ones that get wound up about stuff. He always takes the strain when work gets hectic rather than pile it on to us.'

'Greg looks out for us,' Dwayne added. 'We're just trying to do right by him this time. His ex–girlfriend has sent him into a tailspin.'

Herb nodded so hard his fluffy blue ears bounced emphatically. 'If he had a lovely lady like you as his date for the wedding, maybe Brie wouldn't have a chance to fry his heart and skewer it.'

Before she could reply, Greg walked back in.

Dwayne grabbed her empty plate and ran off with it, while Herb hurried to refill her cup with coffee.

'Let me top that up for you.' Herb poured fresh coffee into her cup, and cast a glance at her, hoping she wouldn't rat on them for trying to set her up on a date with their boss.

Greg frowned, suspecting they were up to something. 'Everything okay?' he asked Lucie.

She smiled at Greg. 'Hunky–dory,' she lied.

Greg's phone rang and he smiled when he saw the caller ID. 'Ana. How are you doing?'

'I'm at home, having last minute alterations done to my dress,' Ana explained. She lived with her parents. Several women, including her mother, were bustling around her, making sure the wedding gown was perfect. Ana was in her late twenties, attractive with a usually calm nature, but Greg knew her well enough to sense the tension in her voice. 'Are you handling the cupcakes okay?'

'Yeah, everything's on schedule. I'll deliver the first load of cupcakes to the lodge before lunch, then take the rest round later in the afternoon.'

'That's great. I can't thank you enough for helping me, Greg.'

'It's not every day one of my best friends gets hitched. Oh, and — Lucie's here.'

'At the cafe?' Ana asked.

'Yes, I cooked her breakfast. I'll explain later.'

'Okay. Tell Lucie I'm looking forward to seeing her tonight at the party.'

'I'll tell her,' Greg promised.

After he hung up, Greg relayed the message.

Lucie smiled and stood up. 'I guess I better let you guys get on with your work.' As she said this, a couple of customers wandered in and sat down in the cafe.

Lucie went to settle her bill, but Greg shook his head. 'Breakfast's on me.'

'Are you sure?'

'Yes.' He walked her to the door. 'Enjoy browsing through the stores.'

'Is Virginia's dress shop nearby?' she asked him.

Greg pointed across the street and further along. 'It's over there. The one with the pretty floral canopy and a little tree outside the front door.' The tree was decorated with ribbons and Easter egg baubles that shone in the morning sunlight.

'Thanks,' Lucie said chirpily. 'And thanks for breakfast, Greg. It was delicious.'

'Any time, Lucie.'

In the daylight she noticed the genuine warmth in his lovely brown eyes, and wished that his ex–girlfriend wouldn't want to hurt him unnecessarily.

She went to walk away and then hesitated. 'Listen, if you get stuck for someone to help bake all the cakes today I'd be glad to give you a hand.'

'That's very kind of you, but hopefully we'll manage, and I wouldn't want you to spend your time in town working.'

She nodded and waved as she left and headed along to the dress shop.

Greg watched her for a moment, seeing the sun catch the golden highlights in her silky, shoulder–length brown hair, and the way she moved, like she was filled with excitement at being here. His heart felt warmth towards her, and he hoped he'd see her at the party later.

Dwayne peered over Greg's shoulder as she walked away. 'Lucie's nice, isn't she?'

Greg nodded thoughtfully. 'Yes, Dwayne, she is.'

Greg closed the door and started serving the customers, while Herb took another batch of cupcakes out of the oven.

Lucie paused outside Virginia's shop to admire the three dresses on display in the window. The designs were beautiful — a pretty floral dress with a daffodil print, a lilac chiffon cocktail dress that looked like someone had sprinkled stardust on the fabric, and a classy deep blue satin number that just might be going back home with her. Matching purses and other accessories were also on display, and she was definitely buying one of the beaded purses.

She'd been so taken with the dresses and it wasn't until she stepped inside that she noticed the shop was busy. Women were chattering, trying on dresses, and there were so many customers in the small shop that it was quite crowded.

Lucie recognized Virginia from her online store photograph. She was wrapping up dresses and hanging others up, and basically run off her feet. And yet the atmosphere was light and filled with women giggling and gossiping.

Lucie was about to slink back out when Virginia smiled over to her from behind the counter. 'There's always room for one more, if you don't mind chaos and bedlam.'

'I'm right at home with both of those,' said Lucie, and proceeded to browse through the dresses on the rails. She picked up a silver and pearl beaded purse and wouldn't let it go. Although totally impractical, she loved it and intended to buy it.

Once she'd settled into the throng of activity, Lucie realized that some of Ana's bridesmaids were part of the chaos and were trying on last minute dresses for the party. The shop had a changing room at the back, but with so many women trying things on, they'd spilled out into part of the shop area.

Quite a tall and beautiful blonde admired her lavender silk cocktail dress in a full–length mirror. She had a great figure and the silky fabric emphasized this.

'Hmmm, I'd like a different color,' she complained. 'My bridesmaid's dress is this tone, and of course we all have to wear what Ana likes, but for the party I want something nice.' She pointed to the classy blue dress in the window. 'I'd like to try that one on.'

Virginia left what she was wrapping and hurried to take the dress out of the display. 'I'll get that for you, Brielle.'

Lucie's heart sank as the dress was carried through to the changing room. She guessed it wasn't going home with her after all. And she didn't immediately recognize Brielle's name.

A beautifully manicured hand reached out and accepted the dress from behind the privacy curtain.

Lucie sighed, realizing that dress was gone, and continued looking through the numerous designs. She needed a pretty full–length dress for the wedding, and held up a pale blue satin gown that she hoped would fit her. Joining in with the throng, Lucie went to the back of the shop and tried it on. It was a classic style and fitted well. The length skimmed her ankles, so it was ideal for the wedding and the dance that followed. She also tried on a cocktail–length yellow dress that shimmered under the shop lights. The prices were a bargain, so she decided to buy them.

'Are you here for the wedding?' one of the women asked Lucie as they rummaged through the racks.

'Yes, and Ana has invited me to the party tonight,' Lucie told her.

The woman's face lit up with glee. 'It's all so exciting. I love a wedding, don't you?'

'I really do,' said Lucie.

Brielle stepped out from the changing room wearing the blue dress. Lucie sighed and had to admit that it suited her.

The cafe started to become quite busy with customers coming in because the diner was packed. This set Greg's baking schedule into slow mode, and he was starting to wish he'd closed the cafe so he could finish Ana's cakes. People were there wanting everything from soufflé omelets with melted cheese to fresh baked fruit pancakes. Normally Greg would've welcomed the extra trade, but today of all days the overspill clashed with his baking.

Dwayne whispered to Greg. 'You should've taken Lucie up on her offer to help.'

Greg sighed, whisked the eggs for the omelets and glared at Dwayne.

Dwayne held his hands up and stepped back. 'Just saying, bud.'

Greg was starting to wonder if he should've accepted her help, especially as another two customers walked in looking hungry.

Herb nudged him while slicing tomatoes. 'Call her.'

Greg eyed him, swithering whether or not to relent.

'Go on, phone Lucie,' Herb urged him.

Greg nodded then realized, 'I don't have her number.'

'She went to Virginia's dress shop,' Herb reminded him.

Greg checked the time. 'That was almost an hour ago. She could be anywhere by now.'

Herb shook his head adamantly. 'Nope. That dress shop lures ladies in and nobody escapes in less than two hours. And you know that. Even Dwayne knows that, don't you?'

Dwayne nodded firmly. 'Oh, yeah. That day I ran in to buy a dress for my wife at Christmas, I was lucky to make it out of there.'

Greg took a deep breath and handed the whisk to Herb. 'Hold the fort while I go get the cavalry.'

'Yeah!' Dwayne and Herb said in unison and fist bumped their bunny paws to cheer Greg on.

With his bunny ears flapping in the breeze, Greg ran full pelt up the street to Virginia's shop and peered in the window. Through the bedlam he noticed Lucie buying dresses. Her back was towards him paying for three dresses and a purse. She didn't notice him, but Virginia did, especially as he waved frantically to get Lucie's attention. He didn't want to go inside as several ladies were in a state of partial undress.

'Greg's jumping up and down and waving in the window,' Virginia announced, causing every woman in the shop to stop what they were doing and look round at him. 'And he's wearing Easter bunny ears.' She smiled. 'He looks cute.'

Brielle stepped out of view, even though Greg hadn't noticed her. 'Ignore him. He's trying to get my attention.' She sighed in mock exasperation. 'I knew he'd do something like this if I came back here. He just won't accept that we're over.'

It was then that Lucie realized that Brielle was Greg's ex–girlfriend. The skewering his heart made sense now.

Lucie looked out at Greg and he nodded frantically at her. Yes, she thought. She was the one he wanted to talk to.

'Don't encourage him to come in,' Brielle instructed everyone.

Lucie picked up the dress shop bag and commented to his ex on her way out, 'You must be Brie.'

'Brielle,' she corrected Lucie. 'I don't go by Brie these days.'

'Well, Brielle, you can relax. It's me he's looking for.'

His ex gave Lucie an incredulous look. ‘You? What are you to Greg?’ There was a hint of jealousy in her tone.

She smiled brightly. ‘I’m Lucie, Greg’s date for the wedding.’

The look in those cold blue eyes iced her to the core.

Leaving the women wide–eyed and wondering what was going on, Lucie hurried from the shop and approached Greg.

‘Smile like you’re pleased to see me,’ she said with a tight grin.

He spoke through his smile. ‘I am pleased to see you, but what’s going on?’

‘Don’t look now, but Brie’s in the dress shop.’

He went to look, then forced himself to focus elsewhere.

‘What’s she doing?’

‘Buying up half the dresses in the shop and complaining that you were trying to get her attention.’

‘I *wasn’t*,’ he objected strongly. ‘I was trying to get *your* attention. I’m busy with customers and need your help with the cakes at the cafe. I didn’t even know she was in the shop.’

Lucie saw the stress tear through him as he gazed down at her. Standing beside him, he was taller than she’d first thought.

‘It’s okay,’ Lucie assured him. ‘I told her it was me you were waving at.’

This seemed to ease his stress. ‘What else did you tell her?’

Lucie bit her lip and looked guilty. ‘I’ll tell you on the way to the cafe.’ Knowing the women were watching them from the dress shop window, she linked her arm through his and hurried him away.

Out of earshot of the shop, Lucie told him.

‘My date for the wedding?’ he gasped.

She explained about the guys suggesting this. ‘It was the only thing I could think of. A spur of the moment thing.’

Greg shook his head in dismay.

By now they were outside the cafe. Greg knocked on the front door, opened it and called in to the guys, ‘Is this Dwayne and Herb’s dating and matchmaking services?’

Two guilty looking bunnies stared at him as they continued cooking.

Greg led Lucie inside the cafe, disregarding the customers who were too busy enjoying their food to understand the nuances of Greg’s chatter.

'Let me introduce you to Lucie,' he said to the two guys. 'She's my date for the wedding.'

Herb gave him a sheepish grin. 'We were just trying to make you feel better.'

'Oh, I feel better, don't you, Lucie?' Greg's chirpy tone said otherwise.

'I don't have to be your date,' Lucie whispered to him.

Chapter Three

Lucie took off her coat, pinned her hair up, put on an apron, washed her hands and started to help bake and decorate the cupcakes, working alongside Dwayne and Herb.

Greg watched her while he continued cooking menu items for the cafe's customers. Lucie was fast, efficient and clearly she was used to this type of work at the bakery in New York.

She caught him watching her a couple of times, and finally said, 'Am I doing okay? Anything I'm getting wrong with these cupcakes?'

Greg shook his head while cooking red and yellow peppers for an omelet order. 'Nope. Faultless.'

She laughed as she expertly piped champagne vanilla frosting on to a tray of cupcakes. 'Nobody's faultless.'

Greg frowned and disagreed. 'Not when it comes to you, Lucie. I just feel guilty that you're not outside enjoying the morning and relaxing.'

'To tell you the truth,' she confided, 'I don't know how to relax in the mornings. I'm up early to start work at the bakery. Usually it's still dark when I head into work. Often it's dark when I finish up. I haven't had a break from work in months, and it's difficult to switch from hectic to relaxation in a weekend.' She added sprinkles to the cakes. 'Working here this morning might be the ideal way to ease myself into winding down.'

'Ready for a lively party tonight with Ana and the girls?' he said, grinning at her.

Lucie laughed again. 'The women in Virginia's shop were so excited about the party. They said it's going to be a wild night of giggling, gossip, dancing and...' She held up one of the cakes. 'Eating cupcakes.'

'I've advised Ana to have a midnight curfew,' said Greg. 'Even if it's only for herself. She doesn't want to be a tuckered out bride. I know the wedding isn't until the afternoon, but from the weddings I've attended in this town, the morning will whiz by and before you know it, everyone will be heading to the ceremony.'

Lucie nodded. 'Weddings are like that.'

Greg looked at her. 'What about you? Any plans for a fairytale wedding of your own?'

Lucie scooped more frosting into a piping bag and continued working while she chatted. 'No, I never met the right guy to make me think that way.'

'Your peppers are sizzling,' Herb reminded Greg, while hurrying past with a tray of cakes.

Greg blinked out of his conversation with Lucie and managed to salvage the peppers in time to add them to the omelet.

'Maybe I should stop distracting you with all my chatter,' said Lucie.

'Nope. You're the nicest distraction I've had in a long time.'

'I'll take that as a compliment. I'm usually tagged with being a troublemaker.'

'You?' He seemed surprised. 'You don't strike me as that.'

Lucie gave him a look like he was so wrong. 'Trust me. I have a reputation.'

He sighed while preparing the next order as Dwayne swiped the hot omelet away to serve to a customer. 'Okay, name three words to describe yourself.'

'Three words?'

He nodded firmly and held up three fingers.

'All right,' she said then listed them off. 'Troublemaker.'

He nodded. 'We've established that one. What else?'

'Mischief–maker.'

'That's two words,' he said.

'One word if it's hyphenated,' she said.

'Hmmm, okay, but that's bending the rules a little,' he conceded.

'And...rule breaker,' she said finally.

'Two words again,' he reminded her.

Lucie shrugged and held her arms out. 'See what I mean?'

Greg smiled. 'So you really are a troublemaker?'

'I try not to be, but I was reprimanded twice last month at work for being bad.'

'What did you do?' he asked her.

'Well, customers had been complaining about the glacé cherries on the cakes, so one day I exchanged them for chocolate dipped strawberries.'

Greg gave her a scolding look. 'That was bad.'

'The customers loved them.'

'I bet they did,' he agreed.

'And then...I added sprinkles to the chocolate brownies.'

Greg pretended to be shocked. 'Unforgivable.'

'I like sprinkles on my brownies,' Dwayne said as he went by with two mugs of hot chocolate topped with whipped cream.

Greg and Lucie smiled at each other, and were about to continue their light–hearted conversation when a woman hurried into the cafe and approached Greg. She was in her fifties and seemed to know her way about the cafe. 'Here's the buttermilk and cream you ordered.' She noticed how busy they were. 'I'll pop them in the refrigerator for you.'

Greg introduced her to Lucie. 'This is Nancy. She owns the grocery store next door with her husband Nate.'

'I met Nate this morning,' Lucie said, smiling at Nancy. 'He gave me a leaflet for the weekend's events.'

'Everyone's gearing up for the wedding,' Nancy enthused, and then asked, 'Are you working here now?'

Greg jumped in to explain. 'No, Lucie's a wedding guest. She's also an expert baker from New York, and kind enough to help me out of a pickle. We've got extra customers with the diner being so busy, and loads of cakes to bake.'

'That's very good of you to pitch in,' Nancy told her.

Dwayne decided to throw in some more news. 'And she's Greg's date for the wedding.'

Nancy looked surprised. Happy, but wondering about this new couple. Nancy was renowned as knowing everyone's business in town.

'I'll tell you all the details later,' Greg promised Nancy, and gave her a look not to pry right now.

Nancy nodded and took the hint to leave. 'Okay, I'll see you later.' She waved and hurried back out.

'I really don't have to be your date,' Lucie said to Greg while she measured out more butter for the frosting.

'Too late,' Greg said chirpily. 'Nancy knows now. And although we all love her dearly, she's the town's go–to person for everything that's going on locally. What Nancy doesn't know, isn't worth knowing.'

Lucie blinked. 'Oh. So we're definitely a date now. But not a real date,' she emphasized.

'Real or not, we're going to be the hot topic of gossip in Snow Bells Haven this weekend. Get ready for living up to your troublemaking reputation, Lucie.'

There was humor in his tone. Wasn't there? Lucie wondered if Greg was trying to hide his true reaction. He'd probably wanted to be free and available when he met Brie, or Brielle, or whatever she now called herself. How quickly his plans to impress the love of his life, when he was looking handsome in his suit at the wedding, were crumbling like the biscuit base Herb was trying to make for a cheesecake.

Sensing Lucie's trepidation, Greg leaned close to her and whispered. 'Don't worry. If the meringue hits the fan, and there's nothing but chaos for us this weekend, at least you'll be able to escape on the bus back to New York.'

He was joking, wasn't he? The mischievous twinkle in his eyes and heart–warming smile made her wonder, especially as she realized that her own heart had jolted at the thought of going back to the city. She was rushed off her feet working in the cafe when she should've been relaxing or out shopping, and yet she was the happiest she'd been in a long time.

Hiding her feelings behind a flurry of efficient but frantic baking, she continued to help Greg and the guys catch up with their work.

Greg's car was now loaded with cakes. 'Want to help me deliver these to the lodge?' he asked her.

'Sure.' Lucie wiped the flour from her hands.

'We'll be back in five, guys,' Greg told Dwayne and Herb.

Forgetting that she was still wearing her apron over her sweater and jeans, Lucie jumped in the car with him — and off they went on the two minute drive to the front door of the lodge.

They both laughed as Greg parked out front.

'We could never have carried all these trays back and forth,' he said.

They got out and started to unload the car. Lucie followed Greg inside the lodge.

Penny did a double take when she saw Lucie walking in along with Greg and carrying a tray of cakes. Several guests were checking in at the reception desk.

'You're not hallucinating. This is Lucie and I'm to blame for everything,' said Greg.

Penny smiled. 'That's fine by me, Greg.' She looked around. 'Kyle was here a moment ago.' She saw him heading through to the dining room and called out to him. 'Kyle, could you please give Greg and Lucie a hand to bring in the cupcakes for Ana's party?'

Kyle came striding over. 'Lucie?' He frowned, eyeing her apron and the cupcakes — and Greg.

Lucie nodded towards Greg. 'He's to blame.'

Greg feigned a hangdog expression. 'No arguments about that from me, Kyle.'

Although wondering what they were up to, Kyle strode out to the car and began carrying in the cakes.

Kyle hurried to keep pace with Lucie as she carried a tray into the function room and sat it down on one of the tables that had been covered with white linen tablecloths ready for the evening buffet. She placed the cakes down and when she turned around she bumped straight into Kyle, not realizing he was there.

'Oops!' she gasped. Her hands had instinctively come up and were now pressing on a wall of chest muscle beneath his shirt. She quickly pulled her hands away as if she'd been burned.

'I understand we got off to a rough start earlier, and I apologize for my behavior,' Kyle began. 'But I was wondering if you'd like to be my date for the wedding tomorrow?'

'Too late, Kyle,' Greg called to him, walking into the function room and overhearing what he'd said.

Kyle spun around to face him. 'What do you mean, Greg?'

'Lucie is my date.' Greg couldn't have stated it any plainer.

Kyle was taken aback. 'Oh, Aunt Penny said Lucie was new in town. I assumed she didn't know anyone. I didn't think she had a guy here.'

Greg stepped closer and almost matched Kyle's height. He certainly matched him in shoulder width. Greg had a really fit build, not surprising with all the hard work he did. Lucie's heart squeezed just looking at him.

A flush of color rose in her cheeks and she hurried from the function room. 'I'll bring more cakes in.' And off she went, leaving Greg and Kyle standing facing each other.

Greg put his tray down and ran after her. He caught up with her at the car.

'Are you okay, Lucie?' Those eyes of his were filled with genuine concern.

She forced at smile. 'Yes, fine.' She picked up another tray, waited for Greg to do the same, and then went back in alongside him.

They passed Kyle in reception. Nothing else was said about dating as the three of them brought all the cakes in.

'We'll be back later with the rest of the cakes and other bits and pieces,' Greg said to Penny.

Kyle leaned casually against the reception desk and gave Greg a challenging smile. 'Fast work, Greg.' He clapped his hands and applauded.

There was a double meaning to Kyle's compliment, but Greg refused to be baited. 'Thanks, Kyle. I've always enjoyed baking — and a challenge.'

Kyle's expression was the one that showed uncertainty now.

Greg waved nonchalantly, swept Lucie with him, and together they left the lodge.

Lucie explained to Greg what had happened earlier when she'd first met Kyle at the lodge. She'd only just finished telling him as they pulled up outside the cafe. Greg took a moment in the privacy of the car to talk to her.

'Kyle is an okay guy. He is. Penny is a total sweetheart, and she's hoping Kyle will forget his wandering ways, never settling in any one place, and come back home and work in the lodge as their head chef. Everyone thought Kyle would end up at the lodge, and for a long time he planned to do that, then...he left to train as a chef in the city and sort of forgot how great it is to live here.'

'What about Kyle's family? Is Aunt Penny all he's got?'

'Penny and her husband are his closest relatives. He's Penny's sister's boy, and she moved to Australia a while back. She never had a lot of time for Kyle, and Penny was more like a mother to him than she ever was.'

'Is there some sort of rivalry between you and Kyle?'

Greg sighed long and hard. 'Kyle is competitive, not only about his culinary expertise but sports and outdoor stuff. I'm not that type, even though my dad's a park ranger up north. I'm happy with my cafe, baking and quilting. When I inherited the cafe a few years ago from my grandfather, who is happily retired, Kyle was kind of envious that I had a business — and I could cook.' He took a breath and admitted, 'Kyle could beat me hands down in cooking fancy cuisine for a main course dinner, but he's never going to win any prizes for baking.'

'So Kyle's envious of your baking ability?'

Greg shrugged. 'I don't want to say anything nasty about the guy. We just rub each other's feathers up the wrong way.' Greg left it at that.

Lucie understood.

As they got out of the car a couple, similar in age to Lucie and Greg, were walking down the street towards them. The young woman, Sylvie, waved excitedly when she saw Greg. Holding hands with Zack, her tall, handsome guy, she came over to chat to him.

'Greg, I've got something to tell you.' Sylvie looked like she was bursting with joy and couldn't wait to tell him.

Zack smiled and nodded.

Then she held up her hand to show that she was wearing a sparkling diamond engagement ring. The facets glinted in the sunlight. It was a beautiful ring.

Greg gasped and smiled, clearly delighted for her. 'You're engaged? When did this happen?'

'Last night. He surprised me.' Sylvie gazed up at her new fiancé. 'Zack proposed during dinner. It was so romantic.'

'Congratulations!' Greg wrapped Sylvie in a hug and shook hands with Zack. 'I wish you both all the best.'

'Thanks, Greg,' said Zack.

Swept up in the happy news, Greg suddenly realized he hadn't introduced them to Lucie.

'Sorry,' he apologized, 'this is Lucie, Ana's friend from New York. And this is Zack and Sylvie, another example of this town's reputation for romance.'

Lucie smiled. 'Pleased to meet you.'

'Sylvie's a fabric designer originally from New York,' Greg explained to Lucie. 'She was like you, new in town, then she fell in love with this guy. Zack's a local architect.'

'Are you here for the wedding?' Sylvie asked Lucie.

'I am. I'm only here for a few days, then heading back to the city.'

Zack smiled at Lucie. 'Be careful you don't fall in love with this town. You might never want to go back to New York.' It was a light–hearted comment, but it made Lucie wonder. Could she ever settle in a small town?

'I will,' Lucie said to Zack, and then asked Sylvie, 'Have you lived here long?'

'No. I came to town at Christmas for a short vacation, met Zack and all the great townsfolk, and now...' Sylvie smiled and glanced at her ring.

'When's the engagement party?' Greg asked. 'I assume you're having a party.'

'We were thinking of next weekend,' said Sylvie.

'We don't want to steal Ana and Caleb's thunder tomorrow,' Zack explained, 'but Nancy knows, so...'

Greg pressed his lips tight and nodded. 'Okay. I'll start thinking about baking you a cake.'

'I don't want to put you to any more work, Greg,' said Sylvie. 'You've done so much for Ana's wedding.'

Greg shook his head. 'Nope. I'm baking you a cake. We'll talk about a theme later.' He held his hands up and wouldn't let Sylvie persuade him otherwise. 'Besides, I've got Lucie helping me with the wedding cupcakes. She's a baker.'

Sylvie gave Greg a warm hug. 'Okay, I'll see you tonight at Ana's party.' And off she went, linking arms with Zack.

'They make a terrific couple,' Greg said to Lucie as they unloaded the empty trays from the car. 'Zack's even got a cute dog.'

'Sounds like an ideal match. The cute dog is a bonus. I love animals.'

'Did you know that Brie worked at the local rescue center? Animals loved her.'

'Really?' Lucie sounded surprised. The woman she'd encountered in the dress shop didn't seem to have time or empathy for anyone but herself.

'That's why she left — to train for more qualifications in New York. And she wanted to experience life outside of a small town. I gave her the time she needed, hoping she'd come back. But she stayed away more often than she was ever home. Eventually we drifted and she made a life for herself in the city.'

'Did you consider moving to New York to be with her?'

'No, city life's not for me.' He shrugged as if realizing something. 'Maybe I didn't love her enough?' He looked right at Lucie. 'They say you'll live anywhere as long as the person you love is there with you.'

'It doesn't always work out like that, Greg.'

He nodded. 'But it worked out pretty well for Sylvie.'

Lucie conceded the point, and followed him into the cafe.

The cafe was busy but Dwayne and Herb were coping well. One of the ovens pinged, and Lucie pulled another batch of cakes out while Herb served up crispy bacon rolls to customers. Dwayne piled pancakes on to a plate and added a side order of maple syrup and chocolate sauce.

Greg had taken a folder from his recipe book shelf and was hurriedly flicking through it. It was filled with pictures of cakes he'd made, and notes about the recipes and construction. He stopped at one of the pictures and studied it, then showed it to Lucie.

'What do you think of this as an engagement cake for Sylvie?'

'Oh, that's lovely. I love the sugar paste flowers,' Lucie enthused. It was a single layer square cake with a previous couple's name iced on the top, and decorated with fondant icing and flowers.

Greg grinned excitedly at Lucie. 'I think a variation of this could be perfect for Sylvie and Zack. Floral fabric prints are her signature design, so flowers would be the theme.' He closed the folder. 'I'll pop it in the car so I can show it to her later tonight. I've so many things to remember, I'll forget it if I don't do it now.' And off he went.

Dwayne and Herb hustled Lucie aside. Dwayne whispered to her. 'Kyle phoned after you and Greg left the lodge.'

'Kyle phoned the cafe? What did he want?' she asked.

'Information about you,' said Herb.

Dwayne waved the spatula he was holding. 'We told him nothing.'

'What did he want to know about me?' She couldn't even begin to figure this out.

Herb summarized the phone conversation. 'He knew you and Greg wouldn't be back, so he thought he'd try and wangle the information out of us.'

Dwayne gave Herb a look like Kyle had no chance.

Herb continued, glancing out the window to see if Greg was heading back in, but he'd been waylaid by Nate. 'He wanted the low down on your relationship with Greg. I think he sounded jealous.'

'What did you tell him?'

'Nothing,' Dwayne assured her.

'We told him you were an expert baker and helping Greg with the cakes,' said Herb. 'We said the only people in town you knew were Ana and Caleb, and the three of us.'

'Then we said we were too busy cooking pancakes to chat,' Dwayne added.

Herb tapped the side of his nose. 'We thought you should know, but don't tell Greg until later. He's got enough on his plate right now.'

Lucie nodded quickly, and the guys scattered back to their cooking as Greg walked back in and started to help with the orders.

Lucie whipped up the last bowl of frosting they'd need to finish the cupcakes, and wondered why Kyle was being so nosy.

Customers were coming into Greg's cafe for lunch.

The last trays of cupcakes were loaded into the car and ready to be taken to the lodge.

Lucie took her apron off and put her coat on.

'Want me to help you take these to the lodge?' she said to Greg.

'No, it's fine. You've done more than enough.'

Lucie lifted up the dress shop bag. 'I'm heading there anyway to try these on.'

Greg peeked inside the bag and saw the lilac dress that had been on display in Virginia's front window. The sparkle on the fabric glittered under the cafe lights.

'Lovely dress,' Greg commented.

'Three dresses.' Lucie showed him the gorgeous yellow shimmer dress underneath it, and the long pale blue satin dress at the bottom of the bag. 'And a purse.'

Greg pretended to be dazzled by the sparkle of the fabric.

Lucie laughed.

'Can we have a look?' Dwayne asked, pushing his way over along with Herb.

Herb nodded his approval. 'Very nice.'

Dwayne agreed. 'All the dresses in Virginia's shop are pretty. My wife is wearing one to the party tonight.'

'Which one are you wearing to the party?' Greg asked her.

She hesitated. 'I'm not sure. Maybe they're too fancy. I brought a little navy blue dress with me.'

Greg shook his head. 'Nothing's too fancy here. Ana has stitched glitter beads on her dress. Be prepared to be out–sparkled.'

Lucie smiled at him and the guys. 'All right.' She picked up her things and got ready to leave.

'I'll be back in ten minutes,' Greg told Dwayne and Herb.

Lucie waved to the guys and went out to the car with Greg.

'I really can't thank you enough for all your help, Lucie,' Greg said as they drove off.

'It's been fun.'

He glanced over at her. 'It has.'

'Any plans on what to do about Brielle? How to win her back?'

Greg sighed and shook his head, and any sense of lightness disappeared from his expression.

'Is she still single? Does she have a boyfriend in New York?' asked Lucie.

'Ana said Brie's single. No current boyfriend.'

'So there's a chance the two of you might get back together?'

'Brie isn't interested in me. For her, we were over a long time ago. I was a fool for hoping I could impress her at the wedding.'

'You still could.'

'I think the bunny ears sank that boat before it even sailed.'

'Remember, I don't have to be your date. It doesn't matter if Nancy and everyone else expects us to go together. You're free to go on your own, Greg. No ties from me.'

He sensed her words were meant to reassure him. Instead, they caused him to feel...he wasn't sure, empty, adrift, not the same as he'd felt before. He smiled at her anyway. Lucie was kind. A troublemaker perhaps, but kind.

Within minutes they were parked outside the lodge and she helped Greg carry in the cupcakes.

Kyle was in the function room setting up tables around the small dance floor for the party. He smiled when he saw Lucie and hurried to grab the two trays of cakes she was carrying.

Greg put his trays down and headed back out to the car while Lucie put her dress shop bag aside and quickly set the cakes on the plates. Rather than help Greg, Kyle busied himself helping Lucie.

Greg made another few trips in and out of the room, and then put the last tray of cakes down.

Lucie quickly lifted them from the tray and set them on a cake stand. 'I'll sort these out for you, Greg.'

'You sure?' Greg asked.

'Yes, you go back to the cafe. The guys will be busy,' she said.

Greg nodded and yet seemed reluctant to leave her alone with Kyle.

'Lucie and I will be fine,' Kyle assured him.

Greg's steps were heavy, like the soles of his shoes were stuck to molasses, and he walked away, looking back a couple of times, hesitant. 'I'll see you tonight, Lucie,' he called to her.

She smiled and waved at him.

The moment Greg left, she looked straight at Kyle. 'Why did you phone the cafe?'

Kyle was taken aback by her challenging and forthright manner. 'I, erm...' He couldn't think of an excuse, so he told her the truth.

'I don't think Greg's the right guy for you.'

'He's not my guy,' she corrected him.

'Sure seems like things are heading that way.'

'And what business is that of yours, Kyle?'

'I was going to ask you to accompany me to the wedding.'

She frowned at him. 'You don't even know me.' Inwardly, she knew that Greg didn't either, but she'd instantly clicked with him and gotten on so well that she felt comfortable with him.

Kyle shrugged his broad shoulders. 'Sometimes you just know who you like when you see them. And I felt that the instant I met you, Lucie.'

Chapter Four

Penny walked into the function room and smiled when she saw Kyle and Lucie.

'Oh, there you are, Kyle.' She nodded to Lucie. 'It's so sweet of you to help out with the party.'

Lucie finished setting up the cupcakes on one of the long buffet tables. 'You're welcome.'

'I was trying to persuade Lucie to take a trip up to the cove this afternoon,' said Kyle. He glanced out the patio doors on to the sun–filled garden. 'It's not warm enough to go swimming, but it's a great place for a picnic.'

Penny agreed with Kyle. 'You should try and make time to pop up to the cove. It's not far.'

'I'll try,' Lucie promised vaguely, not wanting to be roped into a picnic date with Kyle, or wishing to brush aside Penny's well–meaning suggestion. 'Today's been pretty packed, and I'm planning to relax before it's time for the party.'

'Don't miss the start of it at seven tonight. There's a champagne celebration toast for the bride– to–be and everyone's promised to be there.'

'I wouldn't miss it,' Lucie promised.

'You'll meet all the girls from Snow Bells Haven, and some from out of town, like Brielle.' There was no insinuation in Penny's comment. She was just being friendly, but the mention of Brielle jolted Lucie.

'I met Brielle at Virginia's dress shop,' she told Penny.

'She's beautiful, isn't she?' said Penny.

'Oh yes,' Lucie replied.

Penny glanced at her nephew. 'She's another one who skipped town to live in the city. Yet, here she is, still single and not settled down. However, that's her choice and she's probably quite happy. Anyway, Lucie, you'll have a chance to meet all the girls. It's going to be a heap of fun.'

Lucie nodded.

Kyle frowned. 'It doesn't seem right that it's girls only.' He gave his aunt a mischievous grin. 'I'd be glad to assist with the buffet catering this evening, and maybe steal a dance or two.' He flicked a glance at Lucie. She pretended not to notice.

'Oh, no, Kyle.' Penny vetoed his idea. 'Caleb's having a party for the guys, so you can march on over to his house if you want to celebrate with them.'

Kyle wasn't enamored with this idea. 'No, I think I'll stick around the lodge tonight, just in case I'm needed. Besides, Greg's going to be here and Dwayne and Herb.'

'That's different,' Penny told him. 'Greg's part of Ana's special party catering. He won't be hanging around long either. The guys are bringing some of the buffet food, then leaving us girls to enjoy ourselves.'

Kyle gave his aunt a lopsided grin, like he heard her but had plans of his own.

Penny turned to Lucie. 'I see you've got a dress shop bag there. Did you buy something fancy for tonight?'

Lucie picked up her bag and gave Penny a peek inside. 'I did. Greg said I should wear one of these because everyone really dresses up.'

'We do. My dress has more sparkles than a Christmas tree,' she joked. 'Just kidding. But for girls nights we tend to pull out all the stops, and when it comes to party dresses, you can never have too much sparkle.'

'Greg's advice was right then,' Lucie remarked, admiring the glittering dresses in her bag.

Kyle looked mildly annoyed. 'Suddenly Greg's a fashion advisor now too.'

'Oh, hush, Kyle.' Penny waved a dismissive hand at him. 'Greg's a creative type of guy. And not just because of his beautiful cake designs.' She smiled at Lucie. 'Have you seen his fabulous quilts?'

'Greg's quilts? No. He told me he's a member of the local quilting bee, and made the table covers and drapes for the cafe.'

'His quilts are beautiful. He has a great eye for color and design. I'm surprised some fine young woman hasn't snapped him up by now.'

'Greg can't see past Brielle,' Kyle reminded Penny.

Penny sighed. 'That's such a waste of a good man.' Then she brightened. 'Never mind. I'm sure he'll win her back one day, or settle for someone else eventually.'

Kyle stepped in with another comment. 'Surely that wouldn't be fair on the woman he settled for. She'd always be second best.'

Penny shrugged. 'Life's a quandary at times, Kyle. We all do the best we can to find our own type of happiness. One day, you may be lucky enough to find yours.'

'Well,' Lucie said, 'I'm going to my room now to try on my dresses. I'll see you later.'

Penny waved happily, but Kyle tagged along after her.

'Lucie,' he called to her.

She paused in the hallway outside her room and looked round at him.

He ran a frustrated hand through his thick blond hair. 'I'm sorry. I didn't mean to sound like a fool. I hope you enjoy the party.'

She nodded.

'I'm serious. I apologize. I don't usually behave like this. I think I'm just feeling pressured by my aunt.'

'Penny doesn't seem to be anything other than supportive of you.'

'She is, but she really wants me to settle down and work here at the lodge.'

'You could have a worse future,' Lucie said bluntly.

'That's true,' he agreed. 'I've been thinking this past year about coming home again for good. I'm the closest to ready that I've ever been, just not quite ready yet.'

'You should be telling your Aunt Penny this, not me.'

He nodded and looked down, thoughtful. 'You're right. I've tried to tell her, but she doesn't listen.'

'Maybe you should try telling her again. She seems like a kind–hearted woman who really cares about you.'

He nodded again and swept his unruly hair back from his brow. 'Thanks, Lucie. I appreciate the advice.'

He walked away.

She went into her room, hung her coat up, kicked her shoes off and flopped down on the bed. The morning had not been anything like she'd expected. She'd thought that she'd book into the lodge, amble around the town, enjoy a relaxing time and then get ready for the party. She took a deep breath and sighed. Despite the hectic time since she'd arrived, she had enjoyed herself, especially at the cafe with Greg.

Pushing herself up again, she tried on the dresses and padded around the room wondering what one to wear for the party. She looked at herself in the closet door mirror wearing the lilac dress. Behind her the view of the sunshine in the garden reflected in the mirror with the crocus peeping through the grass and the flowering cherry trees. For a moment she saw herself and the life she could have here in Snow Bells Haven. Could she settle in a small town like this? She'd been brought up in New York by her elderly aunt who'd passed a number of years ago. Her aunt had advised her to follow her heart and she wouldn't go far wrong, or regret the things she never did.

Lucie had never considered living anywhere except the city, but oh how pretty this town looked. A sense of excitement made her hang the dresses up and head out into the main street to take a look around.

The main street was pleasantly busy. It was a town that seemed to have plenty of things going on. Nate's leaflet listed the wedding events, but there was an Easter Egg hunt with stalls selling coffee, hot chocolate and cakes, and of course chocolate Easter eggs, and special picnic events this weekend at the cove. The picnic event that afternoon was the one Kyle had mentioned to her.

Jessica's quilt shop was now open and she headed over and went inside.

Jessica, a woman in her forties, was serving a couple of customers. One was buying fabric to sew a quilt and the other was purchasing a quilt she'd ordered.

'Take a look around,' Jessica said to Lucie. 'I'll be with you in a moment.'

Lucie recognized Jessica as one of the women in Virginia's dress shop earlier buying a purse and joining in the laughter amid the busy shop.

Lucie smiled, and then gazed at the beautiful selection of fabrics, mainly cotton prints for quilting. What a lovely shop this was to browse in. Everything from the fat quarter bundles to the rolls of fabric piled on the shelves tempted her to buy them.

She ventured over to where quilts were on display and marveled at the stitching and designs. There was a floral patchwork quilt that looked so cozy and comforting, and she knew she'd definitely buy it. The price was reasonable for the quality and she imagined this would be something she'd keep for years as a reminder of her trip to Snow Bells Haven.

Lucie lifted the quilt up and took it over to the counter, staking her claim on it, while Jessica finished serving the other customers.

Waving them off, Jessica smiled at Lucie. 'Didn't I see you in Virginia's dress shop? You bought that lovely lilac dress.'

'Yes. I'm thinking of wearing it to Ana's party tonight.'

'You should. I bought a purse to match the dress I'm wearing.'

'There were so many gorgeous dresses I could've bought up several, but settled for three, and a purse. And now I'd like to buy this beautiful quilt. Did you make it or was it sewn by another quilter?'

'I made that one.'

'It's so pretty. I wish I could make quilts like this.'

'Come along to our quilting bee at the community hall. We welcome new members.'

'Unfortunately, I'm only here for the weekend, for Ana's wedding.'

'Oh, that's too bad.' Jessica reached into a drawer on the counter. 'Here's my quilt shop card. I post patterns and sewing tips on my website. It's become an online quilting community where we all share handy hints and talk about quilts. Pop on sometime. It's free, and such a friendly community. You'd be made very welcome. I'm sorry, I don't know your name.'

'Lucie,' she said, accepting the card and putting it in her purse.

'Well, Lucie, I hope you'll join in. We all have different levels of quilting and sewing skills. We post videos too, so you can see how things are finished. You'll meet all the ladies from the local bee. Lots of friendships are made sharing quilting skills online. It's a very friendly community.'

'That's how I became friends with Ana, chatting to her online.'

Jessica nodded firmly. 'There you go then.'

'I'll definitely do that when I get back to New York.'

'New York? That's where I met my husband. I was at a quilting event. He moved here and he's the town sheriff now.'

'That's so romantic.'

'He's a great guy. I was lucky to find him. Quilting helped me meet the man I married.'

'Does he share your love of quilting?' Lucie asked.

'He loves wrapping himself up in one and sitting cozy by the fire after a long day,' she said, smiling. 'But he's not into sewing at all. He leaves that to me. The only male member of our local quilting bee is Greg.' She paused. 'What was he doing this morning? If you don't mind me asking. He was jumping up and down outside the dress shop and then the two of you hurried off arm in arm. Brielle's face was a study.'

'I offered to help him out with baking cakes at the cafe. It was extra busy.'

'You're a baker?'

'Yes. I work in a cake and bakery shop in New York.'

'Do you have family there?'

'No. I've no one left. I was raised by my aunt. She taught me how to sew and the basics of quilting. I wish I'd learned more, but at the time I started to take an interest in baking cakes and made a career out of it. Anyway, Greg accepted my offer to help bake Ana's cupcakes.'

'You must be very skilled. He wouldn't let just anyone bake his cupcakes. Greg's a great baker. Have you seen the wedding cake he's made?'

'Yes, it's so beautiful. The sugarcraft flowers are perfect.'

'Greg's very creative. In his baking and quilting. A really talented and genuinely nice guy.' She sighed and put Lucie's quilt into a bag. 'It's such a shame about him and Brielle. She broke his heart. He's never dated seriously since they broke up.'

Even though they were alone in the shop, Lucie spoke in a confiding tone. 'Do you think she still has feelings for him? Is there any chance they'd get back together? He was hoping to impress her at the wedding.'

'I would never tell him, and I trust that you won't either,' said Jessica, 'but Brielle was never really into Greg. He loved her, but she wasn't serious about him. We all knew that.'

'I won't tell him,' Lucie promised.

'Brielle said she wanted to train for qualifications in New York and experience life in the city. She kept making excuses not to come home, and the weeks became longer and then a year went by.' Jessica considered this. 'I think Greg would've handled the split if it had been a clean break. She kept him hanging on, hoping she'd come back, and I think that's why he never fully got over her.'

'No proper closure?' said Lucie.

Jessica nodded. 'We're concerned what will happen this weekend. Brielle's a beautiful young woman. Maybe not the warmest or sweetest nature, more self absorbed. We're worried it'll tear open the old wounds Greg has tried to heal. He's too nice a guy for her.'

'Hasn't he ever met someone else in town? Maybe at the quilting bee?'

'Most of the ladies are married or taken, like Ana. We thought there was a budding romance between Greg and Sylvie. She arrived here at Christmas for a vacation and never left. But it's just friendship between them. And Sylvie and Zack are together now.'

'I saw Sylvie's engagement ring this morning. It's lovely.'

Jessica's eyes lit up with excitement. 'I haven't seen it yet. Nancy hasn't either, but she told me Zack has just asked Sylvie to marry him.'

'Sylvie said he proposed during dinner last night. I'm sure she'll tell us all the details at the party tonight.'

Jessica handed her the bag with the quilt. 'I can't wait.'

Promising to keep each others confidences, and to chat again at the party later, Lucie waved and left the quilt shop.

As she walked along the street towards the flower shop, Nate came ambling towards her still dressed as an Easter bunny.

'I hear you were baking up a storm at Greg's cafe,' Nate said, giving her a broad smile.

'Just helping with a bit of baking.'

'Are you going to the picnic at the cove this afternoon?'

'No, I'm browsing the shops and then putting my feet up and relaxing at the lodge.'

'That sounds sensible, especially as you'll be up dancing into the early hours.' He went to walk away and then paused. 'Not even tempted to join in the Easter egg hunt? It's right over there. A couple of minutes walk from here.'

Lucie looked over to an area of grassland where stalls draped with bunting were set up. People were starting to buy items from the stalls and everyone from kids to adults were carrying baskets ready to collect the eggs they found during the hunt. A wave of excitement rippled through her, and the urge to join in made her smile.

'You're smiling, Lucie,' he said.

Lucie tried not to smile and failed. 'I have other things to do and I really should relax before this evening. I'll be tuckered out.'

'Fun won't tucker you out. Heavy thoughts and responsibilities are far more tiring.'

'Hmmm, that's quite a good sales pitch, Nate.'

He knew she was joking with him, and played along. 'Okay, how about this for the kicker.' He gazed up at the clear blue sky. 'The sun is shining and it's a perfect day to have fun searching for Easter eggs and drinking hot chocolate.'

Lucie laughed. 'You win, Nate. I'm sold on the idea.'

'Come on,' he said, smiling. 'Let's head over.'

Nancy was manning one of the Easter egg stalls and waved when she saw Nate and Lucie.

'Are you joining in, Lucie?' said Nancy, offering her a little basket to collect her eggs in.

'Definitely,' said Lucie, and dropped a monetary donation into the tin requesting help to raise funds for the local animal rescue.

'A couple of the ladies are looking after the store or us,' Nancy explained to Lucie. 'Everyone helps out on days when we've events going on.'

'Looking at the list on the leaflet, there's always something happening,' said Lucie.

A family waved Nate over because the kids wanted to meet the Easter bunny, and this left Nancy to chat to Lucie.

'Greg seemed happy with you at the cafe,' said Nancy. 'He's been kind of tense recently because of Brielle coming back for a visit.'

'I can understand. He really loved her.'

'He did, but she was never the one for him.' Nancy smiled her. 'It's great that you're his date for the wedding. I popped into the cafe and he told me what happened.'

'It's obviously not a real date–'

'No?' Nancy cut–in. 'I thought the two of you looked fine and happy together.'

Lucie felt a blush rise in her cheeks. 'I'm not...I mean...I've only just met Greg...'

Nancy smiled knowingly. 'You like him though, huh?'

Lucie tried to sound nonchalant. 'He's nice, good company and everyone seems to like him. Well, except Kyle,' she corrected herself.

Nancy shook her head at the mention of Kyle. 'That young man needs to settle down. His Aunt Penny frets about him. He's never settled in the city, yet won't come back home. A talented chef though. He'd be an asset to the lodge, or maybe open up his own restaurant in town. Local folks would support him.'

Lucie looked around her at the people having fun. 'It's a very supportive community.'

'A lot of people from out of town have the wrong idea about living here. They think because it's a small town it's quiet, relaxing, and that the city offers a bigger life. But we're a full–on, busy little town, filled with folks who enjoy knowing each other. Every time I've been to the city, I'm glad to come back home. In the city people walk past folks they don't know and never will. That feels like a lonely life to me.' She paused. 'Some of us, like me,' she admitted, 'are busybodies, but better that than not caring about the people living in your own town.'

Lucie found herself agreeing to the things Nancy was saying, and a sense of loneliness hit her. She hadn't realized the sadness she felt showed on her face.

Nancy reached out and placed a hand on her shoulder. 'I'm sorry, Lucie. I didn't mean to comment on your life in the city. Each person to their own. I apologize for upsetting you.'

'It's fine,' Lucie assured her. 'I'm not as settled in New York at the moment as I used to be. I'm moving out of my apartment soon and thinking of heading to Long Island to work in a cake shop there.'

'What about settling down? Making a real home. Finding yourself a nice young man, raising a family of your own. Do you want anything like that?'

Lucie nodded and an unexpected rush of emotions swept through her, causing her to almost cry. She realized no one had asked her anything like this in a long time. Not since the days when she'd sit and chat to her aunt.

Nate came back over.

'Is everything okay?' he asked.

'Everything's fine, Nate,' said Nancy.

Lucie brushed away her unsure thoughts and forced a happy smile. 'Just girl talk.'

'Better pick up your basket, Lucie,' Nate encouraged her. 'There won't be any eggs left to find if you don't join in.'

Lucie grabbed her basket and hurried to join the search. She found a couple of little chocolate eggs in the lush grass near one of the trees, surrounded by bright yellow daffodils, and committed the moment to memory. The sound of the laughter and squeals of glee, and how much fun she was having being part of the event were things she wanted to recall. She'd never taken part in something like this before even though there were events in Central Park that she'd seen.

'How are you doing there, Lucie?' Nate called to her.

She held up her basket triumphantly. 'Half full. More chocolate eggs than I've ever had.'

Nate gave her the thumbs up and then continued to play his role as the Easter bunny.

From where Lucie was standing, she could see part of Greg's cafe on the main street, with the pretty awning above the front window fluttering in the light breeze. Her heart ached a little just thinking about him. She paused for a moment and gazed up there, wondering how he was coping with the baking and cooking. He was one of the nicest guys she'd met in a long time. She hadn't dated anyone in over a year, and even then it hadn't been serious. True love was something she'd had no luck in finding. And the last place she expected to find any hint of romance was in Snow Bells Haven.

Shaking herself out of thoughts that were unlikely to lead to anywhere except disappointment when she had to leave soon, she continued to join in the hunt.

'Would you like a cup of hot chocolate?' one of the stallholders asked Lucie.

'Yes, thank you.' She stopped to sip her drink, looked around her and breathed in the lovely sunny day.

Lucie carried her Easter eggs in a paper bag and walked back up to the main street. There were still lots of stores to visit and she meandered along looking in all the windows.

As the afternoon wore on, she decided to head back to the lodge to rest up. Penny was busy checking guests in and there was no sign of Kyle, so she was free to go to her room to relax without stopping to chat.

Lying back on her bed, she thought about all the things that had happened since she'd arrived in town. And she was looking forward to seeing Ana at the party.

After a few minutes, she supposed she'd better unpack her duffel bag to check she'd packed everything she needed, including her fancy shoes. Flats and boots were her normal style, particularly as she spent most days standing baking, but heels were more suitable for the party and the wedding.

Unpacking everything, she placed her shoes down and hung her clothes in the closet. Then she jumped in the shower and emerged refreshed, and towel dried her hair.

The lodge felt homely, but she wondered what it would be like to live here in town, in a house, a real home. Ana had sent her pictures of the house she was planning to move into with Caleb. He was a painter and decorator by trade, and they'd spent months making it into a home for the two of them. It was a detached house with a veranda and a garden. Lucie hadn't lived in a house for years, just apartments, moving from one to the other, and now moving out of her current address when her friend got married.

She earned a decent living from her work at the bakery, and she baked cakes in her spare time and made extra money from that. Fancy birthday cakes and Christmas cakes were her specialty. She budgeted well and had managed to put some savings aside, but not enough to afford to buy herself a house in New York.

Gazing out the window, she noticed the sun was still shining, but it had deepened like burnished gold streaming across the garden as the day became late afternoon. Not long now until the party.

She set the timer on her phone in case she fell asleep, and relaxed on the bed wearing a robe provided by the lodge.

Moments later, there was a knock at the door, so she got up and went over to open it.

'I hope I didn't disturb you, Lucie,' said Penny.

'No, is everything all right?'

Penny hesitated. 'Erm, no, we've had a slight mix–up with some of the cupcakes for Ana's party tonight.'

Lucie frowned. 'Greg said the cakes were exactly what Ana ordered.'

Penny sounded tense. 'They were. Unfortunately, one of our waiting staff served two platefuls up to our regular guests during afternoon tea. So we're short of cakes now for the party. I'm really sorry to ask you, but is there any chance you could whip up some more at our kitchen in the lodge? We've got everything you'd need, a well–equipped kitchen and all the ingredients, but we don't have anyone capable of baking cakes.' Penny shrugged. 'I've never been good at baking.'

'Okay, give me a few minutes to get dressed and I'll be right there.'

'I'm so sorry to put this stress on your shoulders, Lucie.' Penny sounded genuinely upset.

'It's fine,' Lucie assured her, perking up. 'We've still got time to bake them for the party.'

Leaving Lucie to get dressed, Penny hurried away.

Lucie jumped into a pair of jeans, pulled on a clean white T–shirt, tied her hair in a ponytail and headed to the kitchen.

When she walked in she was surprised to see Kyle standing there preparing the baking trays, flour, sugar, bowls. He was wearing a white chef's jacket and a casual smile.

Penny smiled happily. 'Kyle said he'd help you.'

Lucie smiled tightly. 'That's great.'

'I'll leave you two to get busy baking.' Penny smiled again and hurried out of the kitchen.

Lucie glared at Kyle suspiciously.

Kyle held up his hands. 'I didn't plan this if that's what you're thinking. One of the waiting staff made a mistake. Aunt Penny thought it was better to ask you to do the baking because you know how to make them, especially the champagne vanilla frosting.'

She believed him, but he was pleased at the predicament.

'We don't have the recipe, but we thought that Greg would panic if we phoned to ask for it.'

Lucie sighed and nodded, picturing Greg's reaction if he'd found out.

'So my plan is to use this.' He'd opened a cook book at a recipe for cupcakes.

She scanned the ingredients. 'This will do nicely.'

'Do you want me to start measuring out the ingredients?' he offered.

'Yes, I'll sieve the icing sugar.'

They started working together in the kitchen, and the tension she'd felt started to melt as his capability as a chef made the process easy. She had no plan to tell him this. No way.

'This is fun,' he said, smiling at her, as they popped two batches of cupcakes in the oven. 'We work well together.'

Lucie nodded and began to prepare the butter, sugar and vanilla extract for the frosting.

'I'll open the champagne.' Kyle held up a bottle of champagne and expertly popped the cork.

'We don't need a lot, just enough to flavor the frosting.'

Kyle smiled happily and grabbed two fluted glasses from a shelf. 'In that case, let's indulge in a toast to celebrate.' He began to pour two glasses full, then hesitated and looked at her. He held up the bottle. 'Will you take a glass?' he checked before filling one for her.

Her first reaction was to refuse, but then she reconsidered. 'Yes, I think I will.' She wasn't one for drinking, and certainly not champagne.

'Great.' He poured a glass full and handed it to her, picking up his glass and holding it up in a toast. 'To us, and to new beginnings.'

She tipped her glass against his and sipped the refreshing bubbles.

At that moment Greg hurried in and was taken aback when he saw them.

'Greg!' Lucie gasped.

Chapter Five

'I heard about the cupcakes,' said Greg, looking at the two of them standing there drinking champagne.

'Would you like a glass of champagne?' Kyle offered him. 'We're drinking a celebratory toast.'

Greg frowned at Kyle. 'What to?'

'To us and new beginnings,' Kyle told him, pouring a glass for Greg and handing it to him.

Greg held the glass but didn't drink the champagne. 'What happened to the cupcakes? Someone came into the cafe and said that guests at the lodge had eaten them.'

'Staff served some of them up by mistake,' Lucie explained. 'Penny asked me to make some more. She knew you were busy at the cafe and didn't want you to stress out.'

Kyle gestured towards the oven. 'We've got two batches baking and Lucie's about to whip up the frosting. Everything's in hand. So you can go back to the cafe, Greg.'

Greg was obviously stressed and had hurried from the cafe to the lodge. It was a relief that only some of the cupcakes were missing, and it seemed like Lucie could handle the situation. But what really took him aback was his reaction when he'd seen her with Kyle, drinking champagne and looking...cozy together.

Greg put the glass down, and nodded, trying not to show the mix of jealousy and resentment he felt. It made no sense to feel like this, and yet, he didn't like seeing Lucie with Kyle. He didn't like it one little bit.

'I'll leave you both to it,' said Greg. He smiled briefly at Lucie. 'I'll see you tonight at the party.'

She smiled at him. 'Yes, see you then.'

She watched him walk away and fought the urge to run after him, yet she wasn't sure why.

Kyle continued as if they hadn't been interrupted by Greg. 'Let me help you mix the frosting.'

Greg walked back to the cafe feeling deflated. Kyle was probably sweet talking Lucie right now, plying her with champagne and maybe trying to make a date with her. He saw the way he looked at

Lucie. Kyle liked her. He didn't blame him. He liked Lucie too. He sighed heavily and tried to shrug off the urge to run back up to the lodge and be there with her.

He went into the cafe and started to help Dwayne and Herb with the orders. The cafe was still busy with customers.

Dwayne nudged Herb and they exchanged a knowing look. Greg was whipping up eggs and working fast behind the counter.

'Everything okay with the cupcakes at the lodge?' Herb asked him.

'Yeah. Lucie and eh...Kyle, are baking them.' Greg didn't even look up as he told them.

Herb glanced at Dwayne, then said to Greg, 'Kyle's baking the cupcakes?'

Greg nodded, still working fast and efficient, cooking up the orders. 'A few cakes got eaten by mistake and they're making up the shortfall.'

'I hope Kyle's not sweet talking Lucie,' Dwayne said bluntly.

The whisk Greg was holding almost slipped from his grip, but he pretended not to have reacted. 'I don't think Lucie's interested in Kyle.' Nothing in his voice suggested this was true.

'I've heard women say a few times that Kyle's a good looking guy,' said Dwayne.

Herb iced Dwayne with a look.

Dwayne tried to backtrack. 'But he's never around town for long. He'll be heading back to New York after the wedding.'

Greg's shoulders tensed. 'So is Lucie.'

Herb made a face at Dwayne, urging him to shut up.

Dwayne sighed, knowing he'd made things worse.

Herb spoke up. 'You'll see Lucie at the party, Greg. We're the only three guys allowed in. You could ask her to dance.'

Greg shook his head. 'We're there to drop off the tray bakes, make sure everything is ready for Ana, and then we're out of there. Girls only, remember. Rules are rules.'

Herb scoffed at this. 'When did you start living by the rules, Greg? You're often the first guy to break or bend the rules. Never in a bad way, just you being you, buddy.'

Greg glanced over at Herb.

Herb shrugged and picked up a pot of coffee to serve to customers. 'If Kyle really has been trying to sweet talk Lucie, all bets are off as far as rules go.'

Nancy was back working at the grocery store when Nate walked in.

The store had a great selection of grocery goods, fresh fruit and vegetables, and a deli counter with a delicious range of cheese.

Nancy was eager to give Nate the latest news. 'Penny just phoned me from the lodge.' She went on to explain about the cupcake scenario.

'Does Greg know?' said Nate.

'Yes, he ran like the wind up there when he found out.' She spoke in a confiding tone. 'Lucie was drinking champagne with Kyle in the kitchen while the cupcakes were baking. One of the waiting staff saw them.'

'Well, that's none of our business now, is it, Nancy?'

'No, but Penny said that Kyle seemed to take an instant liking to Lucie when he first met her at the lodge. And he is a handsome one.'

'It's not our place to interfere,' he said, knowing that no matter how many times he told his wife this she paid no heed.

'Dwayne and Herb think Greg likes Lucie, and we both know how Greg and Kyle have always been at loggerheads. I know that Greg's been all in a pickle over Brielle being here, but what if Lucie is just what he needs to finally get over that girl?'

'Nancy, honey, you know I love you, but don't go meddling in these young folks lives. It could mess things up for all of them.'

Nancy pressed her lips together and said no more about it, but this was no guarantee that she wouldn't meddle later on.

Lucie piped frosting on to the last of the cupcakes as Kyle tidied things up around her and chatted casually.

'Ana and Caleb have been sweethearts for a long time. I didn't want to miss their wedding. They're a great couple,' he said.

'They are,' she agreed, concentrating on swirling the frosting on.

'What about you? Any special guy waiting for you in New York?' He looked at her, but she kept working on the cakes.

'No. Maybe one day. I've been busy with work.'

'You should make time for romance,' he said. This time she caught his glance.

'I plan to.' She nodded, as if trying to convince herself.

The lodge's catering and waiting staff started to come in to work in the kitchen, and Lucie took the chance to lift one of the trays of finished cupcakes through to the function room.

Kyle picked up the second tray and followed her through.

The lights had been switched on in the function room ready for the party, and lilac and silver balloons were added as decorations. Lanterns lit up the garden and the whole venue was looking lovely.

Lucie put the tray down and arranged the cakes on a couple of the large plates. Kyle did the same with his tray of cakes.

Stepping back to admire everything, Lucie gazed around her. The buffet tables were all set with party food, and Greg would be arriving with tasty tray bakes and a few other items to add to the buffet.

'Would you like a cup of coffee?' Kyle offered her.

She checked the time. 'Thanks, but I need to get dressed for the party.' She started to walk away.

'I'll see you later, Lucie,' he called to her.

She glanced back, smiled and nodded, then continued on to her room.

The champagne celebration toast for the bride was due to start in ten minutes. The function room was busy with women, all dressed up for the party. It seemed like everyone had arrived on time.

Lucie, wearing her lilac dress, hair down and silky smooth, walked into the room. Ana saw her, squealed with delight, and ran over to give her a hug.

'It's so good to see you, Lucie. Thanks for coming,' said Ana, hugging the breath from her.

'I'm glad to see you too,' Lucie said, smiling.

Ana wore a dress she'd made herself, a yellow chiffon cocktail–length dress. It sparkled with beadwork. Ana's hair was pinned up, and she beamed with excitement.

'Come and meet all the girls, and my mother.' Ana clasped Lucie's hand and led her over to the hub of the group and introduced her. Lucie had already met some of them including Nancy, Jessica, Virginia and Sylvie, so this made her feel part of the group straight away. Their welcome was warm and genuine, like most things in this town, Lucie thought to herself.

Sparkle was certainly the order of the night when it came to the dresses. Most of them had been made by Virginia and the women who were part of her dressmaking team from the shop, including Ana. With Lucie wearing the lilac dress from Virginia's shop, she fitted right in as one of the girls.

Any tension Lucie had felt lifted just being there with them. The energy was contagious, and soon it was time for the party to start with the celebratory toast.

Glasses of champagne were poured and soft drinks of sparkling lemonade. With their glasses in hand, the women stood listening to a few words of introduction by Penny.

'Welcome to Ana's party. I hope you'll raise your glasses and drink a toast to our wonderful bride–to–be. Ana was born and raised in Snow Bells Haven, and we're proud and happy to celebrate her forthcoming wedding.' Penny lifted her glass high. 'To Ana.'

'To Ana!' the women said in unison, and drank a toast to her.

Cheers, applause and smiles filled the room.

Music started playing and glasses were topped up with more champagne and wine as the party got underway. Waiting staff were on hand to serve at the buffet tables.

Brielle arrived late, and walked in looking stunning, wearing the deep blue satin dress she'd bought earlier.

Penny and Nancy exchanged a disapproving look. Brielle was staying at the lodge and knew fine what time the party started. However, her attempt to steal some of the limelight from Ana failed because everyone was too busy enjoying themselves to notice her making an entrance.

Brielle flicked a glance at Lucie and then went over to get a glass of champagne.

Greg arrived, as agreed, a few minutes after the toast, accompanied by Dwayne and Herb. They carried in some of the catering food, including his specialty — sweet potato fries and his savory dip. The fries were piping hot in metal catering containers. Penny immediately instructed the waiting staff to take the fries through to the kitchen to keep them warm, while Greg put one large container of fries on a hot plate at a buffet table. These started to be served up right away.

Ana waved to Greg. 'Thanks, Greg.' Then she beckoned to the girls. 'Come and try these sweet potato fries.'

Dwayne and Herb put their trays down containing a selection of mini pizzas. The toppings varied from cherry tomatoes to yellow peppers and red onion. Then they hurried back out to bring in more items from Greg's car.

Greg was looking handsome in his cream shirt, tie and smart but casual pants. Lucie's heart squeezed when she saw him. No bunny ears. Clean shaven, showered, hair swept back smooth. Oh yes, Greg cleaned up real nice.

Not that he hadn't looked good earlier, Lucie thought, but she had the impression he'd made an extra effort this evening.

Dwayne and Herb were still happy to wear their bunny outfits. Dwayne waved to his wife on his way out. She was chatting to Nancy and Penny.

Lucie noticed Greg glancing around, as if looking for someone. She assumed he was probably looking for Brielle, but she was wrong.

Greg smiled across at Lucie. He'd been looking for her. She smiled back at him and her heart felt a warmth towards him that made her pause and watch him as he hurried back out to bring more food in.

Amid the laughter, music and squeals of excitement as some of the party balloons were untied, Lucie thought about Greg and how she felt towards him.

By now Dwayne and Herb were heading back in carrying more trays of food, but the tall figure of Kyle emerged from a side door and swooped in to snatch a tray from Dwayne.

'Let me take one of those for you,' said Kyle, without giving Dwayne a chance to refuse.

Kyle then walked along with Dwayne and Herb as if he was part of the catering, giving himself an excuse for being at the party.

Dwayne tried to take the tray back off him, but Kyle side–stepped and carried it to one of the buffet tables right beside Lucie. With it being so crowded, she couldn't easily get out of Kyle's way.

'You're looking beautiful, Lucie.' Kyle took his time placing the items from the tray down on to the plates.

She smiled and looked around, wondering if Penny saw that he was here, but his aunt was too busy talking to Nancy. Lucie supposed it was fine that Kyle was at the party even though it was a girls only night, but she felt he'd used his privileged position as

Penny's nephew to wangle his way into the hub of it. Certainly, Greg and the guys were there, but only to drop off the food. Kyle had quite a nerve making himself look like he was part of their hard work.

'I know I shouldn't be here,' Kyle confessed to her, giving her a smile that made it difficult for her to be mad at him. 'But as you're only in town for a few days, I thought I'd ask you to dance with me. We may not get a chance to dance at the wedding.'

Lucie stared up at him. He had a great smile and blue eyes that were filled with warmth and humor. She could see how Penny adored him, and yet he was incorrigible.

As she hesitated, Greg came back in carrying melted cheese vol-au-vents and reacted when he saw Kyle clearly chatting up Lucie. He hadn't expected to see Kyle at the party and the surprise showed on his face, along with a flicker of resentment.

And that was the moment it happened...

Greg walked right past Brielle and headed straight for Lucie and Kyle.

Lucie saw Brielle blink in disbelief. Brielle's expression showed she was insulted — how dare Greg ignore her, especially as she was looking beautiful in her new dress.

Kyle was so intent on leaning down and smiling at Lucie, cajoling her to dance with him, that he didn't notice Greg approaching.

And maybe it was a guy's instinct type of thing — Greg knew from the way Kyle was leaning in to Lucie, giving her his full attention and warmest smile, exactly what was going on.

'Quit sweet talking Lucie, Kyle!' Greg shouted louder than he'd intended.

At that precise moment the music paused, changing to a different song, and in the lull Greg's voice sounded loud and clear.

Everyone stopped talking and stared at Greg, and then at Kyle. And at Lucie. Even Dwayne and Herb paused and wondered what to do.

Realizing instantly what he'd done, Greg looked like he wanted the dance floor to open up and swallow him. The embarrassment burned across his face, and yet, he was still prepared to stare Kyle down until he stepped away from Lucie.

Kyle held up his hands, stepped back and tried to make out that everything was fine. But Lucie was close enough to him to see the muscles tighten in his jaw as he suppressed his reaction to argue with Greg.

Penny came running over, pushing through the balloons, and scolded Kyle. 'You've no business being here, Kyle. The guys' party is over at Caleb's place.'

Kyle gave her an innocent smile. 'I was just trying to help with the–'

Penny spoke in a hissing whisper. 'I know fine well what you were trying to do. Now, off you go, and don't be causing any more friction at Ana's party.'

Kyle moved away from Lucie, but continued to linger near the dance floor, pretending to sort some of the balloons.

Greg mouthed over to Ana that he was sorry, but she wasn't concerned about it. With a room full of women enjoying gossip and mischief, it only gave them more romance to speculate about.

Not knowing what to say to Lucie, Greg hurried out again. Lucie stood on her own where she was as the melee circled around her.

'There's something wrong with Greg,' Herb whispered to Nancy.

Nancy frowned and whispered back. 'Greg seems okay to me. He sounds quite feisty in fact. I haven't seen him like this is a long time.'

Herb nodded. 'Exactly. He even walked straight past Brielle without giving a hoot about her to get to Lucie.'

Nancy's eyes widened. 'I get your drift. You're thinking that he's...'

'Finally over Brielle,' said Herb.

Nancy's face lit up with a smile. Herb and Dwayne both grinned at her, and Dwayne's wife joined in with an acknowledging nod.

'Well, that's great!' Nancy sounded so happy. 'It's about time Greg let go of the past and found fresh happiness.'

Herb wasn't smiling, and Dwayne wasn't sure what he was supposed to do.

'What's wrong?' Nancy asked Herb.

'Lucie leaves on the bus on Monday,' Herb reminded her.

Nancy's smile changed to a frown. 'We'll have to do something to make her want to stay.' She motioned towards Sylvie. 'Look at Sylvie. She stayed here instead of going back to New York.'

‘Yeah,’ Herb agreed, ‘but Sylvie was here on a Christmas vacation. Lucie’s only here for a wedding weekend. We’ll need to do something real fast.’

‘I have an idea,’ Nancy said to them. ‘But it could cause chaos and calamity.’

Dwayne smiled and shrugged. ‘What’s new about that in Snow Bells Haven?’

Gathering several of the girls, including Penny, Jessica, Virginia and Dwayne’s wife, along with Dwayne and Herb, Nancy quickly told them her plan.

‘The sugar could hit the fan,’ Nancy warned them, ‘but I think it’s worth stirring things up a little while Lucie’s here.’

Penny winked. ‘I’ll handle Kyle.’ And off she went to shoo him from the party.

‘I just wanted to dance with Lucie, Aunt Penny,’ he said in his defense.

‘You can go and dance your socks off with Caleb and the boys.’ Penny flapped her hands at him to go. ‘Now on you go. Have fun.’

Brielle sidled over to Penny. ‘Is there something going on that I should know about?’

‘No, I’m just making sure that this is a girls only night.’

Brielle eyed Dwayne and Herb who seemed to be deep in cahoots with Nancy and several other women. ‘If I’m not mistaken, Penny, that’s two guys over there right now.’

‘They’re Easter bunnies, Brielle. That’s a whole different category.’ Penny flicked her hair and walked away to join Nancy and the others.

Greg sat outside in his car slumped in the front seat, sweeping his hair back from his brow and hoping to clear his thoughts. How could he have been so stupid? He’d more or less announced to everyone that he had feelings for Lucie. No wonder Lucie was stumped for what to say to him. When she’d looked at him with those lovely hazel–green eyes of hers, he’d wanted to hug her and say he was sorry. Instead, here he was, sitting outside the lodge, feeling like a jealous fool and with his stomach flipping like a butter churn. And he had to go back inside to deliver the rest of the food so the girls could enjoy it.

He sighed heavily and forced himself to get out of the car and take the food in.

He saw Kyle driving off and shook his head. Maybe Lucie liked Kyle. They'd seemed happy drinking champagne when baking cupcakes. What if he'd got things wrong? What if Lucie really wanted to date Kyle?

Deciding he needed to stop thinking about things that made him even more stressed, he carried the last two trays of food into the party.

The sounds of the party filtered out into the reception as he headed inside. The music and dancing had notched up a few levels and lots of photographs were being taken by the women using their phones.

In the midst of it all were Dwayne and Herb, happy to be pulled into the photos as the girls wanted to snap a picture of themselves with an Easter bunny.

Nancy, Penny, Lucie and Ana were up dancing to a lively song, and he was able to slip past and put the tray of food down on a table without them noticing him.

On the way out, however, Greg got pulled on to the dance floor by Ana.

'Come on, Greg,' Ana encouraged him, though giving him no option but to join in.

Soon several of the women were dancing with Greg in the middle of them. He wasn't a natural dancer and didn't have much rhythm, but gave it his best for Ana.

There was no escape, he thought, giving in to the fun of the moment, especially when Lucie joined them. Everyone seemed to forget about him shouting at Kyle and making a fool of himself.

Dwayne and Herb waved at Greg and gave him the thumbs up. Yes, Greg thought to himself. Sometimes breaking the rules was a whole lot of fun.

Greg finally managed to escape back to his car, missing only his tie and the top button from his shirt. Even though he was capable of doing his own mending, Jessica promised to sew it back on for him, if they ever found it.

Dwayne and Herb came running out moments later and got into the car. Herb sat up front while Dwayne flopped exhausted in the back.

'Drive!' Herb shouted jokingly at Greg. 'Let's escape while we still can.'

Laughing, Greg started up the car and drove off, right past the cafe where they were supposed to be headed. The lights in the cafe were off and everything was secure. Buzzing with adrenalin Greg wasn't ready to call it a night. Not yet, not when there was a party in town.

'Where are we going?' Herb asked him.

'I'm going to Caleb's party. I can drop you guys off home if you want.' He smiled as he said this, knowing their reaction.

'No way, buddy,' Herb told him. 'If you're up for partying, so are we.' He glanced back at Dwayne.

'I'm in. Let's go!' Dwayne punched the air with one of his bunny paws, and off they went, heading to Caleb's party.

Lucie was enjoying the party, and it was great to be with Ana and the girls, but she felt a pang of sadness, picturing Greg and the guys back at the cafe. No doubt they were clearing up and getting it ready for the next day, then locking up and going home.

Ana was right to want a girls night before her wedding, but she wished Greg and Dwayne and Herb could've had fun too. They'd worked so hard.

Greg pulled up outside Caleb's house. Caleb lived with his uncle. The lights were on and music was playing.

Caleb was the first to welcome them in. He was a few months older than Ana and a fine looking young man.

Nate was there too. 'We've promised Ana that Caleb will be tucked up in bed around midnight.'

Caleb shook hands with Greg and the guys. 'Glad you could make it, boys. Come on in.' He smiled at Nate. 'Don't worry, Nate, I've also promised Ana I'll get some sleep tonight.'

'All ready for your special day?' Greg asked him, feeling happy for him.

'Yep. I can't wait to marry Ana. She means the world to me.'

It was then that Greg saw Kyle over at the food table, helping himself to a coffee and something to eat.

'We heard what happened between you and Kyle at the party,' Nate confided to Greg.

'I won't be causing any trouble,' Greg promised. 'We're just here to celebrate with Caleb.'

Greg meant every word he said, but Kyle had other ideas, especially when it came to Lucie.

Chapter Six

Nancy and the ladies were busy conspiring while Lucie was up dancing with Ana and several other girls.

'You know the effect this town has on people,' said Nancy. 'If Lucie is here for more than a few days, the town will start to have its effect. She'll want to stay.'

The ladies nodded.

'When does she leave?' Jessica asked. 'Should we invite her to our quilting bee night? Greg will be there.'

'Lucie is booked into the lodge for a long weekend,' Penny explained. 'Then she's leaving on the bus. She won't be here for the quilting bee. But I can extend her room booking for the next two weeks. She's welcome to stay at the lodge.'

'Perfect,' said Nancy. 'We'll encourage her to extend her visit and invite her to the bee. It'll give her a chance to see how much fun we have here, and it's something else that Greg's involved in.'

'Greg seems to be smitten with her,' Jessica remarked.

Nancy nodded thoughtfully. 'I think the reason Greg was so receptive to Lucie is because he was amped–up about Brielle coming back. It put him in a head space he hadn't been for a while. He was already in a lovey–dovey frame of mind.' She paused. 'Brielle crushed his confidence outside the cafe, and then Lucie walked in and was just kind and selfless.'

The women agreed with Nancy.

'Lucie was the right girl at the right time,' said Penny.

'Yes, so we can't let Kyle spoil things,' Nancy added.

Penny sounded adamant. 'As much as I love Kyle, he's not right for Lucie.'

'We're going to have to tell a few little white lies,' said Jessica, 'for Lucie's own good you understand.'

Nancy nodded firmly. 'Think of it as emergency skulduggery.'

'What about Lucie's work at the bakery in New York?' Virginia asked.

'She's not happy there,' Nancy explained. 'She's moving out of her apartment soon, and is thinking of leaving her job to work in another cake shop.'

'There are shops in town she could work in,' said Jessica. 'She could even help Greg at the cafe. Or start her own cake shop. We'd all pitch in to help her I'm sure.'

The women nodded.

'Lucie is going as Greg's date to the wedding,' said Nancy, 'so they'll see each other then, and we can talk to Lucie and convince her that Snow Bells Haven would be a wonderful town to move to.'

Penny nudged Nancy. 'Lucie's coming over.'

'So I'm looking forward to seeing Ana's wedding dress...' Nancy said, making it sound as if they hadn't been planning Lucie's future for her.

Lucie smiled as she approached. 'I haven't danced like this in ages. It's a great party.'

'It is. We have great parties here,' Nancy told her. 'Isn't that right, girls?'

'Oh yes,' said Jessica. 'And lots of fun things to do — like our quilting bee. Greg's a wonderful quilter.'

'I love the quilt I bought from you, Jessica,' said Lucie. 'It's going to remind me of being here when I go back home.'

'You should stay in town for a while,' Nancy said, 'and enjoy yourself here for a week or two.'

Lucie smiled apologetically. 'I'd love to, but I have to go home.'

Penny sparked up the conversation. 'You're an independent young woman. You can do what you want. Okay, so you've got a job in the city, but...' she shrugged, 'you don't love working at that bakery, do you?'

Lucie hesitated. 'Well, no, not really, but I—'

'You said you were thinking of changing jobs and working for another cake shop,' Nancy prompted her.

'I erm...I did, and I am, but—'

'There you are then,' Nancy concluded. 'You could work anywhere you want if you put your mind to it. You could move here and work in Snow Bells Haven.'

All the women nodded as if this was totally feasible.

Lucie wondered if it was the second glass of champagne, or the fun of the party, but suddenly she felt herself seriously think about this.

Nancy saw the expression on Lucie's face and continued to encourage her. 'You'd love living here. You could maybe open up your own cake shop.'

Lucie blinked. 'My own cake shop?'

'Yes, why not,' said Jessica. 'I've got my quilt shop, and Virginia has her dress shop.'

'And Nate and I have our grocery store,' Nancy chipped–in. 'We all know how to set up a shop here. We'd help you.'

Lucie was deep in thought. She pictured the types of cakes she'd bake and what her front window display would look like. 'When I was a little girl, my aunt bought me one of those toy cake shops that kids enjoy. I used to spend hours in my room playing with that shop, pretending I was baking cakes and selling them to customers.' She laughed at the thought. 'I used to daydream that one day I'd have a shop like that.'

'You could do it for real right here,' said Nancy. 'Opening a little cake shop and bakery in the city would be hard. Finding premises you could afford wouldn't be easy in New York, or establishing enough regular customers. But you could do it in this town.'

Lucie nodded. 'You really think I could make a go of it here?'

'Definitely,' Nancy assured her. 'If you decided not to open your own shop right away, you're a fine baker and would find a job, especially with our help.'

Lucie looked at them. 'I'd need time to think about it.'

'And so you should,' Penny agreed. 'That's why you should extend your visit to town. Stay at the lodge while you think things over.'

And suddenly, Lucie was more convinced than ever. 'I'm due a vacation from work.'

Nancy smiled at her. 'Great. Now we've got something extra to celebrate.'

Sylvie joined them. 'What's that?'

'Lucie's staying in town for a longer vacation,' Nancy told her.

Sylvie looked pleased. 'Oh, you'll love it, but fair warning, if you're anything like me, you'll never want to leave.'

There were smiles and hugs all round, and then Nancy realized something. 'I haven't had a chance to see your engagement ring, Sylvie.'

Sylvie held out her hand and the diamond ring sparkled under the lights. 'I still keep looking at it. I didn't expect Zack to propose last night.'

'You said he proposed during dinner?' said Jessica.

'He did. He designed the ring and had it made locally. I didn't know a thing about it until he popped the question to me last night. It was so romantic.'

'Any date planned for the wedding?' said Lucie.

'We're thinking of the summer, or maybe waiting until Christmas, a year since we first met.' Sylvie shrugged and smiled. 'But I don't think either of us want to wait, so probably a summer wedding.'

'If you don't mind me asking you,' said Lucie, 'you met Zack during your Christmas vacation?'

'I did. He was the first person I met when I arrived in Snow Bells Haven. I didn't know anyone. I wanted a small town, cozy Christmas away from New York. I'd finished work for the holidays, had split from my boyfriend, Conrad, and it was my Christmas gift to myself. I thought I'd relax, but the moment I arrived...well,' she grinned at Nancy.

'We pulled her into all the activities and she never stopped to relax while she fell in love with Zack.' Nancy laughed. 'And his cute dog, Cookie.'

Lucie found herself smiling at the thought of Sylvie getting involved in the town's business. 'Snow Bells pulls you right into the hub of it.'

'It does,' Sylvie agreed. 'So be prepared to have the most fun–filled, whirlwind of a vacation. And don't pack your bags. You may never go home.'

Lucie smiled broadly. 'I'll keep that in mind.'

Sylvie slipped her engagement ring off. 'Plenty of the girls have made a wish on my new ring. Do any of you want a wish?'

All of the women present were keen to do this, and as the ring was passed around, starting with Nancy, Sylvie finally handed it to Lucie.

Lucie, having seen what the others did, placed the ring carefully on one finger and turned it three times, closed her eyes and made her wish. Then she handed it to Sylvie.

'I hope all your wishes come true,' Sylvie said, smiling at them.

As they were all about to head on to the dance floor, Lucie's phone rang. She was surprised to hear Greg's voice as she picked up.

'Lucie? Hi, it's Greg. I got your number from the lodge.'

'It's Greg,' she whispered to the girls.

They gave her the thumbs up and went off to dance, leaving Lucie to chat to Greg.

'Is that a party I hear in the background?' she asked him. It sounded lively.

'Yeah, I'm with Dwayne and Herb. We're at Caleb's party. Nate's here, all the guys, and eh...Kyle. Though we're pretending to ignore each other at the moment.'

She thought this was a good idea.

'But that's not why I'm calling. I wondered if you're busy tomorrow morning. Early morning.'

'Really early?'

'Eh, yeah.'

'I'll most likely be sleeping off this hectic party. I haven't danced like this in years. And the night is young.'

'That's okay. Just thought I'd ask.'

'What were you thinking of doing?'

'I have to take Ana's wedding cake to the community hall and set it up for the reception. I didn't have time today. I thought perhaps with your baking expertise, you'd like to come along and help me put it together.'

'Oh.' He'd really taken her by surprise. 'Well, yes, of course. I'd be glad to help you with the wedding cake.'

'Great. I'll see you at the cafe in the morning.'

'I'll be there early,' she promised.

He heard the sounds of music and laughter in the background. 'Your party sounds lively. Wilder than ours.'

'It certainly is. This is a girls night. We are not behaving ourselves. We've eaten most of the food, including your sweet potato fries and they are tasty by the way.'

'Thank you.'

'And now we're continuing to dance, have fun, gossip about you guys and make wishes on Sylvie's new engagement ring.'

'We can't compete with that,' he conceded.

'So you're not causing any trouble with Kyle?'

'Nope. He baited me a couple of times earlier, but I didn't bite.'

'You're the better man.'

'I'm trying to be, but he doesn't make it easy. I think he intends asking you out on a date before you leave town.'

She brightened. 'I have some news to tell you.'

His heart sank. 'You're not going to accept a date with Kyle, are you?'

She laughed. 'No, silly. I'm taking a vacation.'

'A vacation? Where? When?'

'Here in Snow Bells Haven. Starting sort of now. Nancy and the other women convinced me I needed a break, and Penny is happy for me to stay on at the lodge.'

Greg's heart soared. 'That's great, Lucie!'

'I'll tell you all the details in the morning.' She laughed. 'Once I figure them out myself. Perhaps when I wake up I'll blame the champagne for making me take a chance here. Not that I've been drinking much. Two glasses, and one of those was just a sip.'

'So, Nancy and the girls put some thoughts into your head, and now you've decided to take a vacation in town?' He loved that she was staying, but he knew the shenanigans that Nancy and the others got up to.

'Yes, but I've been thinking recently of making a fresh start. Nothing is planned further than an extended visit, just a vacation.'

'I'm happy you're not leaving anytime soon.'

'And if even part of my wish comes true, I may even open a cake shop in town. Anyway, I'll talk to you tomorrow.'

'Okay, Lucie. Enjoy your night. See you in the morning.'

'Goodnight, Greg.'

He didn't want to hang up, but forced himself to click the call to a close. His mind was whirring with hopeful thoughts that Lucie was perhaps going to settle in town.

He should've resisted telling Kyle. He really should, but he was bursting to tell the guys at the party the news.

All the guys were delighted, except Kyle. His reaction wasn't pretty.

Maybe it was the fact that Greg couldn't stop grinning, especially when Kyle realized he was the only one going back to the city.

Kyle pointed an accusing finger at Greg. 'You planned this, didn't you?'

Greg balked. 'Don't blame me. I had nothing to do with it.'

Kyle sneered at him. 'Yeah, right.'

Greg held up his hands. 'Lucie has only just told me.'

Kyle refused to believe him, and as he moved forward to continue berating Greg, it looked like he was going to punch him. He wasn't, but that's how it seemed to Dwayne and Herb and the others watching the face–off unfold.

Dwayne stepped in to defend Greg and body–slammed Kyle on to the rug in a takedown worthy of a champ.

The thud sounded worse than it was, and the speed of it was impressive, especially as Dwayne's bunny paws prevented him getting a tighter grip.

Herb was ready to sit on Kyle's chest to restrain him if he tried to get up and retaliate, but this back–up was unnecessary.

Kyle had the fight knocked out of him. He pushed up from the floor, dusted himself down and tried to look like it didn't bother him one iota that he'd been beaten by a bunny.

Dwayne was a fair match in height and weight against Kyle, and everyone was surprised that Dwayne's judo classes when he was a kid had finally come in handy.

Kyle's cheeks burned with more embarrassment than anger, and he marched off, casting a snippy comment to Greg as he left. 'Having your buddies watch your back won't impress Lucie.'

'Being taken down by an Easter bunny won't impress her either,' Herb shouted at him.

Kyle left the party.

'Anyone got that on their phone?' Herb asked.

No one had, except Nate. He slipped his phone into his pocket and didn't own up to having captured the footage. He thought it would cause nothing but trouble, so why he decided to send it to Nancy he'd never know. He did underline that she wasn't to show anyone. But Nancy had a mind of her own, and soon all the girls at the party were crowded round watching Kyle get a hiding from Dwayne.

'Oh! I felt that.' Nancy winced and so did some of the others.

'Kyle's getting up and trying to look like it didn't faze him,' Penny reasoned, 'so I think the only thing that's hurt is his pride.' She shook her head in dismay. 'What a silly thing to do — picking a fight at Caleb's party. That young man needs to learn how to behave properly.'

Lucie was distressed. 'I feel like this is my fault.'

Nancy put a reassuring hand on her arm. 'No, it's not. This is Kyle's doing.'

Dwayne's wife tried to suppress how proud she was of her husband. 'I didn't know my Dwayne had that type of power in him.'

Several of the women nodded, and Jessica spoke up. 'It's the quiet ones you have to be careful of. Dwayne's such a nice guy, but it seems like he was up for defending Greg.'

'Greg handled the situation well,' said Nancy. 'He didn't start the fight. Kyle seemed set on blaming him for Lucie staying in town.'

'It'll all blow over,' Ana remarked. 'Greg isn't a troublemaker and Dwayne is a sweet guy. Kyle's just rankled that he can't get his own way.'

'Is the sheriff at Caleb's party?' Penny asked Jessica. 'I'm sure he'd calm things down.'

'No, my husband's on duty tonight. He's working extra shifts until we get a new deputy.'

'Nate's there,' said Nancy. 'He won't put up with any nonsense. And he'd have phoned if there was any further trouble.'

Ana smiled and sighed. 'Well, if tussling with an Easter bunny is all the guys have gotten up to, I'm glad we have our own party.'

Nancy spread her arms wide. 'Party on, girls?'

'Oh, yes,' said Ana, and led the way back on to the dance floor.

While the girls partied the night away, Brielle left early because she wanted her beauty sleep so she didn't looked tired for the wedding. No one tried to convince her to stay.

Ana was the second to leave, along with her mother, keeping her promise of a Cinderella curfew.

After hugs all round, the girls waved Ana off, while they continued to enjoy themselves for another hour.

Lucie paused to catch her breath and sipped a glass of pink lemonade. Nancy, Jessica and Virginia joined her and talked about Ana's wedding dress.

'Ana had her final fitting today,' Virginia revealed.

'Ana and Virginia designed the dress,' Jessica told Lucie. 'It's beautiful.'

'She said that she wasn't sure whether to go for white or creamy white fabric,' said Lucie.

'She went with white satin,' Virginia explained. 'Ana wanted a fairytale dress, and that's what we aimed for. The design is based on a vintage pattern that belonged to my grandmother. We updated it, and Ana encrusted the bodice with beadwork that sparkles like stars. We also covered her shoes in matching satin and added beads to those. Her train sweeps beautifully, and should look brilliant in the early afternoon sunlight.'

'It sounds wonderful,' said Lucie. 'It's great that you sewed it yourselves.'

'The women at the quilting bee helped sew the bridesmaids dresses too,' Virginia continued. 'The members also made a special wedding quilt for Ana and Caleb. And Greg has been quilting gifts for their new home.'

'I love Greg's quilted cushions,' said Nancy.

Lucie sipped her lemonade and listened as the chatter swirled around her. Greg's quilting and sewing were included a few times in the conversation, and she found herself thinking about him deeply. She hadn't met a guy like Greg in a long time, probably never.

'I admire the things you do here,' Lucie told them. 'It's a great community.'

'That's why Ana wanted the wedding reception in the community hall so that most folk could attend,' Nancy explained. 'The actual ceremony is being held outside in the garden at the back of the hall. It'll be all set up with a white bridal arch and chairs tied with white chiffon bows. Nate and several other guys, including Zack, are organizing the set–up. Weddings take place there quite often, and Nate and Zack are among the hall's volunteers.'

Lucie took in all the things about the town, and was glad she'd decided to extend her visit. For all the events that went on in the city, most of them had bypassed her, whereas here, she felt part of everything.

Greg was cooking up burgers at Caleb's house. The guys had eaten their way through the potato chips and sandwiches. The party food was adequate for the guys, but nothing fancy like Ana's catering. However, in need of a late night snack, Caleb offered them burgers and fries, washed down with cool beer and hot coffee.

Caleb started cooking, but Greg stepped in to help. 'No cooking Caleb. This is your night. I'll rustle up some burgers and fries.'

It didn't take long for Greg to cook up all the burgers needed, and Dwayne and Herb took charge of the fries and buns.

Soon, the guys were all sitting around eating their food, and more coffee was consumed than beer. Greg had added melted cheese and onion slices to some of the burgers as they sizzled cooking, and the savory aroma filtered out on to the patio where the guys ate their food under the stars.

Caleb sat back and looked up at the velvety night sky. 'A fine last night as a single guy, but I sure am looking forward to being a married man.'

Nate sat down nearby and gazed up too. 'I felt like that the night before I wed Nancy. I was so excited I thought I wouldn't sleep a wink. Don't remember if I slept at all. I just kept waiting until it was time to go and marry her.' The guys listened as Nate continued. 'I didn't have a lot of confidence in myself back then. I was worried she'd change her mind. But when I saw her walk down the aisle looking like a princess, I knew I was the luckiest man in the world. It was the best day of my life, and every day since that I've been married to Nancy.'

Several guys drank a toast to that.

Dwayne joined in the conversation. 'My wife thought I'd be the one to chicken out. But I always thought she was too good for me, and I was the lucky one. I fell for her the first time I ever saw her. Never cared for any other woman since.'

'Folks talk about love at first sight,' said Nate, 'but that's what happened the night I met Nancy. I asked her to dance with me. By all accounts she almost said no, but her girlfriends encouraged her to take a chance on me. And I'm glad she did.'

Caleb nodded thoughtfully. 'I've always loved Ana. We grew up together in this town, and it was like we were waiting for the day when we could get wed.'

'I live in hope,' said Herb, dishing up more fries to the guys. 'I've got a date for the wedding.' He shrugged. 'It's a start.'

'Tell them what happened,' Dwayne encouraged him.

Herb took a long breath. 'She'd been coming into the cafe for weeks. I thought it was because she liked Greg's pancakes.'

Dwayne jumped in to tell the rest of the story. 'But it was Herb that she really liked. I asked her if she'd like to go with Herb as his date to the wedding.'

'I wanted to hide behind the counter,' said Herb. 'I didn't expect him to come right out and ask her. I thought she'd laugh at me, or stomp out. Instead, she said yes, she'd love to.'

'Sounds promising,' Nate told Herb.

Herb nodded. 'She's real pretty, but she's only ever seen me dressed as an elf, a cook and an Easter bunny. I'm hoping she recognizes me when I'm wearing a suit.'

'I'll make sure she knows it's you,' Dwayne assured him.

Herb thumbed over at Dwayne and smiled. 'Listen to my matchmaker, huh?'

The guys laughed.

Caleb smiled at Greg. 'What about you? There's a lot of talk going around town about you and Lucie.'

Tactfully, none of the guys brought up the subject of Brielle.

Greg shifted uncomfortably in his chair, feeling the focus on him, wondering what to say. So he decided to tell the truth. 'I like her, obviously. She's beautiful and sweet and kind, and she's great at baking...'

'And she's single and has extended her stay here,' Nate added.

Greg nodded.

'She's also your date for the wedding,' Dwayne reminded him.

'She sure is.'

'That's your chance to impress her,' said Caleb. 'What's your plan?'

Greg looked vague. 'I don't have one.'

Caleb shook his head. 'You've got to have a plan. Do something that women really like.'

Greg frowned. 'What would that be?'

None of them knew.

Dwayne had a suggestion. 'Just think what any of us guys would like, then don't ever do that.'

Greg frowned. 'There's a weird logic in there somewhere, Dwayne, but I don't quite get it.'

'Don't do anything we would do,' Dwayne summarized.

Greg nodded. 'Okay. I guess I have a plan.'

The last of the girls' party guests headed home. Lucie had somehow acquired two party balloons tied with long ribbons. Several women left with balloons too, and Lucie had shared the Easter eggs she'd collected earlier.

Nancy walked with Lucie out of the function room. 'That was a great night.'

'It was,' Lucie said, starting to feel tired. 'I'd better get some sleep. I'm up early tomorrow morning to help Greg assemble Ana's wedding cake at the community hall.'

Nancy smiled. 'It's wonderful that you're happy to be involved, though I'm guessing that Greg is pleased to have an excuse to ask you to help out.'

Lucie felt a blush warm her cheeks. 'I didn't expect to meet anyone special here.'

'Greg's a great guy.'

'He is, but I came here for the wedding. I wasn't looking for romance. I've been so busy since I arrived, I'm not sure how I feel. I don't want to leave here with a broken heart just because I got caught up in the romance and excitement of the wedding.'

'Since you're staying longer, slow things down, make sure you want to become involved with Greg,' Nancy advised, though her expression didn't convince Lucie.

Lucie frowned at her to tell her the truth.

'Okay, I'm glad I took a chance on Nate. He was from another town, and here for one of our town's summer dances. We met and fell in love that evening, and started dating pretty soon. I've always thought that you know in your heart when you've met someone special. Take things easy with Greg by all means, but honey, don't let the possible love of your life slip through your fingers.'

Lucie smiled, and Nancy gave her shoulders a comforting squeeze.

Nancy spoke in a confiding whisper. 'Is it Brielle that's concerning you?'

'Yes. Greg loved her. What if he still does?'

'It sure didn't look like he gave two hoots about her tonight. There she was, all dressed up and looking beautiful, and Greg walked right past her to get to you. We think the feelings he had for her were wrapped up in thoughts from the past. Once he saw her again, really saw her, he was free of whatever love he'd felt for her.'

'But everyone in town knows about him and Brielle. I don't want to look like he's with me to make her jealous.'

'Credit the people here with plenty of savvy. We can all see that Greg's smitten with you.'

Lucie sighed wearily. 'It's been so long since I cared about a man. Sometimes it's easier to only concentrate on work.'

'It is easier. Love can be complicated. But work doesn't give you a hug after you've had a hard day. Or hold your hand at night for comfort during a winter storm. Or smile at you with loving eyes even on days when you're not looking your best. I wouldn't have missed a day with my Nate.' She paused. 'Nothing worthwhile is ever easy.'

'That's what my aunt used to say to me.'

'I reckon she was right.' She looked at Lucie. 'You miss her, don't you?'

'I miss her a lot.' She smiled at Nancy. 'It's nice to have someone to talk to about things. Everything in my life in New York is so fast–moving. It's all about surface. I'm friendly with some of the people at work, but we don't talk, if you know what I mean.'

Nancy knew exactly what she meant. 'I wouldn't want to burn through years of my life skimming on the surface of it. I'd take a chance and dive right in.'

Lucie sighed. 'The company won't even care when I tell them I'm taking a vacation. Others will happily work my shifts for the extra money, and everything at the bakery will keep on spinning.'

'How long have you worked there?'

'Too long. I tend to get stuck in a rut.'

'Greg says you have a reputation as a troublemaker, but you don't seem like that to me. You seem to have lost your way and need time to find a better road. You're not a mischief–maker.'

Lucie gave her a doubtful glance. 'Kyle might disagree with you.'

'I shouldn't laugh, but oh my, that body–slam from Dwayne...'

'No, we shouldn't laugh,' Lucie said, trying not to giggle.

'I wonder if the guys are still enjoying their party, or if they've called it a night?'

Chapter Seven

The guys were singing their hearts out, enjoying one last rousing song together before heading home.

A cheer rose up as they all wished Caleb a happy marriage.

Caleb smiled at them. 'Cheers, guys! Thanks for coming, and I'll see you at the wedding.'

'Are you going on honeymoon?' Dwayne asked Caleb.

'No, we're planning on taking a short vacation in the summer. Ana and I knew if we went away on honeymoon we'd both be itching to get back to our new house. We're moving in after the wedding. Spending our first night as a married couple under our own roof.'

'You've worked hard on making a real nice home,' Greg complimented Caleb.

'It's a house we've wanted for years. Ideal for raising a family. It's everything we both want. So although we considered going on a honeymoon, we decided we had what we wanted right here. We'll spend time up at the cove with the picnic season starting. And we're planning a housewarming party. I hope you'll all be coming along to that.'

'Wouldn't miss it,' said Nate. 'With you being a painter and decorator, I'm sure your house is looking fantastic.'

'Ana picked out the color scheme and I just did the painting. It's looking amazing.' Caleb smiled. 'Ana knows what she likes, and I seem to like whatever she does. So that works out just fine.'

Greg started to quickly tidy up the kitchen, knowing how to clear chaos easily, throwing stuff in trash bags, and wiping surfaces clean. Dwayne and Herb helped him, and then Nate the other guys mucked in and within ten minutes they'd left the house fit for a groom to wake up to the next day.

Greg had been drinking coffee for most of the evening and wasn't tired as he drove Dwayne and Herb home. He was also anxious about how to impress Lucie.

'Buy her flowers,' Dwayne suggested. 'Something she can pin on her purse or wear on her wrist for the wedding.'

Greg glanced at Dwayne. 'That's a great idea.'

‘The flower shop will have them,’ said Herb. ‘I saw things like that in their window. You know Ana’s color theme for the wedding, and the shop will tell you what’s appropriate.’

‘It’s like giving a girl a corsage if you’re taking her to the prom,’ Dwayne added.

Greg nodded. ‘Yeah, I think she’d like that.’

Dwayne was the first to be dropped off, and received a welcoming hug from his wife at the front door. Greg imagined them talking about what he’d done to Kyle, and smiled to himself.

After dropping Dwayne and Herb off at their houses in the heart of the town, Greg drove home. His house was a bit further out, situated in the middle of a substantial piece of land.

He parked outside and sat for a minute looking at his house. He liked living here, but somehow tonight he felt all on his own and thought how great it would be to come home to someone like Lucie.

These past couple of years he’d felt a longing to settle down, but kept busy with work. He hoped he’d meet someone in town, however, that never panned out for him. And the memories of Brie had still lingered in his thoughts.

He picked up the folder from the back seat of the car and stepped out. There hadn’t been a spare moment to discuss Sylvie’s engagement cake. The easiest way was to email the pictures to her, which he intended to do before going to bed.

He should’ve been tired, but he wasn’t. Standing for a moment, he breathed in the night air. He loved the quiet out here and the scent of the plants and the trees. The air had a wholesome quality that always made him feel like he was home, where he was supposed to be, where he felt settled, except for someone to share it with.

The vast night sky arched above him and the house. He gazed up at it and smiled. He’d seen enough evenings here to sense that the following day was going to be a warm and sunny one. Perfect for the wedding.

He went inside and closed the door to a day that had surprised him in many ways. When he’d left for work that morning, he’d been worried about meeting Brie, and now he realized that in the past few hours he’d barely thought about her. And he was glad. Thinking about Brie had never brought him anything other than heartbreak. Hopefully, things would be different with Lucie.

After emailing the cake details to Sylvie, ironing his shirt and sorting his clothes out for the wedding, he finally went to bed.

From his upper floor bedroom window he had a view of the lights in the town in the near distance. The main street was aglow every night from the street lamps and the store windows, and he wondered if Lucie was sound asleep at the lodge. He was looking forward to seeing her in the morning.

Lucie lay in bed, snuggled up under the patchwork quilt she'd bought from Jessica. Although there was a lovely quilt on the bed, she'd needed some extra comfort, and unfolded the new quilt to put on top.

The previous night she'd slept on the bus, now here she was at the lodge — and planning to stay a while longer.

She snuggled further under the quilt. She'd kept the curtains open so she could gaze out at the garden. The lanterns flickered in the moonlight and it looked quite magical. It was so quiet compared to the city. But the excitement she sensed was something she hadn't felt in a long time — like the feeling of Christmas Eve and knowing it was Christmas Day in the morning. She wondered how she would sleep.

And she wondered about Greg...

Was he asleep? How would their day go in the morning assembling the wedding cake? She'd made several wedding cakes and hoped to do her best to help him. There wasn't a lot to do except transport it safely to the community hall and set it up.

Then there was the wedding to attend as his date. Her heart rate rose just thinking about it all.

Brielle was one of the bridesmaids and that was surely trouble in the making. Not her doing thankfully. Everyone from Ana's mother to Nancy and Jessica wouldn't let Brielle upset Ana's special day.

Brielle had cast Lucie a warning glance at the party. She had the feeling that Brielle wasn't interested in Greg, but resented being overshadowed by anyone. Yes, she definitely sensed trouble brewing from Brielle.

There was also Kyle to contend with. She didn't even want to start thinking about him.

Then she remembered some of the things Nancy had said. Nancy was right about advising her not to waste her life skimming the surface. A rush of determination went through her. It was time to dive right in and make a better life for herself, starting with her date with Greg. No matter what Brielle tried to do to sink her, or any ripples caused by Kyle.

Sink or swim, Lucie, she told herself firmly, before drifting off to sleep.

The early morning sunlight shone in a clear blue sky as Lucie walked to Greg's cafe. Her hair was tied back in a neat ponytail and she'd kept her makeup to a minimum, relying on the waves of excitement inside her to give her cheeks a blush of color. She wore jeans and a white sweater, and felt the warmth from the sun on her face. Not a cloud in the sky. Ana's day was set to be sunny.

The cafe door was open and Greg was busy inside. The aroma of fresh coffee wafted in the air. He looked round and smiled at her as she walked in, and her heart reacted like before, thinking how handsome he looked. He was clean–shaven, hair swept back, wearing a blue shirt and black pants. The sleeves of his shirt were folded up and revealed his strong, lean forearms as he lifted the top layer of Ana's wedding cake from the glass cabinet and placed it down carefully into a white cardboard box on the counter.

'What can I do to help?' she asked.

'If you could wrap the cake tiers when I put them in the boxes, that would be great. Then I'll load them into the car and we'll head up to the community hall. Oh, and we have to remember all the silver decorations and ribbons.' He motioned to where these were.

'I'll put them in one of the small boxes.' She started to wrap the silver bell decorations in tissue paper and rolled up the satin ribbons.

He made sure he didn't break any of the sugar paste flowers from the second tier of the cake as he lifted it into a box. 'Did you enjoy the rest of the party last night?'

'I did. It was so much fun.' She hesitated then decided to clear the air regarding Kyle and Dwayne. 'I eh, saw what Dwayne did to Kyle. Nancy had it on her phone.'

Greg kept his head down, concentrating on the cake. 'Yeah, Nate told us Nancy showed it to all the women at the party.'

'They thought you handled the situation well.'

He looked up. 'They did?'

'Yes, it was obvious that Kyle was spoiling for a fight, verbal or otherwise.' She couldn't stop a small smile forming. 'Dwayne certainly took him by surprise.'

'Dwayne took us all by surprise.' He shook his head. 'I didn't want any trouble at Caleb's party, but it all sort of worked out fine after Kyle left.' He glanced over at her. 'How did Penny react?'

'She thinks Kyle was way out of line. She doesn't blame you.'

Greg nodded. 'That's good to know. I get on well with Penny and I don't want any ructions between us because of Kyle. I supply the lodge with cakes and other food when they have functions. The lodge has catering staff to prepare the regular meals for guests, but they don't cook anything fancy. That's why she keeps hoping Kyle will come home and join them. They could use a professional chef. Penny's husband deals with the admin side of their business. He's not into cooking. He's away at a business convention and won't be here for the wedding.'

Lucie looked out the window. 'It's going to be a lovely sunny day for it.'

'From some of the things Caleb said last night, even if it was a snow storm in winter, he'd be happy to trek through it to marry Ana.'

A wistful feeling swept over her. 'It must be wonderful to have someone love you like that.' The moment she said it, she wished she'd kept it to herself. She looked away, hiding the blush that was starting to burn her cheeks, reaching up to a shelf for more tissue paper. She wasn't quite tall enough and even standing on tip–toe she had to really stretch...

'Let me get that down for you.' Greg stepped close, and she tensed as his body inadvertently pressed against her. She felt the strength in him. Greg didn't look muscle–bound, but all the hard work he did gave him a taut, leanly–muscled build. For a man who said he wasn't into sports, she could be forgiven for thinking otherwise. Greg was fit.

She accepted the tissue paper from him, averting her gaze, hoping he didn't sense the reactions his closeness caused in her. Hiding her feelings was something she'd become accustomed to, but working together in close proximity in the cafe made it difficult to keep to her own space. Not that she wanted to keep her distance from Greg. She was comfortable in his company, and the sparks of attraction she felt led her to hope that he liked her too.

But she had to keep reminding herself that her date with him stemmed from convenience rather than him asking her to go with him to the wedding.

She realized she'd been holding her breath and momentarily lost in her thoughts, so it jarred her when Nate called in to them. 'Morning!'

Lucie turned and looked over her shoulder at Nate, while Greg was still standing near her. Her expression must've shown what she was feeling, because Nate smiled and apologized, thinking they were fooling around. 'Oh! I didn't mean to intrude, folks.'

'No, Nate!' Lucie yelled, inflaming the situation even further. 'You're not interrupting.'

'We're just wrapping up the wedding cake,' said Greg.

Nate wasn't easily fooled, but went along with the pretence that he hadn't interrupted a private moment between them. 'Zack and I are heading to the community hall to set up the chairs.'

'We'll be there with the cake soon.' Greg pointed behind him. 'Coffee's fresh made if you'd like a cup.'

'Thanks, Greg.' Nate waved Zack to come in. 'Come and grab a coffee before we start.'

Greg poured four cups of coffee and they chatted about the wedding.

'Ana's decided to give a showing of her wedding presents at her housewarming party,' Nate explained. 'A lot of the gifts wouldn't fit into the community hall anyway, especially those from Zack and Greg,' he said to Lucie.

'What did you get for them?' She sipped her coffee while they told her.

'Several of us got together to build Caleb a large work shed for his back yard,' Zack began.

'Zack designed it specially to suit Caleb's painting and decorating work,' Greg added, giving the credit to Zack. 'He built most of it too.'

'That sounds like a fine and practical gift.' Lucie started to understand why Ana would show the gifts at the housewarming, especially when Greg told her what he'd bought for them.

'I got them a swing seat for the front porch of their new house.'

‘That’s a lovely idea,’ she said, picturing sitting outside and swinging on it, relaxing after a busy day.

Lucie had bought them a set of vintage cake tins. Ana wanted these for her kitchen, and Lucie found them in a store in New York. She’d sent them a couple of weeks ago, and received a thank you note from Ana and Caleb.

Finishing their coffee, Nate and Zack headed to the community hall, while Greg and Lucie packed the last tier of the cake.

Lucie reached across to add another couple of silver decorations. Her hand brushed against Greg’s and a spark of excitement charged through her. She pulled her hand away and tried to look like he hadn’t affected her like this.

Greg continued to pack the boxes, hoping she didn’t sense how strong his heart was beating just being close to her. He liked Lucie, he really did.

‘I’ll start putting these boxes in the car.’ He picked up the largest box and carried it outside.

She tidied things up and watched him through the cafe window as he loaded up the car. Then he beckoned her to come out.

She got into the passenger seat while he locked the cafe door, and they drove the short distance to the community hall.

Wedding streamers wafted in the light breeze above the entrance as they arrived.

The front door was open and she helped Greg carry the cake boxes.

The main hall was all set up for the wedding reception with white and silver balloons tied with ribbons. There was a stage area, and long tables with white table covers ready for the buffet.

Lucie gazed around. ‘Oh, this looks lovely.’

‘It does,’ he agreed. ‘I can almost sense the excitement in the air.’

They put the boxes down on one of the tables and Greg started to carefully unpack each tier.

Once the three tiers were assembled, Lucie helped him decorate the cake with the silver decorations and ribbons.

‘It’s such a beautiful cake, Greg.’

‘It’s a traditional fruit cake recipe with raisins, currants, sultanas, glacé cherries, nutmeg, treacle and lots of delicious hints of lemon and orange.’

'I love fruit cake.'

'I'll bake one for us.' He blinked, realizing he may have given the wrong impression, or the right impression too soon. Either way he started to fluster and backtrack. 'What I mean is, I'll bake a fruit cake for us to enjoy with a cup of coffee, not bake a wedding cake for us...not that I wouldn't if...what I'm trying to say is...'

'I know what you mean. And I'd love to try one of your fruit cakes. So yes, please do bake one.'

He sighed so hard it sounded in the quiet hall.

Lucie pretended not to notice, but his hands were unsteady and he almost dropped one of the silver bell decorations.

She looked up at him. 'Really, Greg. It's fine.'

He bit his lip and concentrated on adding the fondant flowers to the top tier.

She hardly dared breathe as he placed each flower with their beautiful petals and leaves on to the top as the finishing touch.

He stepped back to look at his work. 'What do you think?'

'It's perfect.'

Greg gazed at her. 'Quite perfect.'

She knew he meant the cake, or did he?

He looked right at her. 'I really have to thank you for helping me — and for being my date for the wedding.'

'Not a real date though, a date as friends.'

He shrugged. 'Yeah, sure. Good friends.'

He wanted to tell her so many things. That he really liked her, that maybe they could go on a proper date. Friends with potential. And he was about to tell her when Nate popped in and called to them.

'Come and take a look at the wedding arch and decorations we've set up in the garden.'

The moment was broken, and as Lucie smiled at Greg, he accompanied her outside to see Nate and Zack's handiwork.

The garden looked gorgeous, all done up like the hall with ribbons and balloons. A white wedding arch was set where the couple would stand to take their vows. Chairs tied with white chiffon bows were lined up to form an aisle where the bride would walk down on the arm of her father.

'What do you think?' Nate asked them.

'Ana and Caleb will love it,' Greg enthused. 'You've done them proud.'

Zack smiled. 'I'm thinking of having something like this when I marry Sylvie. Seeing it all done up, it's ideal for a wedding.'

'It's so pretty.' Lucie admired the arch and gazed around her. The early morning sunlight made everything look bright and fresh. The crocus and daffodils and other flowers in the garden added a touch of lilac, yellow and springtime color. 'Spring is such a wonderful season for a wedding. And summer too, and the colors of autumn can be amazing.' She laughed, realizing she thought that most times of year were ideal to get married.

The guys were smiling at her, especially Greg.

'We had a winter wedding recently,' Nate told her. 'It looked like a wonderland, covered with snow and the trees sparkled with frost.'

Greg and Zack nodded. They'd been guests at that wedding too.

'I was there with Sylvie, and I think that's one of the reasons she was thinking of waiting until later in the year for our wedding,' Zack explained. 'But I'm happy she's going to marry me in the summer. I can't wait to start a new life with her.'

Greg was happy for Zack and Sylvie, but he couldn't help feeling a slight pang of longing for that type of happiness. He watched Lucie wandering around, enjoying being there, and for a moment he wondered if he'd ever stand here with her for their wedding?

'Is the cake all set?' Nate asked Greg.

Greg blinked out of his thoughts and beckoned Nate and Zack inside the hall. 'Yes, come and have a look.'

Nate and Zack admired the cake and complimented Greg on his work.

Zack grinned. 'We'll be getting you to bake our wedding cake, Greg.'

'I'd be happy to.'

'Sylvie got your email with the engagement cake suggestion. She loves it.' Zack gave Greg the thumbs up.

'Great, I'll talk to her about it later.'

With the cake set, Greg drove Lucie back to the cafe.

She hadn't realized there was a sign in the window stating that the cafe was closed all day for the wedding. But it made sense, she supposed. Dwayne and Herb would be busy getting ready, and Greg couldn't do everything on his own and still make it to the ceremony on time.

Greg pulled up outside the cafe. 'Coming in?'

'I thought you were closed for the day.'

'I am, for customers. We're friends. I thought I'd cook you breakfast.'

She perked up at the sound of a delicious cooked breakfast from Greg. 'Are you sure? I could have breakfast at the lodge.'

He was shaking his head. 'How does eggs, bacon, waffles, tomatoes, the works sound to you?'

'It sounds like a lot of trouble to go to for me.'

She was now following him inside the cafe. He locked the door behind them.

'Cooking is easy, Lucie. The only trouble in here is you.'

'I haven't caused any trouble so far this morning,' she argued playfully.

'The day is young,' he told her, starting to heat up the stove. 'Besides, I was thinking of joining you for breakfast.'

'In that case. I'll set the table and make the coffee.'

Greg rustled up a hearty breakfast while Lucie prepared the coffee and set the plates out on a table for two. She noticed the various quilted items in the cafe and told him about Jessica's invitation.

'Last night, Jessica invited me to join in the local quilting bee evening. She said I don't need to be skilled at sewing quilts because the ladies will help me.'

Greg divided the scrambled eggs between them, and added the bacon and tomatoes. 'I hope you'll come along. I'll probably be there.'

She poured the coffee. 'It sounds like fun.'

He scooped the waffles on to their plates. 'It always is.'

They sat opposite each other and tucked into their breakfast.

Lucie pointed her cutlery at her food. 'This is tasty.'

He smiled at her. 'So, what are you doing for the rest of the day, until it's time for the wedding?'

She shrugged. 'I'm not sure. Maybe browse the stores in the main street. There are so many pretty shops.' She gazed around her. 'Though I love this cafe.' She loved the warm, welcoming, atmosphere, the colors Greg had used for the decor — fresh cream, white and yellow, from pale lemon to buttermilk, and the yellow and white gingham table covers. And the quilted wall hangings instead of pictures added splashes of bright colors. 'Did you sew those quilts?'

He sipped his coffee and nodded.

'I'd love to sew little quilts like that. They're so cute, but I bet they're tricky to stitch, especially those neat borders.'

'I start by making the main quilt block. Those are about twenty inches by fifteen inches. Then I sew on the borders, framing the block as if it's a picture. I like to finish it with binding using fabric that brings out the colors of the whole design.'

Lucie was nodding, taking in all the little details. 'I wish I could do that.'

'I'd be glad to show you. If you come along to the quilting bee, we'll make a start on one.'

'Yes.' She sounded enthusiastic. 'I'll buy a fabric bundle from Jessica's shop.'

'You can if you want, but I have a fabric stash that is up to here.' He held his hand up to indicate how high it was.

'Okay,' she said, accepting his offer. 'Maybe you could advise me what colors work well. You seem to have a great eye for color and design.'

He smiled at her. 'I'd be happy to. And speaking of colors, what color is the dress you're wearing to the wedding?'

She blinked. 'It's eh...blue. It's one of the dresses I bought from Jessica.'

'Oh, right. You gave me a glimpse of those in the bag. It was pale blue, wasn't it?'

'Yes,' she said, flattered that he was taking an interest in what she was wearing.

'What about accessories? What color of purse are you planning to take with you?' He smiled and tried to sound casual.

'My purse is sort of creamy white, same as my shoes. I brought these with me as I thought they'd work with whatever color of dress I bought from Jessica's shop. That was my plan — to buy a dress to wear for the wedding here in town rather than bring a load of clothes with me.'

'Creamy white accessories sounds perfect.'

Before she could ask why he was so interested, he collected their plates and cleared the table. 'Another cup of coffee?' he offered her.

'I'll get it.'

While Greg cleared the plates, she poured their coffee.

He sat back down opposite her. 'This used to be a bakery store.' He started telling her about the cafe.

'Really?'

'Yeah, the bakery folks retired and my grandfather bought the premises and made it into a cafe. There's a large garden out back. I've applied for permission to extend the cafe, maybe include a cake counter to display items like the specialist cakes, wedding cakes, that sort of thing. I could use more room here. The cafe has been thriving, and I've made a substantial profit these past two years, so I was thinking of investing some of the money back into the business. Zack's drawn up designs for the building work.'

Greg got up and went over to a drawer behind the counter. 'These are the plans he's come up with. What do you think?'

He brought the plans over and put them on the table. She studied them, trying to figure them out.

He pointed to the paper. 'This is the cafe's front window, and Zack suggested moving everything back to make room for a few more tables. The cake counter would fit neatly in here, and the storeroom would be extended.'

The plans started to make sense and she began to picture the new look cafe. 'I like Zack's layout. This would work, especially as the baking could be separate from the main food cooking.'

'Zack also added patio doors leading out to the garden so that we could put tables out back when the weather was fine. Zack and some of the local building guys would do the work in a week, so there wouldn't be too much disruption to the cafe. Nate and some of the other guys have offered to pitch in and help.'

'You should do this, Greg. It looks wonderful.'

He rolled up the plans and put them away again. 'I'm glad you approve.'

She glanced at him.

'With you being a baker and looking at it from a practical sense,' he was quick to add.

'What do Dwayne and Herb think about your plans?'

'They're well up for it. We're often too cramped in here, especially as trade has increased. Last summer we were really busy with tourists and Christmas was crazy.'

'I bet the cafe looks amazing in summer and at Christmas.'

'It sure does. I'm thinking of having turquoise and white gingham table covers this summer. Last year I had strawberry pink. And you'd love it at Christmas — twinkle lights, Christmas tree, silver tinsel and gingerbread cookies galore.'

'And fruit cake.'

'That reminds me. I'll make a note to buy more glacé cherries from Nancy's grocery store to bake that cake I promised you.'

She smiled at him. 'Sounds delicious.'

Finishing her coffee, she got ready to leave. 'Thanks for breakfast, again.'

'You are more than welcome.'

She headed out. He walked with her and locked the door behind him.

'I'll pick you up at the lodge around two. That'll give us time to drive up to the community hall to see the bride arriving.'

'I'll see you then.' She smiled brightly and started to walk away.

Greg watched her cross to the quilt shop, and waited a moment before hurrying to the flower shop.

Outside the quilt shop she admired the window display, and glanced over her shoulder for a second to see where Greg had gone.

He ducked out of view behind a tree near the ice cream parlor, then made a dash for the flower shop.

The shop was busy with people collecting their flower orders for the wedding, including the type of corsage he had in mind for Lucie. He hoped they had some left, or could make one up for him.

'Hi, Greg,' the flower shop owner said to him. 'What can I get for you?'

'I need a corsage for Lucie. I'm taking her to the wedding, and want to surprise her with the flowers.'

'Do you know what color of outfit she's wearing?' the woman asked.

'Pale blue, with a creamy white purse and accessories.'

The woman smiled, delighted. 'I have something that would be ideal. Creamy white roses.' She selected the corsage and placed it on the counter. The roses were tied with white ribbons. She brought out a roll of pale blue satin ribbon. 'I could add a piece of this to match her dress.'

'Yes, thank you.' The excitement washed over him. Now all he had to do was go home and get showered and dressed.

With the flowers wrapped up carefully, Greg hurried from the shop, keeping a lookout for Lucie. He saw a glimpse of her further along near Jessica's dress shop.

Putting the corsage safely in his car, he drove off home, looking forward to seeing Lucie later.

Chapter Eight

Lucie stepped out of her room at the lodge a few minutes before two in the afternoon. Greg had arrived at reception and smiled when he saw her walk towards him. He had the flower corsage in his hands, and he was smartly dressed in a dark gray suit, white shirt, silk tie and a cream rose buttonhole. His hair had been tamed back from his brow and he looked the most handsome she'd seen him.

'You look beautiful, Lucie.' The words were out before he could restrain the strength of his compliment. His feelings for her were loud and clear. The reception was busy with guests bustling around getting ready to head up to the community hall, but Greg and Lucie only had eyes for each other.

'Nice suit, Greg.' She smiled, genuinely happy to be accompanying him. She hadn't given too much thought to going on her own when she'd accepted Ana's invitation. She'd assumed she would be fine attending the ceremony as a single guest. But it was great to have a partner for the wedding, especially a guy like Greg. She felt comfortable with him, as if she'd known him a lot longer. Some people just fitted together naturally, and Greg seemed really pleased to see her.

The pale blue dress felt special to wear. She wore the single strand of pearls her aunt had given to her for her birthday one year, and had pinned her hair up with a pretty pearl barrette. Her court shoes had reasonable heels and were comfy to wear, especially as there was a dance after the wedding.

Greg handed her the corsage.

She was taken aback. She hadn't even thought of wearing flowers. 'This is lovely!' she enthused.

He helped her pin the corsage on to her purse.

'The ribbon matches my dress.' She looked at him. 'So that's why you were so curious about my outfit.'

He shrugged. 'I wanted to surprise you.'

She admired the flowers pinned to the front of her purse. 'You certainly have.'

He looked outside the entrance. It was packed with cars. 'If you want to wait here, I'll bring my car round to the side of the lodge. It's outside the cafe.'

The sun was streaming in, and she could feel the pleasant heat of the afternoon. 'No, I'm happy to walk to the community hall. It's not far.'

'Are you sure?'

'Yes. It's a lovely day.'

They stepped outside and started to walk together towards the community hall. The sun was warmer than the previous day, and the main street was busy with people heading up to the wedding, all dressed in their finery.

Lucie looked up at the ribbons that were tied to the street lamps. They wafted in the light breeze, and storekeepers had added flowers to their shop window displays in celebration. Silver and white balloons were everywhere, and townsfolk were starting to line the main street where the wedding party were due to drive along.

Lucie shivered with excitement, sensing the anticipation buzzing through the town, like someone had sprinkled happiness into the air.

Greg clasped her hand. 'Are you okay?'

The warmth of his hand sent a further flood of emotions through her. 'Yes. There's such a feeling of excitement. I've never experienced anything like this in the city.'

Greg continued to hold her hand, knowing she was fine, and she made no attempt to break away from him. Again, she felt comfortable with Greg, and innocently holding hands while walking up to the community hall felt totally natural.

'Wait until there's the summer parade. It's even more lively. You'll love it.'

He spoke as if he she would be a permanent resident by then, and strangely, she didn't jolt at the idea. Extending her visit here by two weeks was a start, a short vacation, but with everything that had happened, picturing Snow Bells Haven as her home town felt like something she could do, something real.

Nate and Nancy were the first couple Lucie recognized standing outside the community hall. Nancy had her arm linked through Nate's, and she carried a basket brimming with flower petals ready to scatter when the bride arrived. Both of them were smartly dressed, and it seemed like all the male guests had worn similar flower buttonholes as part of the wedding theme.

Sylvie and Zack were nearby. Lucie loved Sylvie's light floral dress. As Sylvie was a fabric designer, she reckoned the print was her own design. Zack was bandbox handsome standing beside her.

Two women were interviewing people and asking them for quotes. The more mature of the two was the town's local newspaper editor. She was also one of the guests. She'd brought along a staff photo–journalist. The journalist wanted a group photograph of the crowd outside the hall, and she took several pictures of the happy gathering for the next issue of their paper's social news page.

Along from them Lucie noticed Jessica chatting to her husband, the sheriff. Jessica's dress was the palest gray, a few shades lighter than the one Nancy was wearing with elegant lilac accessories. Virginia was there too, although on her own, and wore a blossom pink dress that suited her well.

Caleb stood with his uncle, waiting for Ana.

'Caleb looks happy,' Greg said to Lucie, finding them a place to stand and watch the bride arrive. 'I'm sure I look more nervous than he does.'

Lucie smiled and nodded.

Caleb wore a gray suit that befitted a well–dressed groom. His buttonhole had a spray of greenery with his white flower, as did the one worn by his best man — his uncle.

Caleb's uncle whispered a few words to bolster his nephew's spirits, though this seemed unnecessary. Caleb clearly couldn't wait for his bride to arrive, and kept looking down the main street where the traffic had been cleared to allow the three horse–drawn open carriages to ride along.

Hearing the crowd cheer, Caleb's uncle ushered him inside so that his first glimpse of the bride would be when she walked down the aisle.

'Here they come!' Nate announced, waving to Zack and Greg.

Greg squeezed Lucie's hand reassuringly. 'I volunteered, along with Nate and Zack, to be one of the guys to help the bridesmaids from the carriages. Stay where you are. I'll be right back.'

She smiled at his care for her and willingness to get involved in everything for Ana and Caleb, right down to the last minute duties giving the ladies a supporting hand as they stepped from the carriages.

Nate was in charge of the bride's carriage, leaving Zack and Greg to attend to the other two carriages filled with the bridesmaids. Greg hoped to make it to the second one, but Zack had already stepped forward ready to greet them. This left Greg in charge of the third carriage. His heart sank a little. Brielle was in the third carriage. Despite not wanting to connect with her, he'd have to do his duty.

The bride waved as people cheered her on. A chestnut horse pulled the traditional carriage and the smartly dressed driver sat up front. Beside her, Ana's father sat proudly, smiling at all the well–wishers for his only daughter's special day.

The carriage pulled up outside the community hall, and Lucie got her first glimpse of Ana's beautiful wedding dress. The beadwork sparkled in the sunlight, and the white satin design was fantastic. Ana's hair was pinned up with lots of clips that matched the beaded pearls and crystals on the dress, and her bouquet of white and cream roses, lily of the valley and spring flowers had a trail of greenery and ribbons.

Lucie cheered along with the others as Nate opened the carriage door and helped Ana step down. She loved that Ana's father fussed with his daughter's dress, adjusting the train so it swept unhindered behind her.

Nancy cast a handful of flower petals high into the air and they fell down around Ana, creating a perfect picture. Ana's designated photographer snapped the moment. The woman was armed with a camera as the official photographer and was also capturing special moments on film for Ana and Caleb's wedding memory video.

Zack assisted the bridesmaids and Ana's mother to step from the second carriage. The heliotrope satin of the dresses looked gorgeous, Lucie thought, and their bouquets of lilac, yellow and white flowers were lovely.

Greg held his hand out to steady the bridesmaids stepping down from the third carriage. Their dresses were full–length and it made it easier for them to alight without faltering. A couple of the girls giggled nervously, knowing so many people were watching them. Brielle was the last to leave the carriage. Unlike the others, Brielle exuded confidence, and she was unquestionably beautiful in her dress. Greg had been right. The heliotrope color suited her. She wore her blonde hair swept up in a chignon pinned with lilac pearl clips, and her makeup emphasized her blue eyes and model–like features.

Greg did the right thing, offering his hand for support. He tried not to meet her gaze, but when she spoke to him, he instinctively looked at her as she stepped down and stood close to him. 'Thank you, Greg. You're looking handsome in your suit.'

His body tensed, waiting on the pithy comment that would spoil her compliment, but instead she smiled at him and walked on to join the other bridesmaids.

Lucie saw what happened, but as Greg's back was towards her, she hadn't seen his tense expression. Instead, she felt an unwanted pang of jealousy that she tried to shake off.

As if sensing Lucie's reaction, Greg spun round and saw her looking at him. More importantly, he caught the hint of unease on her face, before she forced herself to smile.

He hadn't done anything wrong, she told herself firmly. Nothing at all. Brielle was a tease, a beautiful distraction, and knew how to wield her looks to full effect.

Greg walked quickly to Lucie, wanting to be by her side, to brush off the feeling Brie had created in that brief moment.

Neither of them mentioned Brielle as they fell in step with each other and walked into the hall to take their seats in the garden.

Everyone was seated and ready for the wedding ceremony. Caleb stood at the arch waiting for Ana. The music started playing to announce the arrival of the bride. Looking radiant, Ana walked down holding on to her father's arm.

Caleb couldn't resist glancing over his shoulder to take a peek at his wife–to–be. It was obvious from his expression that he loved her more than anyone, and she smiled at him as she approached.

Greg sat next to Lucie, glancing at her now and then, smiling, and she smiled back, as Ana and Caleb exchanged their vows.

At one point Greg reached over and took Lucie's hand, giving it a gentle squeeze. She made no attempt to pull away, and they listened to the last few moments of the ceremony holding hands.

A cheer and applause rose up as Caleb kissed his new bride, and the couple embraced for the first time as man and wife.

It was only when they needed to applaud that Lucie let go of Greg's hand. Then he escorted her into the hall where the reception was due to begin after the new couple had their photographs taken in the garden.

'They're a beautiful couple,' Lucie remarked as Greg was about to get them a glass of champagne to toast the married couple when they came in.

Nate came hurrying over to Greg. 'Ana's asked if you'll come out to have your photo taken with her and Caleb and some of the others.'

'I'll wait here,' Lucie said to Greg.

Nate frowned. 'No, Lucie, you're included.'

'Oh,' she said, not realizing she was to be pictured together with Greg, as well as three other couples, all close friends of the bride and groom.

With Ana and Caleb in the middle of the picture, Greg and Lucie stood to one side of them along with Sylvie and Zack. And on the other side were Nate and Nancy with Jessica and the sheriff.

'Everyone smile,' the photographer called to them, but it was unnecessary because they were all grinning happily. She then captured them on video as well.

Ana hugged Greg as he congratulated her.

'I saw the cake as we walked in,' she confided to him. 'It's perfect. Thanks for everything, Greg.'

He hugged her again. 'I'm so happy for you and Caleb.'

Caleb shook Greg's hand and gave him a manly hug. 'You've been a true friend to Ana and me.' He glanced at Lucie, and then smiled at Greg. 'I hope you find the type of happiness I have.'

Caleb gave Lucie a hug, thanked her for coming along to the wedding, and hoped she'd go to their housewarming party soon.

'I'd love to,' said Lucie. It was great to feel part of a community like this, even though it was slightly overwhelming. But she could get used to this type of open–hearted friendship. Being part of a town like this would be great.

Lucie stood with Greg and watched Ana and Caleb have more photos taken in the garden. The sun shone bright and there was only the lightest breeze, barely felt because the trees shielded them.

The couple posed under the branches of one of the trees in full blossom, and Lucie had the strangest feeling. A sense of longing, of maybe finding where she truly belonged, with people she seemed to fit in with easily. They'd made her welcome from the moment she'd arrived, and she couldn't imagine feeling this excited and yet content anywhere else.

New York crossed her mind, and in that second, her heart lurched. Even the thought of going back to her old life jolted her uneasily. She'd only just left her life in the city, and now she wanted to drag her heels for as long as she could to avoid going back anytime soon.

As the guests filtered inside the hall, Greg chatted to Lucie about the wedding and other occasions he'd celebrated at the community hall — from the harvest festival events to Christmas parties.

'And this is where we hold the quilting bee each week,' Greg added.

'They're going to cut the cake!' Nancy called to Greg and Lucie. They were the last to leave the garden. They'd been standing talking and so wrapped up in each other that they had to hurry in to see the cake being cut.

Lucie laughed as Greg grabbed her hand and they ran into the hall. It looked lovely with the buffet tables all set up.

Ana and Caleb held the knife, hands together, to officially cut their wedding cake.

A cheer rose up, and champagne and lemonade toasts were enjoyed by all those present.

Greg handed Lucie a glass of champagne. 'To the happy couple.'

Lucie tipped her glass against his and smiled.

Dwayne and his wife waved over to them. They were standing with Herb and his new girlfriend.

Lucie barely recognized the guys without their bunny outfits. And then she felt someone watching her, eyes boring into her back. She glanced round and saw Brielle staring coldly at her. Lucie pretended not to notice and swept her gaze past Greg's ex to look around. She noticed Kyle with his Aunt Penny, but looked away before he saw her.

One of the wedding caterers Ana had hired, expertly cut a tier of the cake and pieces were handed out to the guests. Although Greg and others had volunteered to help with the catering, Ana wanted all her guests to enjoy the wedding reception without having to cook. This especially included Greg. He was always helping her out.

The buffet was a hearty feast including roast chicken, baked ham, salad, fresh fruit, cheese and pickles, rustic bread and an array of sweet treats from deep baked apple pie with whipped cream to chocolate gateau and strawberries and ice cream.

Greg gave Lucie a piece of cake.

She bit into the sweet icing and then tasted the rich fruit cake. 'This is delicious, Greg.'

'I'm still going to bake you a fruit cake,' he promised.

A voice spoke over Greg's shoulder. 'Compliments on the wedding cake, Greg. It tastes great and looks beautiful.'

Greg was surprised to see Kyle standing there.

Before Greg could respond, Kyle offered him his hand. 'I don't want any bad feelings about what happened recently.'

Greg hesitated, then reached out and shook hands with Kyle.

Kyle smiled at him. 'It's a small town, and although we've never been best buddies, we've gotten along okay.'

Greg had to agree on that. 'We have. And I don't want to upset Penny.'

'Neither do I, especially as I'll be hanging around town for a bit longer than I originally planned. My uncle has extended his business trip, so I'm staying to help her run the lodge. Mainly the cooking.'

Lucie was glad that Greg and Kyle were going to try and get along, and yet...she wasn't sure that Kyle's motives were as straightforward as he was telling them.

Kyle flicked a glance at Lucie, gauging her reaction, and seemed pleased to see her smile back at him. What else was she supposed to do? She couldn't stand there looking awkward, and surely it was better that they all tried to get along.

Unfortunately, Kyle took their friendship pact one step too far, too quickly. He smiled at Lucie and held out his hand, not to shake, but to step on to the dance floor.

'Would you care to dance with me?' said Kyle. Couples were starting to join Ana and Caleb as they enjoyed their first dance together as a married couple.

Lucie looked at Greg, and he seemed as unsure as she was, but to refuse felt awkward, so she accepted Kyle's hand.

In her heart she was disappointed that her first dance at the wedding wasn't going to be with Greg. And judging by Greg's expression he felt the same, like he'd missed out on the chance to ask her first.

Greg watched Kyle take Lucie in his arms and start to waltz with her. He hated to admit it, but Kyle was a capable dancer and they looked like a well–matched couple. Kyle's dark suit emphasized his tall, broad–shouldered, rangy build, and Lucie was so beautiful. Yes, he thought, his heart sinking fast, they were a fine match, just like Sylvie and Zack who were dancing near them. He felt slightly nauseous, as if he'd taken a realistic step back and saw Lucie in proper perspective. She was too good for him. He was lucky that her kind nature had brought her into his world. He cringed, thinking how he'd taken advantage of her willingness to help with the cooking at the cafe. How dare he do a thing like that to a young woman new to town and only here for the weekend wedding. And then he'd asked her to get up early to help assemble the wedding cake. What had he been thinking? But when they'd held hands, he sensed that she was comfortable with him. He jolted. Maybe that was the answer. Lucie didn't think of him as a potential boyfriend. She was like Ana and Sylvie and other women at the quilting bee. He was the guy you were friends with while you dated the guys you intended to marry. How could he have been so wrong? No wonder he was still single in a town renowned for romance. Geez! Here he was at another wedding as a single guy with no prospects of settling down.

'Are you okay, Greg?' Dwayne's familiar voice interrupted his destructive thoughts.

Greg looked round at him. Clearly, he wasn't okay.

'Come on, buddy. Let's get you a coffee and a crepe.' Dwayne put his arm around Greg who looked like his world had sunk like a flattened soufflé. Greg let Dwayne lead him over to one of the buffet tables.

Herb was by Dwayne's side in seconds offering back–up. 'Is Greg all right?'

Dwayne whispered to Herb. 'Something must've happened between him and Lucie. He looks like his hopes have crumbled like a cookie.'

Greg heard what they said, but didn't have the impetus to care. They were probably right.

Herb nudged Dwayne. 'Lucie's dancing with Kyle.'

Dwayne's caring expression for Greg morphed into a tiger's snarl when he looked at Kyle. 'What's he doing dancing with her?' he snapped.

'Calm down.' Herb pressed a restraining hand on Dwayne's chest, worried his friend was going to barge on to the dance floor and rescue Lucie from Kyle's possessive clutches. 'They're just dancing.'

Dwayne wasn't happy. 'He's smooth–talking her. Look at the way he's dancing, as if he's good at it.'

'Kyle is a good dancer,' said Greg.

Herb gave Greg a rousing punch on the shoulder. 'Get in there, bud, and ask her to dance with you.'

Greg shook his head. 'I can't dance for toffee.'

Dwayne and Herb exchanged a look. There was no point in trying to bolster Greg's confidence. He could cook, bake, sew and grow pumpkins, but when it came to dancing, Greg had no sense of rhythm and always looked like he was dancing to a whole different tune.

Dwayne decided to rally him on anyway. 'It doesn't matter. Most guys can't dance great. I can't, and Herb here, well...he can waltz but he sure can't shimmy.'

As if to prove Dwayne wrong, several couples danced past looking well capable of waltzing around the floor including Nate and Nancy, Jessica and the sheriff, and Sylvie and Zack.

Herb urged Greg to eat something from the buffet, diverting his gaze from the happy couples dancing. 'Have a slice of pie. Dwayne will get you a coffee. Pie always cheers you up.'

'Put a crepe on the side,' Dwayne whispered to Herb. 'He loves those.'

Greg wasn't hungry. Even a mouthful of crepe couldn't buck him up. He looked at his two buddies, and tried not to weigh them down with his woes. 'How's your date going with your new girl?' he asked Herb.

'Terrific. She's agreed to go on another date with me tomorrow. There's a picnic party at the cove.'

'That's great, Herb. I'm pleased for you.'

'What's bugging you?' Dwayne came right out and asked Greg.

Greg blinked, snapping out of his deep thoughts. 'Look at Lucie with Kyle. They seem like a well–matched couple, don't they?'

'Nooo,' Dwayne sounded emphatic. 'She's just being nice. She keeps looking over here at you.'

Greg bucked up. 'Does she?'

Herb agreed with Dwayne. 'Yep. I bet she's hoping you'll man–up, despite being a rotten dancer, and rescue her from Kyle.'

Greg viewed the situation in a whole new light. 'You think?'

Dwayne put a reassuring hand on Greg's shoulder. 'Yeah. Lucie came here with you. She's not into Kyle, but she's too sweet and kind to tell him.'

Herb nudged Greg and took the plate of pie and crepe off him. 'Go on, go and get her.'

At that moment the music changed from a waltz to something far more lively.

'They're going to do a circle dance,' said Dwayne. 'You can handle that, Greg. No one knows whether they're coming or going when the music gets faster. Lucie won't realize you can't dance until she's exhausted and glad to sit down and enjoy the buffet.'

Greg straightened his shoulders. This seemed like a plan. And over he went to Lucie and tapped Kyle on the shoulder. 'Mind if I cut–in?'

Greg's plan would've worked if it hadn't been for the video photographer requesting they play another waltz so she could film Ana and Caleb dancing. 'I want to make sure I've got enough footage of them waltzing and everyone dancing with them.'

The guests were happy to oblige.

And so as Kyle stepped aside and handed Lucie politely to Greg, not only was it immediately apparent to Lucie that Greg lacked any dancing prowess, it was now going to be highlighted in the wedding video.

Chapter Nine

Realizing Greg was floundering on the dance floor, Dwayne asked his wife to dance, and Herb pulled his girlfriend along beside them. They tried their best to cover Greg's attempts to waltz smoothly or at least in time to the music. Failing on all levels, from leading Lucie in the wrong direction and almost bumping into Nate and Nancy, to stepping on her toes and pausing to apologize and ensure she was okay, Greg's dancing was mildly entertaining.

Ana smiled at him, knowing he'd never been able to dance well, and encouraged him to continue despite disrupting the flow of the waltz around the floor.

'You're doing fine,' Lucie lied.

He waltzed with her. 'You blush when you're telling lies, Lucie.'

'Okay, so smile like you're having fun, and let me lead.'

Greg forced a smile. 'I thought you were leading. I'm clinging on for dear life.'

She laughed, and it looked like they were enjoying themselves. She was sure of this because as they danced past Brielle those cold blue eyes glared at her.

'Is this an extra long song or am I just aware of every note?' Greg asked Lucie.

'It's nearly finished,' she assured him. 'Just keep turning and then dip me when we stop. Make it look like a flourish at the end.'

'I can do a flourish. Hold on tight.' He looked so serious.

'Remember to smile.' Her own smile was tense, trying to force them in the right direction. Leading Greg was hard. He was a lot stronger than her. She could feel the muscles in his shoulder as she kept her hold steady.

Greg beamed a smile, and as the music faded, he dipped her with a flourish and leaned down as if he was going to kiss her into the bargain. His lips paused a breath away from hers, and she gazed up into his gorgeous dark eyes, lost in one intense moment between them.

Forcing himself not to give in to temptation, he lifted her up and set her carefully upright. Their bodies were still close, with his strong arms wrapped around her waist ensuring she didn't fall from his grasp.

Unless it was her imagination, everyone was staring at them. She glanced around. Nope. They were staring all right. It wasn't due to Greg's lack of dancing ability. Oh, no. The expression on the faces watching them showed it was the fact that they'd almost kissed, and clearly everyone sensed the attraction between them.

'I think you should have that crepe now, Greg,' Dwayne advised him.

'And a cold glass of lemonade,' said Herb.

'That's a great idea, guys.' Greg smiled at Lucie. 'Shall we?'

Lucie smiled and linked her arm through Greg's and let him lead her over to the buffet.

Neither of them acknowledged their near kiss, and sipped their lemonade. Champagne was available, but Lucie preferred to keep a clear head right now, especially as her heart was pounding from what had just happened.

'Drink up you two,' Nate called to them. 'The circle dancing is about to start.' He beckoned them to join in, and there was no sitting this dance out.

Taking another few sips of the lemonade, Greg led Lucie back on to the dance floor. They held hands, and then joined hands on either side with Nate and Nancy.

Lively music started and they were off, whirling around the dance floor, without a care of keeping in time or doing the right steps. There was no right or wrong in the fast–moving circle dances — just a lot of people having fun together.

In the midst of them all, Ana and Caleb crossed hands and he swirled his bride around and around, with laughter ringing throughout the hall and those still standing at the buffet clapping in time to the uplifting music.

Lucie couldn't remember having as much fun in years. She smiled at Greg and he grinned back at her. Ana's wedding video would be filled with great memories, and Lucie was glad to have memories like this of her own. Snow Bells Haven was a wonderful town, but it was the people that made it great.

In need of some refreshment after all their dancing, Lucie and Greg went over to enjoy the buffet and catch their breath. Lucie helped herself to the roast chicken and salad, while Greg opted for a selection of cheese, pickles, with tomato relish and rustic bread.

Greg poured them both a cup of coffee. 'I'm saving myself for a slice of that apple pie and whipped cream.'

'I'll second that, especially if we throw in a few strawberries and a scoop of ice cream.'

'Sheer indulgence, but that's what celebrations like this are for — having fun, eating tasty food, enjoying great company, and making a total fool of yourself on the dance floor.'

Lucie smiled at him. 'Your dancing will be one of the highlights of the wedding video.'

'That bad, huh?'

Lucie ate a mouthful of savory salad and tried not to laugh.

'You're laughing, Lucie,' he scolded her jokingly.

She shook her head and continued to suppress her giggles.

'Having fun?' Sylvie said to them. Zack was with her. He was carrying their food plates while Sylvie had their coffee cups.

'Lucie is enjoying mocking my embarrassing waltz,' Greg told them.

Zack burst out laughing. 'Definitely one for the archives, Greg.'

Greg smiled at him. 'Thanks for the support, Zack.'

And then they all laughed together.

'Want to join us?' Greg offered.

There was a lack of vacant tables, so Sylvie and Zack were glad to accept.

Lucie budged up with Greg and the foursome shared the table to eat their food.

Sylvie smiled at Greg. 'I love your idea for the engagement cake.'

'I'll personalize it with your names iced on top,' said Greg. 'And I'll add extra fondant flowers, like the colors of the ones on the dress you're wearing.'

Sylvie was delighted. 'That would be wonderful.'

'I'll have it ready in time for your party next weekend,' Greg promised. 'I'm sure Lucie here will help.'

Lucie nodded firmly. 'I'd love to.'

Sylvie smiled at her. 'It really is great that you're staying in town for a vacation. I could never imagine living in the city again. Snow Bells Haven feels like home.' She thumbed at Zack. 'Especially because of this guy here.'

Zack beamed a loving smile at Sylvie, and for a moment, Lucie pictured if this type of happiness would happen for her.

'I showed Lucie the architectural plans you made for the cafe,' said Greg. 'She thinks the design would work well.'

Lucie jumped in to add a comment. 'The cake counter is a great idea, and the patio doors leading on to the garden is a perfect way to extend the cafe.'

'It wouldn't be too hard to do,' Zack explained. 'The original structure of the building, when it was a bakery, is still more or less there. All we'd need to do is restructure part of it and refresh the interior. The patio doors are new, but they could be installed in a day. We'd work quickly, get it all done in a week.'

'I was thinking of asking Caleb to paint and decorate the interior,' Greg added.

Zack nodded. 'Sounds ideal.'

'So if we're all in agreement, when would be a suitable date to start the work?' Greg asked him.

'I could get things organized to start a few days after our engagement party,' said Zack. 'I've got time on my schedule, and I'm working with a couple of building guys who would be happy to do the work. All the material we need can be sourced locally. I'll order beams from the timber yard. The patio doors can be purchased here too. All we're really talking about is the labor, and as I'll be mucking in with Nate and others, we'll get it sorted.'

'Great. I'll let you push ahead with it then.'

Zack nodded, and tucked into his baked ham and salad.

'Nancy says I can put items from the cafe in her storeroom for safe keeping, and the diner is sure to take extra food stuff that isn't used. Nothing needs to be wasted, and that will allow me to keep the cafe open until the last minute.' Greg appreciated having Nate and Nancy's grocery store next door, and the diner one door along. They'd always helped each other out.

With the plans set for the cafe's refurbishment, the conversation veered back to Sylvie and Zack's engagement.

'I hope you'll come to our engagement party,' Sylvie said to Lucie.

'I'd love to, thanks.'

'We're having it here in the community hall,' said Sylvie.

After finishing their food, the foursome got up to join in the dancing. The music and the company was lively.

Lucie kept looking around her, committing it all to memory. All of Ana and Caleb's guests were having a great time, and as the evening wore on, Lucie felt elated rather than tired. Every now and then she'd sit down with Greg for refreshments, and later they wandered outside into the garden to breathe in the calm night air.

The wedding arch and chairs were still set up and wouldn't be cleared away until the morning. Greg and Lucie sat down, sipping long tall glasses of iced lemonade, and took a breather from the dancing.

Twinkle lights were draped around the edges of the garden, and tiny lanterns highlighted the blossom on the trees. Everything had a glow to it, and the evening sky shone with stars.

Lucie gazed up at it. 'The sky is so clear here. I've never seen so many stars.'

Greg looked up too. 'They're always there. You just can't see them like this in the city.'

'I feel like I've missed so much, that I've been living in the wrong place for most of my life. All of it in fact.'

'You've never lived anywhere but New York?'

'No. It always seemed to offer so many variations of things to do, and it does, but this feels like...' She shrugged.

'Like it could be home?' he suggested.

'Yes. Though it's a scary thought to leave everything behind and move here. I'd need to find a job, somewhere to live...'

'People here would help you.'

She looked at him. 'I know. The people I've met here are great, like friends I've known for years.' She paused. 'I called the woman I share my apartment with and told her that I was staying longer. She's happy because she gets to enjoy some private time with her guy.'

'You said they're getting married soon?'

'They are. The apartment is rented furnished so most of the items aren't mine.'

'Packing up would be easy for you.'

She nodded, suddenly feeling quite overwhelmed at the idea of doing something like this so quickly.

Greg noticed her tension. 'You don't need to think about that right now.' He glazed up at the sky again. 'Nights like this are meant for relaxing.'

'And dancing.'

'A lot of dancing.' He stood up and offered her his hand. 'Shall we?'

Lucie took his hand and they walked together into the hall and joined in the dancing.

They were twirling around to upbeat music when Nate came hurrying over to Greg. 'There's a skirmish in the kitchen.' He pointed to the kitchen area at the back of the community hall. 'The caterers have gone home, but we'd run out of fries, so Dwayne and Herb offered to cook some up.'

'So what's wrong?' said Greg.

'Kyle insisted on helping them.' Nate gave Greg and Lucie a look like Kyle was causing trouble. 'Dwayne had him in an arm–lock when he went to take over the deep fryer.'

Greg dashed through to the kitchen closely followed by Lucie and Nate.

They could hear the noise of raised voices as they approached the community hall's small catering kitchen.

Dwayne had Kyle in a solid arm–lock and was attempting to march him out of the kitchen while Herb held the door open.

Kyle's shoes were scuffing on the floor and he was refusing to go without putting up a struggle.

Lucie put her hand up to her mouth to suppress a...she hated to admit it, a loud guffaw. Seeing Kyle wriggle to get free looked preposterous. It didn't seem like Dwayne was hurting him, just restraining him and trying to put him out of the kitchen for his own safety. And she'd only just noticed that Dwayne still had the dark whiskers drawn on his face from wearing the bunny outfit. He'd wiped the white tip from his nose, but the whiskers were still there. Despite wearing a smart suit, he'd retained a cute bunny look.

Meanwhile, Kyle continued to struggle.

'Kyle's tipsy. He's a hazard in the kitchen,' Dwayne shouted to Greg. 'He nearly set the deep fat fryer alight.'

'He's a stubborn fool,' Nate muttered, helping to peel Kyle's hand from the door handle where he gripped it to stop them throwing him out.

'Kyle's been drinking too much champagne,' said Herb.

'Let's get him out back into the fresh air.' Greg grabbed Kyle's other arm and together with Dwayne they wrestled Kyle outside into the garden.

Whatever fight Kyle had left in him faded in the cool night air. One deep breath of it and he stopped struggling and folded like a napkin on to the grass.

'Sit him up on one of the chairs.' Greg pulled him up and Dwayne lifted him on to a chair. Kyle flopped down, breathing deeply.

'I'll get him a cup of coffee.' Lucie rushed off to get it.

There was no coffee ready in the kitchen, so she hurried through to the buffet and poured a cup, strong and black.

Nancy came rushing over to Lucie. 'I heard that Kyle was causing trouble in the kitchen.'

'It's all under control. Kyle's had too much champagne. I'm taking him a coffee outside. Greg and the guys are with him.' Lucie looked over to where Ana was dancing with Caleb. 'We don't want Ana to know or upset her wedding.'

Nancy seemed unperturbed. 'There's always a ruckus at a wedding. If Kyle causing a calamity in the kitchen is all it is, I'd say that's fine.'

Brielle was eyeing them from further along the buffet table. Lucie gave Nancy a knowing look.

Nancy made a show of pretending they were talking about Ana's dress. 'The beadwork on the satin was gorgeous, and I love the bridesmaids dresses.' She smiled at Brielle. 'That color really suits you.' She then went over to chat to Brielle while Lucie hurried away with the coffee.

Dwayne and Herb ran into the kitchen to cook the fries, while Lucie went outside with the coffee.

Nate took the cup from her and handed it to Kyle. 'Drink this up.'

Kyle sipped it, still slumped on the chair.

'He's calmed down,' Greg whispered to Lucie, 'but Nate's going to take him back to the lodge.'

'No, I'll be fine,' Kyle objected, standing up while drinking the coffee. 'I'll go sit with my Aunt Penny and enjoy the rest of the party.'

Kyle sounded like he meant it, so Greg and Nate nodded to each other and they all went back inside.

'You go along with Nate,' Greg said to Lucie. 'I want to check on the guys in the kitchen.'

She knew he was going to help them make the fries. 'Want some help?'

'You shouldn't be cooking wearing a pretty dress like that.'

'I won't mess it up. Come on. We'll get those fries ready in quick time. Dwayne and Herb have probably got them cooked by now.' She paused. 'Why does Dwayne still have whiskers drawn on his face?'

'He made a mistake again and used the marker pen from the cafe. It's indelible ink, doesn't wash off easily. It'll fade the next time he shaves.'

Lucie laughed.

Greg headed into the kitchen with Lucie and together with the guys they served up a whole heap of fries for the buffet.

Ana was at the buffet with Nate. She smiled and shook her head at Greg. 'You weren't supposed to be cooking at my wedding. You're here to enjoy yourself.'

Greg spread his arms wide. 'Nothing I love more than cooking, Ana.'

Ana hugged Dwayne and Herb. 'You two guys are great.'

With guests coming over for hot fresh fries and coffee, the evening continued on with lots more dancing and fun.

During one of the fast–moving circle dances, Brielle wangled her way in and held hands with Greg and the sheriff. With Lucie on one side of him and Brielle on the other, Greg danced around with both of them. He glanced a few times at Lucie, as if wondering what he could do. To let go before the music was finished would break the entire circle and mess things up for everyone. Lucie pretended it didn't bother her that Brielle had intervened, and that in itself seemed to irk Brielle.

When the music finished Brielle gasped, catching her breath and threw her arms around Greg in a supposedly friendly hug, like quite a few people were doing. Greg was forced to let go of Lucie's hand as Brielle enveloped him, laughing and giggling.

'That was fun!' said Brielle.

Dwayne swooped in, spoiling Brielle's plan. 'How about the next dance with me, Brielle? I haven't danced with any of the bridesmaids yet.'

Brielle smiled tightly. 'Thanks, Dwayne, but I promised the next dance to...' she looked around for the nearest target and spotted him. 'Kyle.'

Hearing her call his name, Kyle looked round, and seeing Brielle smile at him, he happily escorted her for the next dance, a slower paced waltz.

Lucie wanted to warn Greg that Brielle was up to something, but didn't want to sound jealous.

Greg shrugged at Lucie. 'I know it's a waltz, but would you like to dance?'

Lucie stepped into his arms and this time she let him lead as they made their way out of step around the floor.

'Either I'm getting better at waltzing, or you're getting better at adapting to my lack of rhythm.'

'You're getting better at waltzing.'

'I can always tell when you're lying, Lucie.' He smiled and pulled her that little bit closer to him as they danced on.

Kyle danced past them with Brielle. Kyle acknowledged them, but Brielle treated them as if they were invisible.

Lucie looked at Greg. 'Nancy and Ana were saying earlier that Brielle has changed since she was last here. Nancy said she's not the girl she used to know. She's a lot less...'

'Likeable?' Greg suggested.

'Something like that. People change though, especially if they're in the city for a few years.'

He frowned as he watched Brielle waltzing with Kyle. 'I don't understand why she came back here, even for Ana's wedding, if she felt this way about the town. It's not like she's particularly close to Ana these days. Ana invited her because she was part of a group of friends from school, and they'd kept in touch at Christmastime, exchanging cards, that sort of thing.'

Lucie took a deep breath. 'Maybe Brielle came back because of you. To see you.'

She felt his body tense, and even the grip he had on her hand tightened, as if she'd jolted him with her suggestion.

'I doubt that.' He sounded like he was telling the truth, but now she wished she hadn't even mentioned it. He almost stepped on her toes. 'Let's sit the rest of this one out.'

Lucie nodded, and let him lead her over to get glasses of iced lemonade.

She sipped her drink. 'I didn't mean to spoil our fun.'

He sat close beside her. 'You didn't. I'm just...I'll be glad when Brie leaves town. She makes me feel uneasy. I don't believe for one second that she cares about me. But I think she'd like me to believe she does. She's playing games. She used to do that. Not everyone saw that side of her. She has changed, but not as much as Nancy and Ana think.'

'The night's almost over.' She was trying to reassure him, but this had the opposite effect.

'I don't want it to be. I wish I could enjoy it all over again with you. I'm happy here with you, Lucie. I can't dance, I mess things up and say the wrong things.' He looked at her. 'But I can't remember the last time I felt so happy.'

He leaned close, gazing at her, and for a moment she thought he was going to kiss her. Instead, he restrained himself, realizing he'd almost overstepped the mark.

Lucie's cheeks were burning, first from excitement thinking Greg was going to kiss her, from her heart racing trying to decide if she'd let him, and from embarrassment knowing that several of the guests had seen them almost kiss. She had wanted to kiss Greg, and yet, was it appropriate so soon, and in front of everyone?

'Sorry, I won't step out of line,' he apologized.

'That's okay, we're both needing time to get to know each other.' She only half believed what she was saying. She felt she knew Greg well, even in a short time. He was what he appeared to be — a nice guy. A really nice guy, lacking in confidence at times, and yet full of strength when it mattered. 'For what it's worth, this is the best night I've had in a long time.'

Greg squeezed her hand and was going to offer her more lemonade when Nate and the sheriff came over to him.

'We're about to tie the wedding bells to Ana and Caleb's carriage ride home,' the sheriff confided. 'We're heading outside now.'

'Oh, right.' Greg put his glass down. It seemed like they'd made a prearranged agreement to get the newlyweds carriage ready for them leaving.

Nate whispered to Lucie. 'Head over to where Nancy and Jessica are standing.'

Lucie nodded, feeling the excitement build as they organized a great send–off for Ana and Caleb.

Greg smiled at Lucie. 'I'll see you outside in a few minutes.'

Lucie saw Nancy and Jessica and several other women chatting to Ana, but as she headed over to them, a disturbance near the side of the stage area caught her attention. She heard giggling and a man's raised voice. Couples were continuing to dance unaware of what was going on.

Lucie went over to take a peek and was surprised by what she saw.

The bridesmaids had Dwayne pinned down on a chair. Brielle was in charge of whatever they were doing to him. Judging by his flailing legs as four of the girls held him steady, whatever they were up to wasn't to his liking.

Brielle wielded a makeup cleanser pad that she'd taken from her purse. 'Hold him down, girls. This won't take long. Oh, hush, Dwayne. Stop whining. You look ridiculous.'

At that moment Dwayne's wife rushed past Lucie. 'Get your hands off my husband, Brielle.'

Brielle smiled sweetly. 'I'm just using cleansing lotion to wipe off his cute little whiskers.'

Dwayne's wife stood with her hands on her hips. 'I'm asking you nicely, Brielle. I won't ask you again.' There was a warning tone in his wife's voice.

Brielle stepped back. 'Fine. He can look like a dork if you're happy with that.'

Dwayne made his bid for freedom. Two of his whiskers were missing and the others were smudged. He touched his face. 'Do I look a mess?'

'No, honey,' his wife assured him, leading him away. 'You look fine. Come on.'

He sniffed the air around him. 'I smell like a perfume counter.'

'I'll make you hot chocolate when we get home. That'll smell so much nicer.' She squeezed his arm. 'But we're getting ready for Ana and Caleb leaving. Greg and Nate are outside decorating their carriage.'

Dwayne perked up and they hurried out.

By now Ana and Caleb were enjoying their last dance of the night. The lights were dimmed to show the twinkle lights around the hall and the music was perfect for a slow, romantic waltz. Everyone cleared the floor to allow the new couple their closing dance together.

Chapter Ten

The sheriff opened the trunk of his car and handed silver bells and a *Just Married* sign to Greg and Nate.

He was parked outside the community hall beside the horse–drawn carriage. The carriage driver sat up top keeping the horse steady.

Greg hung the bells on the carriage while Nate attached the sign to the rear of it.

The last item the sheriff lifted from the trunk before closing it was a folded quilt — a wedding quilt handmade by the members of the quilting bee for Ana and Caleb. The intricate white work and gold work embroidery was exquisite. It had the couple's initials stitched into the fabric and the design was a traditional double wedding ring pattern with a floral bridal border.

The sheriff placed the quilt carefully on the seat of the carriage ready for it to keep the couple cozy on their ride home. Their new house was in the heart of the town, with their garden edging on to the countryside, but not as far out as Greg's property. The ride home was part of the town's traditions for newlyweds, a special part of the proceedings, to send them off to start their new life together.

The lanterns on the carriage, two up front and two at the rear, were lit, and Greg hung the last of the silver bells on to one of them, creating a silvery sheen.

Jessica came running out of the community hall and hurried over to the sheriff. 'Ana and Caleb are about to come out.'

'Everything's set,' the sheriff assured his wife. He gave her a warm smile, and whispered to her. 'I remember the night we rode home in a carriage after our wedding. You're still the best thing that ever happened to me.' He kissed Jessica on the cheek and she gave him a loving hug.

'Here they come now,' said Nate, looking to see if Nancy was with them. And she was, along with the bridesmaids and the other guests.

Ana's white satin dress glowed beautifully in the evening light, and Caleb held her hand as he escorted her from the hall to the carriage. He opened the carriage door and helped his new bride step inside, then sat down beside her.

Nancy cast handfuls of flower petals into the air, and Ana got ready to throw her bouquet into the crowd.

Greg stood beside the carriage to make sure everything went well, but he kept looking for Lucie among the guests. And then he saw her, and waved.

Lucie waved back, and at that moment Ana threw her bouquet into the crowd. It seemed as if one of the bridesmaids near the front was going to catch it, and Brielle made a bid to grab it but missed. The bouquet soared over the heads of the guests nearest the bride and it was Lucie's hands that caught it, as if it had been thrown directly to her. This wasn't true. Ana had thrown it for everyone to have a chance, but somehow it fell into Lucie's hands.

Never thinking she'd be the one to catch Ana's bouquet, Lucie beamed and held it high, delighted. The guests cheered and everyone, except Brielle, was happy for her.

Greg was particularly pleased. Seeing Lucie wearing that beautiful blue dress and standing there holding a bride's bouquet, his heart ached for a life he'd only ever dreamed of. He hoped that circumstances had brought Lucie into his world, and he aimed to do right by her. Planning Ana's wedding had been a mix of fun, laughter, stress, cake baking, and panicking that he wouldn't make everything as perfect as he'd promised Ana. He'd experienced a whole variety of feelings that had ended better than he could've hoped for. And that included taking Lucie to the wedding as his date. Something special he never bargained for.

Caleb unfolded the wedding quilt and tucked it around the two of them as they set off in the carriage.

Cheers and laughter resounded in the calm night air, and Greg came over to stand beside Lucie as they waved them off.

Greg looked at the bouquet and grinned. 'I'm glad you caught it.'

Lucie smiled back at him, neither of them saying that this was supposed to indicate she'd soon be a bride herself.

Their happy moment was interrupted by Brielle. 'You left your purse in the hall, Lucie. Better go and get it before everything's locked up for the night.'

Lucie realized she'd forgotten her purse in her rush to see Ana and Caleb leave. 'Thanks, Brielle,' she said, and hurried inside to get it.

Brielle sighed deeply and stepped closer to Greg. 'It was a beautiful wedding. Makes me want to maybe finally settle down, if I found the right guy.'

Greg's heart twisted. Part of him knew she was toying with him, like she always used to do. And part of him wished he'd never loved her. He'd wasted years loving a woman whose special knack was making you love her so she could break your heart. How different his life might have been if he'd never met Brie.

She stepped closer and put her hands on his chest, gazing up at him and smiling. 'We used to be happy.'

'I'm happy with Lucie.'

Her beautiful blue eyes gazed deeply at him and she shook her head. 'No, Lucie will always be your second choice.'

Her words were a verbal stab through his heart, and he hated that she could make him feel that way, or feel anything. Before he could step back from her, Brielle leaned up, placed her hands around his shoulders and kissed him full on the lips.

Greg tried to pull back, but Brielle kept herself wrapped around him, long enough for Lucie to see them kiss and embrace.

Lucie almost dropped her purse as she watched the two of them together. People were heading home, but in the midst of it all, there was Brielle kissing Greg and he wasn't doing anything to stop her.

Lucie could've wept, but held in her tears for now. Clearly Brielle was seeking a reaction from her. Well, she was out of luck. No way was she going to let Brielle see how upset she was.

Lucie kept on walking, but instead of going back to Greg, she started heading along the main street to the lodge. The evening hadn't seemed cold until now, and she shivered, perhaps from shock and upset, as the night air brushed against her bare arms. The fabric of her satin dress suddenly felt icy cold, but she hurried on.

Somewhere in the back of her mind she heard Greg call to her, but she kept on going, not looking back at him, not wanting to see another second of his closeness to Brielle.

'Lucie, wait, Lucie!' Greg shouted and ran to catch up with her.

'Leave me alone, Greg.' Her voice was unsteady, trying not to cry, but it was tearing her apart inside. How could she have been so stupid?

'It's not how it looked. I know it must've looked bad.'

She didn't even want to glance at him as she replied. 'It looked like you were having a good time from where I was standing.' She continued on.

'Lucie, no, wait.'

'I'm going back to the lodge, Greg.'

'Let me get the car. I'll drive you.'

'I'd rather walk, thanks.'

'Please don't let Brie ruin this. It's been such a great day.'

'It's not Brielle, Greg. She may have made a move, but it was your reaction...I mean, everyone saw the effect she had on you.'

'She took me by surprise, that's all.'

'Greg, you can't explain this away that easily. Dwayne and Herb roped me into this in the first place because you were in danger of getting your heart crushed by her. I was a date to show you'd gotten over her, fake or not. You just showed her and everyone that you're not!'

'I am. Please, Lucie.'

'We barely know each other. I think the romance of the wedding maybe had us both swept up believing something that isn't there.'

'Lucie, don't go. You may be right about how quick this has happened, but today has been the best day I've had in years, and it wasn't the townsfolk, it wasn't my friends getting married, it was spending the day with you.'

She felt the tears roll down her cheeks. 'I can't do this right now, and I can't have my heart broken either. So much is changing in my life back in New York. Everything is uncertain. I think I'm going to go back like I planned.' She walked on, wiping away her tears.

'Wait,' he called to her.

'Please don't follow me. I want to walk alone right now.'

Lucie walked back to the lodge thinking how complicated things felt. She'd been swept up in the happy events. She thought about her life in New York. It wasn't perfect. She knew that. But maybe she was better off with what she knew, the familiar, the routine at the bakery, and yes, then having to move to a new apartment. The thoughts were starting to overwhelm her, and she didn't want anyone in the lodge to see her upset as she walked into the reception.

She hurried to her room and closed the door. Inside, she leaned against it and tried to calm down. The room looked so pretty, lit by a soft lamp, and with the lanterns aglow in the garden. And there was the lovely new quilt on the bed. What memories would that evoke when she took it back with her to New York? Maybe she'd be better leaving it here, leaving everything behind, packing her bags and taking the first bus out of town back home to the city?

Greg walked back to the community hall looking distraught. He wanted to head home, rather than face Nate and Nancy and the others. No doubt they'd seen what happened. But he had duties to attend to before he could go. Ana's wedding cake, the tiers that were left untouched, needed to be packed away again in the white cardboard boxes for safe keeping. He'd promised Ana he'd take them to the cafe after the wedding and she could collect them in the next couple of days.

Most of the guests, including Brielle, had gone, leaving Nate and Zack to secure the hall. Nancy and a few others were tidying things up, but it would be properly cleaned in the morning.

Greg started to pack the cake into the boxes.

Nate came over and shook his head. 'How's Lucie?'

'Upset. And I don't blame her. Brie used to say everything was always my fault. Seems she was right.'

'Brielle's trouble, no two ways about it. She's a disappointment to the folks here that used to think of her as over confident, but still one of us. But she doesn't belong here. Causing mischief seems to amuse her, and we don't enjoy being the source of her entertainment.' Nate's tone deepened. 'That doesn't excuse your behavior tonight, letting her kiss and cuddle you in front of Lucie and all us folks.'

Greg hung his head low as he rewound what happened. 'I know, Nate. You're right. I just...Brie always had a way of manipulating me even when I knew she was doing it. She did that for years, ever since I first met her, even before we dated.' He sighed heavily. 'I wish I could rewind and had stepped back from her, pushed her hands away from me, but...' he shrugged. 'I didn't do it. I was about to, but I didn't do it fast enough. And that's what Lucie's really upset about. I let Brie kiss me and never stopped her. I feel such a fool.'

'You are a fool,' Nate told him straight. 'I'm not going to sugar coat things. You messed up, and you've hurt Lucie. It's gonna take a whole lot of mending to make things right between the two of you again.'

Greg closed the cake boxes and piled one of top of the other ready to carry along to the cafe. 'It's too late. Lucie says she's thinking about going back to New York.'

By now, Nancy had joined them, listening to the last part of their conversation.

Nate gave her a worried look.

Nancy spoke up. 'If we can get Lucie to stay, you could have a proper chance at dating, without all the whirlwind and distractions.'

Greg sounded doubtful. 'I don't think she's going to stay, Nancy.'

Nancy's tone was encouraging. 'Leave that issue to us.'

Lucie phoned through from her room to check with reception. There was no 6:00 a.m. bus to the city the next morning, so she couldn't leave town right away.

She hung her dress up in the closet and got ready for bed. Her aunt used to tell her to sleep on her troubles and that things would be better in the morning.

Lucie snuggled under the quilt and fell asleep going over the events at the wedding, wishing things had ended differently with Greg.

The lights shone from Greg's house in the early hours of the morning. He'd had an unsettled night and was up before the dawn baking a fruit cake for Lucie. A promise was a promise.

As he stirred sultanas and glacé cherries into the mixture he wondered what he could do to make things right between them again. Nancy assured him that she'd contact Penny and they'd be alerted if Lucie checked out of the lodge. He'd had no word that she'd left and hoped he'd have a chance to apologize to her later in the morning.

The aroma of the cinnamon, nutmeg and other fruit cake ingredients filled the kitchen with a familiar homely feeling. But deep down something was missing in his home, and that was Lucie. Sweet, kind, wonderful Lucie. His heart twisted thinking he'd upset her. Maybe she could find it in her heart to forgive him?

Brie was so wrong about Lucie being his second choice.

Lucie was up and dressed. Sunlight streamed through the window of her room, highlighting the wedding bouquet that sat on the bedside table. She felt a pang of sadness seeing it, knowing the flowers would wilt and fade. Nothing lasted. Certainly nothing in her world.

A knock on the door jolted her from her thoughts, and she opened it to find Penny standing there smiling at her.

'Would you like to join me for breakfast outside in the garden? It's a lovely sunny morning.'

Lucie hesitated, then accepted her invitation. 'Yes, thanks, Penny.'

With Penny leading the way, they headed through to the function room. The patio doors were open allowing the lovely warm day to filter in. A table for six was set up outside with a garden umbrella providing shade.

Penny confided to her. 'Brielle doesn't want to be disturbed until eleven this morning. She needs her beauty sleep.'

Lucie relaxed. She'd hoped Brielle wouldn't be around for breakfast.

They sat down at the table. Lucie breathed in the fresh air, letting it clear away the heavy thoughts of the night. 'It's lovely out here.'

'It's a fine way to start the day, isn't it?' Penny glanced into the function room. 'The girls will be here to join us soon.'

Lucie frowned, wondering if she'd been set up.

Penny caught her look. 'We have a tradition here. After a wedding the girls like to get together the next day to chat about all the things that happened. Sometimes we don't have a moment during the reception to discuss the bride's dress, the flowers, the cake. You know what I mean.'

Lucie nodded.

'We enjoy exchanging news and chit–chat. It's kind of like extending the wedding into the next day so we can all still be together.'

'That's a nice idea.'

The sound of voices approaching made Lucie look round. Nancy, Jessica, Virginia and Sylvie had arrived. Their chatter was light, and further brightened the day.

Nancy gave Lucie a little hug and sat down beside her while the others took their seats.

'What a fine morning.' Nancy gestured around the garden. 'It looks like summer already.'

Waiting staff served up a tasty breakfast selection and the girl talk began.

Lucie sipped her coffee and was thankful that no one had mentioned Greg or Brielle. Maybe they wouldn't bring up the incident at all, though she doubted that.

'Tuck in, Lucie,' Penny encouraged her. 'A slice of hot buttered toast with strawberry jelly will get your appetite going.'

Lucie was helping herself to this when a man's voice interrupted them.

'Mind if I join you?' Kyle asked. He looked handsome in his light blue shirt and his smile seemed genuine. Fresh from the shower, he showed no signs of tiredness, and appeared fit and energetic.

Penny put her hand up and stopped him in his tracks. 'This is girl talk time, Kyle. Now off you go and have breakfast elsewhere. It's just us girls here.'

Kyle smiled, taking no offence. 'Okay, I'll catch you later.' Although he said this to them all, it was Lucie he glanced at before walking away.

He paused and called to Penny. 'I was thinking of cooking up something special for the guests later today.'

Penny smiled. 'Great. Thank you, Kyle.'

And off he went, heading through to the kitchen to check they had everything he needed.

While they ate breakfast, the women chatted about the wedding.

'Ana looked beautiful in her dress and the bridesmaids were lovely,' said Jessica.

Virginia nodded, pleased that several women had worn dresses from her shop, and that she'd helped to sew Ana's dress and those worn by the bridesmaids. 'Ana is showing the wedding video at her housewarming party, so we'll get a chance to see everything again in detail.'

'That's something to look forward to,' said Nancy. 'When is the housewarming?'

'Soon, according to Ana.' Virginia smiled at Sylvie. 'She's making sure it doesn't clash with your engagement party.'

Penny rubbed her hands together. 'Another excuse to buy a new party dress. Although I have a few, I'm tempted by all those bargains in your shop, Virginia.'

'New fabric arrived a couple of days ago, and I can't wait to start making new dress designs,' said Virginia.

Nancy's interest perked up. 'New fabric?'

'Pop in and have a look,' Virginia encouraged her. 'Several of my dressmakers are excited to sew with the lovely silk and chiffon. And of course we're loving Sylvie's cotton floral print fabric. Perfect for spring and summer.'

Sylvie smiled, pleased that the ladies liked her fabric designs. 'It's great to see my fabric being used to make things you love. When I lived in New York I rarely saw what happened to it, apart from photographs, and those were mainly of it used for household items. Now I actually see the dresses being worn, and the fabric being sewn into quilts.'

Jessica spoke up. 'Speaking of quilts, remember to bring your ideas for our next projects to the quilting bee. Now that Ana's got her wedding quilt, what else should we start sewing?'

'Sylvie's engagement quilt,' said Nancy.

The women smiled.

'I'll pretend to be totally surprised,' Sylvie joked.

'That's what Ana did while we stitched her quilt at the bee,' said Jessica. She smiled at Lucie. 'Remember, you don't need to bring any fabric with you to the quilting bee. We have plenty from our stashes to share. Just come along and have fun.'

Lucie hesitated, realizing she hadn't told them she wasn't staying in town as planned. 'I, eh...I was planning to leave tomorrow.'

'Oh, nonsense. You can't do that.' Jessica brushed aside such a suggestion. 'Things went a little bit wrong last night, but while the ructions simmer down between you and Greg, you've got us for company. Isn't that right, girls?'

All the women nodded, creating a genuine feeling of warmth and welcoming around the table.

'But I—'

Penny cut–in. 'I've got you booked into the lodge for the next two weeks, Lucie. The tourist season doesn't start for a while and there are rooms vacant, so you're welcome to stay here.'

Lucie went to object again, but Penny wouldn't hear of Lucie paying for her extended stay.

'If you feel the need to contribute for your stay,' said Penny, 'chip–in and bake some cakes for the guests. They'd love that. Our kitchen store cupboards are always stocked with flour, sugar, butter and everything you need.'

'I'd be happy to bake for your guests at the lodge, Penny.' Lucie realized she wouldn't be leaving soon after all, and she felt better about this.

'A few of us are going up to the cove later for the picnic day,' said Jessica. 'Come and join us.' Jessica's quilt shop was closed for the day, as was Virginia's dress shop, and even Nancy was going along for a couple of hours while Nate tended to the grocery store.

'Okay, I'd like that,' Lucie said, feeling her day fill up with lots to do.

Greg was baking apple pies in the cafe. He'd given Dwayne and Herb the day off. They'd worked extra hard, especially helping him with Ana's party and the wedding catering, and they'd both wanted to go to the picnic day with their girls. The diner next door was open and he reckoned things would settle back into their usual routine and he wouldn't be inundated with customers. It was a warm, mellow morning and the town was in a sleepy mood, easing into the day, with many people planning to head up to the picnic day at the cove.

Under different circumstances, he would've put up the closed sign and invited Lucie to enjoy the picnic event with him. After the wedding, it would've been an ideal second date. He sighed heavily. Not that it had ever been a proper first date. He was probably the only guy in town to have messed up a date that wasn't even real. But it sure felt real being with Lucie, holding hands and dancing with her.

He looked at the display cabinet. It seemed so empty now without the wedding cake. He sprinkled sugar on the golden crusted tops of the large apple pies he'd baked and sat them in the cabinet.

Then he smoothed chocolate buttercream on to the rich chocolate cake layers and decorated the top with sugar frosted raspberries. The aroma of the chocolate mingled with the lemon cake that was baking in the oven. He planned to decorate this with icing and slices of crystallized lemon.

He'd left the fruit cake he'd made for Lucie at home, along with his hopes of winning back her trust. And yet...on mornings like this as he gazed out the cafe window and saw the warm sunlight, he still wanted to try to make things right between them. At least Lucie hadn't left town yet, and Brie was due to leave tomorrow. Maybe when his ex had gone, things would level out again, and he could make a fresh start with Lucie.

Kyle walked past the window and nodded in before going into the grocery store. Greg nodded back and sighed. He'd forgotten about Kyle. Even when Brie had left town, Kyle was still going to be helping out at the lodge. He shook his head, wondering if Kyle would take advantage of Lucie being upset and try to sweet talk her into a date. And would Lucie accept?

Before he could twist himself into knots thinking about this, Kyle knocked on the cafe window, wanting to come in.

Greg unlocked the door.

'Sorry to bother you, Greg, but do you have any chocolate liqueur I could buy from you? I tried the grocery store but they've none in stock. Nate said maybe you'd have some to spare.'

'Yeah, come on in.' Greg went over to the counter and opened up one of the cupboards. 'I should have a spare bottle right here. Yep, here you go.' He handed it to Kyle.

Kyle smiled and grasped it like it was a lifesaver. 'Thanks, I'm cooking something special for the guests at the lodge — a spicy chicken dinner. I make a chocolate sauce to go with it to bring out the flavor of the chili.'

'It sounds great.'

Kyle went to take out his wallet. 'How much to I owe you?'

Greg wouldn't accept any money. 'Nothing. I hope your dinner works well.'

Kyle was slightly taken aback. 'Thanks, Greg. I appreciate it.' He held up the bottle of liqueur and waved happily as he left.

Greg continued to get on with his baking, hoping Kyle's special dinner for the guests wouldn't include inviting Lucie.

Chapter Eleven

True to her word, Lucie baked a selection of cupcakes for the guests, remembering how well they'd gone down before when they'd been served by accident. She baked two batches — one of vanilla cakes that she topped with buttercream frosting, and one of chocolate with a rich fondant icing.

By the time she'd finished baking these, Penny was ready to head up to the cove. She was armed with a picnic basket and a quilt for them to sit on.

'Shall we go?' Penny beckoned to Lucie.

Wearing her lemon sweater and jeans, Lucie was ready to venture up to the cove with Penny.

'We could drive up,' Penny told her, 'but it's not far to walk, and it's such a lovely day.'

Lucie insisted on carrying the picnic basket. The basket had a handmade gingham cover that Penny had sewn. Lucie felt the urge to make things like this. She wanted to be part of a world where there was time for picnics at the cove, and time for friends to spend the weekend enjoying each other's company. Right now, in New York, she'd be studying recipes in her apartment, or working at the bakery, preparing cakes for the week ahead. What a different life this town offered her.

A narrow road off the main street lead up to the cove. It was between a little knitting shop and Virginia's dress shop, and so narrow and unobtrusive that Lucie hadn't even noticed it when she'd walked past it the previous day to buy her dresses.

A few cars drove by, but most people were enjoying the walk. The edges of the road were scattered with snowdrops and wild daisies amid the lush greenery.

Lucie and Penny chatted as they walked.

'We're fortunate to have such a varied landscape,' said Penny. 'The cove is like a little hidden niche with a view of the bay.'

'With all this countryside I hadn't realized we were so near the coast.' Lucie breathed in the change in the air, picking up the scent of the sea wafting in the warm breeze.

'It's lovely, isn't it?' Penny said as the road opened up on to the cove.

Lucie gazed at the scene in front of her. Several cabins were built around a small bay where the cove water was deep enough to encourage swimming and diving. A rocky area extended around the far side and beckoned people to go exploring. Families and friends were already having fun, and stalls were set up serving food and beverages on the area of grass that surrounded the cove. Trees covered in pink and white blossom provided shelter from the bright sun, and some of them had swings tied to the branches. Ribbons adorned the swings, and everything from the colorful canopies on the stalls to the bunting fluttering in the breeze made the picnic event look lovely.

Jessica and Virginia waved to Lucie and Penny. 'We're over here. Come and join us,' Jessica called to them. They'd laid quilts on the grass beside the edge of the cove. The deep blue water sparkled in the sunlight.

Lucie put the picnic basket down and helped Penny lay the quilt next to them.

'What do you think?' Jessica asked Lucie.

'It's great. If I lived here I'd never want to leave.' Lucie sat down with Penny.

Jessica pointed to one of the largest cabins. 'See that cabin over there? The one with the floral curtains?'

Lucie nodded.

'That's Zack's cabin. He lives in a house in town, but he built himself a cabin. Sylvie's in there cooking up something for us to eat.'

'I told her she didn't need to go to any trouble because of us,' said Virginia, 'but she insisted. She loves the cabin.'

Lucie smiled. 'I guess Sylvie used her own floral fabric to make the curtains.'

Virginia nodded. 'Having a fabric designer in town is a bonus. We do love our sewing.'

'Indeed we do,' Jessica agreed.

'I've got the baking bug,' said Lucie, 'but I think I'm in danger of picking up the sewing and quilting bug.'

'Oh that's for sure,' Penny told her. 'I skipped the baking bug and went straight to the sewing one.'

The others laughed.

'I noticed a little knitting shop as we walked up here,' said Lucie.

Jessica interrupted Lucie. 'Don't go in there. Do not.'

Lucie blinked at Jessica's warning, then saw them start to smile.

'The yarn in that shop is irresistible. I've bought loads in the past two years,' Jessica confessed. 'I've barely knitted more than a few rows of a scarf. But I keep buying that yarn every time I gaze in the window.'

Penny smiled. 'I try not to look in. The colors and texture of those yarns make me itch to knit. It's all beautifully hand dyed. And I'm not really a knitter.'

Virginia pointed to Penny's picnic basket. 'I've got more yarn than would fit in three of those baskets. But I've no time these days for knitting.' She shrugged. 'But I still keep on purchasing that lovely yarn.'

They were still laughing at this when Sylvie emerged from the cabin carrying a tray piled with sandwiches and cakes.

Lucie got up and hurried over to help her. 'Let me take that for you.'

'I've another tray to bring out,' said Sylvie.

'I'll take this over to the girls.' Lucie walked back and Penny spread out a tea towel for the tray to be laid on.

Sylvie was now heading over with a second tray. 'Here you are.' She put it down. 'I'm making coffee. Everyone want a cup?'

They did.

Lucie went to help her while the others set up picnic plates and napkins.

'Come on in,' Sylvie called to Lucie as she stood in the doorway peeking in the cabin.

Lucie stepped inside, surprised at how spacious it was. 'This is gorgeous, Sylvie. There's so much room and lots of light pouring in.' The chestnut wood was offset by the colorful rugs with their thick pile, and she liked the comfy couches and other little touches of homely living. The fire wasn't lit, but logs were piled up ready and the scent of fresh pine mingled with the coffee brewing. The open plan lounge extended on to the kitchen and a staircase led up to a second floor.

'Zack's architecture designs are wonderful. He built this before I met him, and my reaction when I first came here was like yours. The outside looks like a large cabin, but when you're inside, it's an entire house. He designed the windows to face the sun midday, and the skylight adds even more daylight.' Sylvie smiled. 'Zack has a traditional house in the town near the main street, and I love it. But sometimes I think I love this cabin even more. In the evenings I like to snuggle by the fire and gaze up at the stars through the skylight. It's quite magical.'

Lucie looked up and saw the clear blue sky and pictured it would look equally lovely in the evenings.

By now the coffee was ready. Sylvie picked up the coffee pot. 'I think it will be easier to take it outside and pour it there.' Sylvie smiled. 'This is the first time I've had guests up here. It's so different to my life in New York. I never thought I'd be living in a cabin like this in a small town, but Snow Bells Haven is great.'

Lucie lifted the tray of cups. 'I'll carry this if you take the pot.'

Together they headed out and over to the girls.

'Do you miss the city at all?' Lucie asked. 'You haven't been here that long. Since Christmas is that right?'

'Yes, since my Christmas vacation.' Sylvie laughed. 'It's like I'm still on vacation and I never have to go back to the city. I don't miss it. To tell you the truth, I kind of panic when I think that I almost didn't stay.'

'Really?'

'Yes. So be careful about walking away from Snow Bells Haven.'

'You moved here from New York and left everything behind. You're probably the only person here that understands how I feel.'

'It was a big step, but my situation was a little different. I was the one who had an ex in town trying to mess with my head. Conrad tried to tempt me back with promises of money, houses and a big lifestyle. The thing is, Zack fought for me, he wouldn't give up even though he felt he didn't have the same things to offer, he didn't give up. Don't give up on Greg. Brielle may have been in his head, but it doesn't make you his second choice, it makes you the right one.'

Lucie smiled her thanks to Sylvie for the advice.

Virginia and Jessica reached up and took the tray of cups from Lucie.

Nancy had now joined them. 'I brought chocolate chip cookies. Help yourselves.'

The women sat together sharing the food, drinking coffee and talking about everything from quilting to knitting and Sylvie's forthcoming engagement party.

Lucie smiled as the chatter swirled around her and she tucked into the cheese and salad sandwiches Sylvie had made. The sun warmed the light breeze, and Lucie hadn't felt so content in a long time. Days like this were made for sharing with friends.

Greg crossed her mind of course, especially when they spoke about Sylvie's party. Would Greg still want her to help him bake the engagement cake? Not that he needed her to do this. She pictured him working in his cafe, and her heart ached a little, but she pushed this aside to enjoy the picnic and the laughter with the girls.

Zack drove up and parked outside Greg's cafe. Two customers were leaving after eating a light lunch, and Greg was on his own putting the lemon cake in the display cabinet.

He looked round as Zack walked in.

Zack smiled. 'Some of the guys are heading up to the cove for the picnic. Want to join us?'

Luke, the owner of the art store, was already in the car and waved as Greg looked out. A long–time friend of Zack, Luke was single and similar in age and build.

Greg's first instinct was, yes, he'd love to go, but then common sense kicked in. 'Thanks, Zack, but I'm sort of tied up with the cafe. I gave Dwayne and Herb the day off.'

'Come on, close up for a couple of hours.' Zack looked around. 'The cafe's not busy today, and the diner's open for folks wanting something to eat.'

Greg bit his lip. 'I don't know...'

'We're going swimming. First swim of the season.' Zack grinned. 'You don't want to miss that, even if you're only standing on the sidelines mocking us fools freezing our tails off.'

This brought back memories of when they were all kids. Zack and Luke were part of the running team, with Zack being the leader. Zack could run real fast. Greg wasn't into sports and used to volunteer to slice the lemons for the team's lemonade. But he did enjoy swimming in the cove.

Greg was tempted. 'Swimming, huh?'

Zack beckoned him. 'Come on, lock up the cafe.'

'I don't have any swimming trunks with me.'

Zack wasn't accepting that excuse. 'I've got spare pairs in my cabin.'

'Is the picnic busy?'

'Yep. So I don't think you'll have many customers this afternoon. Everyone's up there having fun.' Zack laughed. 'Sylvie's there with the girls. It's up to us guys to provide the entertainment.'

Greg untied his apron and hung it up. 'If that water's half as cold as I think it will be, I reckon we'll be very entertaining.'

With Greg in the back seat and Luke sitting up front, Zack drove off and stopped a couple of minutes later outside the lodge to pick up Kyle.

Kyle was waiting for them, all set with his trunks rolled up inside a towel. He jumped in the back seat beside Greg, and Zack drove off with them up to the cove.

'I didn't think you'd leave the cafe,' Kyle said to Greg.

'Neither did I.' Greg pointed to Zack. 'But someone persuaded me to bunk off for the day.'

Zack laughed. 'Yeah, I'm a bad influence on you guys.'

'I thought you were cooking a special dinner at the lodge,' Greg reminded Kyle.

'The chicken is marinating in the spices. I'll be back in time to cook dinner.' Kyle smiled. 'At least that's what Zack said when he talked me into going.'

The others laughed.

'What's your excuse, Luke?' said Greg.

'I was lured with the promise of a picnic at the cove,' Luke said lightly. 'I thought I'd be relaxing beside it in the sunshine, not swimming in it.'

'Guess who I'm nominating to go in the water first to test the temperature?' Greg said in a joking tone.

The three guys pointed at Zack, and laughter erupted in the car.

'There's Zack with the guys,' said Sylvie, seeing his car pull up at the cabin. 'It looks like a full car. He must've managed to coax the others to come along.'

Lucie's heart started to beat faster as she looked over to see who was with Zack. She saw Kyle, and then she noticed Greg.

'Oh, look,' said Nancy. 'Greg's with them.'

Lucie tried to keep her smile pleasant, as if seeing Greg there didn't bother her.

'So is Luke,' Jessica added, 'and they've got towels with them, so I guess they're going swimming.'

'Swimming?' Lucie couldn't contain her surprise. It was a lovely sunny day, but she expected the water in the cove to be icy cold.

'Zack says it's a tradition to go for the first swim of the season,' Sylvie explained.

'No one has braved the water yet,' said Virginia. 'I wouldn't dare dip a toe in it until the summer.'

Lucie saw Greg and the guys disappear inside Zack's cabin. 'I suppose they're getting changed and really going to go for it.' She looked around her. People were enjoying the sunshine and picnic food, but no one was actually in the water.

Amid the chaos and laughter in the cabin, the guys got changed into their swimwear. The blue trunks Zack gave Greg to wear fitted fine, but he wasn't sure he felt totally comfortable with what they were about to do, especially now that he knew Lucie was there. He caught a glimpse of her sitting beside Nancy as they'd driven past.

'We're all crazy, you know that don't you?' said Kyle, tightening the cord on his yellow trunks.

Zack gave Kyle a reassuring smile. 'Crazy's better than boring. Besides, it's our chance to impress the girls. I told Sylvie I was doing this. This is her first picnic at the cove. I want it to be memorable.'

Luke smirked. 'I think that'll be guaranteed.' He wished he'd brought the dark green trunks rather than the blue and white striped ones he was wearing. 'I match the stall canopies.'

'All the better if you need to hide,' said Zack.

Luke laughed. 'When we step outside, there's nowhere to hide. Everyone will be staring at us.'

Zack adjusted the waistband of his red trunks. 'Once we're in the water we'll be fine.'

Greg blinked. 'You think?' Even the thought of how cold it could be made him shiver in advance. 'And Lucie's out there.'

Kyle snickered. 'This is going to be a total disaster.' He shook his head and smiled. 'I can sense it.'

Greg looked aghast. 'So why are you laughing?'

Kyle didn't have a reasonable response, and continued to smile.

The guys looked at each other and they all started to laugh, knowing there was a high chance of making fools of themselves.

Greg shrugged. 'There I was icing a lemon cake, all cozy in my cafe, and in walks Zack...'

Zack rubbed his hands together. 'Okay, guys, let's go.' He headed towards the open doorway. The others followed.

Kyle nudged Greg. 'If this all goes pear–shaped, and you embarrass yourself in front of Lucie, remember you won't look half as ridiculous as you did last night when you were waltzing with her.'

Kyle was joking, just guys poking fun at each other.

'Thanks, Kyle,' Greg responded. 'You're cheerleading skills are great.'

With laughter resounding in the cabin, they all stepped out wearing nothing more than their swimming trunks and pasted on smiles.

'They've all got very fit builds, haven't they?' Nancy commented.

The other girls agreed.

Lucie noted that the four guys were all similar in height and build, and that although Greg wasn't noted for being sporty, his torso was lean and strong, and the muscles in his back and arms were honed from years of physical work, even if it was cooking. But he'd probably gained some of his muscularity from working the land at his house.

Kyle's work as a chef and his fitness training had given him a broad shouldered, rangy physique.

Although Zack worked at his desk drawing up architectural plans, he also bore the taut muscles associated with the amount of physical building work he did.

Luke's art store business kept him busy during the day, and in the evenings he enjoyed painting or going for a run. All of this combined to give him a fit build.

Lucie's heart thundered as Greg and the others walked past them to the water's edge. Greg glanced down at Lucie and she saw the hesitation in his expression, wondering whether to smile at her or not. He had smiled, hadn't he? Her pounding heart made it hard for her to think straight, and even harder to disguise the effect Greg had on her.

Nancy took a moment to whisper to Lucie while Virginia was distracted and chatting to Jessica.

'If Virginia looks a bit sad when she sees Luke,' Nancy confided, 'it's because she's had a crush on him for a while, but he doesn't feel like that about her. He likes her as a friend, nothing else.'

Lucie nodded, taking this in.

Zack smiled at Sylvie and she looked excited to see him walk over to the water.

Penny cheered Kyle on and waved happily. He smiled back at her.

With everyone watching them, as if the whole picnic had paused, Zack stood at the edge of the water. Taking a deep breath, he dived right in and emerged punching the air with a triumphant fist. 'Come on in, guys. It's fine.'

Thinking the sun had given some heat to the water, Greg, Kyle and Luke took the plunge.

Lucie wasn't sure which one of the three yelled the loudest and gasped for breath as the icy cold water enveloped them.

Zack laughed. Sucking up the cold, he'd convinced them it was mild instead of breathtakingly cold.

Luke was the first to jump out. He was laughing but shivering too.

People were cheering and clapping them, and they had indeed provided entertainment. They'd shown they had enough fun in them to go swimming in spring cold water. The events in the town were always about participation, about the fun and friendship.

Kyle pushed himself up out of the water on to the rocks at the edge and breathed in the warm air.

Greg loved swimming, and after the initial plunge, he started to enjoy taking a swim, disappearing under the surface and emerging again. Yes, it was cold, but the fun of swimming in the cove's clear blue water outweighed this.

Zack joined Greg, swimming up and down. And then Luke and Kyle decided to join them too.

Further cheers rose up that the first swim of the season had been accomplished.

Amid all the cheering, the delicious aroma of cooking filled the air. Someone was firing up a barbecue.

Lucie looked over to the far side of the cove and saw that it was Dwayne and Herb. Dwayne waved an oven glove to Lucie, indicating that she should come and join them for the barbecue. Dwayne's wife and Herb's girlfriend were already there.

Lucie nodded and waved back to him.

Finally the guys finished swimming and got out of the water. They picked up their towels where they'd left them on the grass and started to dry themselves off.

Sylvie waved Zack over to join her and the girls, and the other guys came with him.

Greg pushed his wet hair back from his brow and sat down beside Nancy and Penny.

Lucie felt a rush of color flood her cheeks and sipped her coffee, trying to hide her blushes.

'The water looks so tempting,' Sylvie said to Zack.

Zack bent down, scooped Sylvie up and ran over with her to the water, pretending he was going to throw her in. She clung to him and screamed and giggled, before he carried her back and placed her down safely again.

Sylvie slapped him playfully, and it was clear to Lucie that these two were another happy couple.

Lucie glanced at Greg and caught him looking at her. They still hadn't acknowledged each other properly, but with all the others around it wasn't awkward.

Kyle sat beside Penny with his towel draped around his shoulders and tucked into one of the sandwiches Sylvie had made.

'That looked like a lot of fun, but too cold for me to go swimming yet,' said Sylvie.

'The water's nice in the summer,' Nancy told her.

'The cove's beautiful,' Lucie commented.

'Do you enjoy swimming?' Kyle asked Lucie.

'I do, but I don't have time for it these days,' Lucie told him. 'I'm sure if I lived in a town like this I'd make time.'

'You'd love it here in the summer,' said Greg.

This was the first thing he'd said to Lucie.

She nodded. 'It's lovely in the spring and I imagine the summers are wonderful.' She looked over at Zack's cabin. 'And that cabin is fantastic.'

Zack smiled at the compliment.

Sylvie gazed around her. 'I love that time stretches out here in Snow Bells Haven. In New York I was working from one deadline to the next on my designs, and barely had time to relax. Now that I'm living here, I'm working on designs, but I don't feel stressed and there's time to enjoy days like this.' She shrugged. 'In the city the mornings were a blur, I ate lunch at my desk when I worked at home, and I felt I was always chasing my tail. Now I can relax while still getting my designs finished on time to meet the deadlines.'

'That sounds ideal,' said Lucie. 'I'm so used to the fast pace of living in the city. That's one of the reasons I was looking forward to coming to the wedding — to relax and unwind.'

Greg shook his head. 'I certainly put paid to your plans to relax. As soon as you arrived, I had you working in the cafe baking cupcakes and then helping me deliver them to the lodge.'

Lucie smiled, and some tension eased between them. The others smiled too.

Greg continued. 'Then I had the nerve to ask you to get up at the crack of dawn to help me take the wedding cake to the community hall.'

Lucie nodded. 'You did.'

'And you baked extra cupcakes to make up for the ones eaten by mistake,' Penny added.

Lucie smirked. 'I've had quieter times.'

'Then later I roped her into helping me bake Sylvie's engagement cake.' Greg smiled at Lucie and she smiled back.

Nancy cast a glance at Jessica and Penny, hopeful that Lucie and Greg were going to make up.

Zack went to pour a cup of coffee, but the pot was empty.

'I'll make more,' Sylvie offered.

Zack stood up. 'No, we should get dried off. I'll bring fresh coffee back with me.'

The guys headed up to the cabin to get changed into their clothes.

The aroma of the barbecue was tempting them to hurry up to enjoy the sizzling burgers and baked potatoes.

'This is a fun day, isn't it?' Nancy said to Lucie. 'And Greg's such a great swimmer.'

'He is, isn't he?' Lucie agreed, watching him walk away, noticing how the lean muscles in his back rippled as he moved. She sighed to herself. He was also a heartbreaker. Was she prepared to risk getting involved with him again? Maybe it was better to be friends.

Chapter Twelve

'At least Lucie's talking to you,' Zack said to Greg.

The guys were finishing getting dressed. Greg buttoned up his shirt. 'It's something.'

'You need to talk to her on her own, away from all of us,' Zack advised him as he made fresh coffee. 'Just the two of you, getting to know each other, talking things over.'

Greg nodded, taking in this advice. The cafe wasn't an option. It was always busy with customers or others popping in. Inviting her to have lunch or dinner with him at the diner or at the lodge would still not be private. Penny would be there, and Kyle. Somebody, even well–meaning, would no doubt join them, make a friendly comment or watch their every move. No, Zack was right. The picnic was a great ice–breaker, getting a chance to make amends with Lucie, but he needed to find a way for the two of them to enjoy time alone. And then he had an idea...

As he walked out of the cabin with Zack and the guys, he decided to ask Lucie to help bake Sylvie's engagement cake, but not at the cafe. At his house.

Zack put a clean tray of cups and the hot coffee pot down beside Sylvie and the girls. Sylvie poured them coffee.

'Dwayne's waving a barbecue fork at us,' Kyle commented casually. 'I guess the burgers are cooked.'

'They sure smell tasty,' said Zack.

Greg gestured to Lucie. 'Shall we head over?'

Lucie nodded.

They all went over to the barbecue taking their coffee, quilts and picnic baskets with them.

Lucie helped Nancy and Jessica spread the quilts on the ground near the barbecue while Greg helped Dwayne and Herb serve up the first batch of burgers and baked potatoes with coleslaw and salad on picnic plates.

Greg sat down beside Lucie to enjoy their food, and the others chatted amongst themselves while the barbecue continued to sizzle.

'I'm hoping you'll still want to help bake Sylvie's cake,' Greg began.

'Yes, I said I would. From the pictures you showed me of the type of cake we'll bake, this is something I'll enjoy making. The fondant flowers will require some work. And I'm interested in your fruit cake recipe.'

'I promised I'd bake you a fruit cake.'

'You don't have to do that.'

'I already have. I baked it today. I was up early. I couldn't sleep.' He gazed right at her. 'I'm sorry I upset you last night. I really am. I wish I could make things right.'

Lucie sipped her coffee. 'We could try starting again as friends.'

Greg nodded. 'Friends sounds promising.'

'No promises though.'

'Okay,' he agreed.

'When do you want me to help bake Sylvie's cake?'

'Would you be free tomorrow night?'

She frowned. 'After the cafe's closed?'

'Yes, but not at the cafe.'

'Where?'

'At my house. And before you assume I'm up to anything, I'm not, well not really. I baked your cake at home and I have all the ingredients there that we need. But I thought it would give us a chance to just be us, you and me, without Nancy or Kyle dropping by, or Dwayne and Herb trying to be our matchmakers.'

She smiled. 'All right.'

His heart filled with hope. 'I'll pick you up at the lodge around six–thirty, drive you out there and drive you back later. As friends. I'll show you the quilts I'm working on and you can help yourself to fabric from my stash. I'll even rustle up dinner for us.'

'Baking, dinner and quilting? You've got yourself a deal.' She could see that Greg was really trying to make things nice.

They smiled at each other, and she felt a sense of excitement at having a second date with Greg. Though this wasn't really a date yet again.

'Hopefully our second date will end better,' he said.

'Remember, it's not a proper date.'

'I know.' He gave her the warmest smile, and her heart squeezed just looking at him.

Lucie gazed around her, glad she hadn't left town, and was enjoying the picnic. According to Penny, Brielle was leaving tomorrow, so perhaps this would be like a fresh start with Greg.

As the afternoon wore on, and some people started to drift home, Greg and Lucie walked along the far side of the cove. The sun shone mellow gold off the water and gave an amber glow to the sky. Dwayne and Herb had packed up their barbecue and headed away, having enjoyed sharing their food with the others. Zack drove Nancy, Penny, Jessica and Virginia home, and somehow Kyle and Luke had squeezed into the car and left with them. Sylvie wanted to stay and sketch the spring flowers before they closed their petals for the day. She sat outside the cabin with her artist's pad and drew daffodils, tulips and crocus for her new fabric designs.

Greg had invited Lucie to linger a little while.

Two new cabins had been built on the outskirts of the cove. Greg pointed to them as they meandered along. 'Zack designed those. One is already sold, and the other has been leased by the town's new deputy. He's a young guy and supposed to be arriving soon. The sheriff says he'll be glad to have a full–time deputy.'

'It's a busy town, so I imagine he would.'

'Zack and Nate and a few others volunteer when needed. There was a snowstorm at Christmas and they helped folks get home safely and gave the sheriff and his men a hand with the rescue work. We used to have a regular deputy, but he left to take a promotion in another town, and it's taken a few months to find a suitable replacement.'

Lucie looked at the vacant cabin. 'It certainly looks like a lovely place to stay.' She wondered if she would've considered leasing it if it had been available. 'Is it furnished?'

'I don't know.' Greg led her over to take a look.

They peered through the lounge windows. Sunlight lit it up, and the polished wooden floor gleamed with warmth.

'Oh, it's gorgeous.' It reminded Lucie of Zack's cabin, but only a few basic items such as a couch and comfy chairs with scatter rugs were in it. The cabin was smaller than Zack's but ideal for a single guy.

'I guess it'll be kitted out for the deputy by the time he arrives. Nate and Nancy bought it as an investment. They have their own home, and they own one of the old–style houses near the main street that they lease out to tourists. That's where Sylvie stayed when she arrived here on vacation. Zack's traditional home is a couple of houses down from there.'

'Is that how Sylvie met Zack?'

'Sort of. The story goes that she'd tumbled into a snowdrift on the outskirts of town and Zack came to her rescue. Then they got to know each other from there.'

'I like to hear how romances start, what brings couples together.' She shrugged. 'I suppose I'm a romantic at heart.'

'So am I.' He smiled at her, and they continued to walk on, enjoying the easy pace of the late afternoon and the breathtaking views.

She recalled the flowers he'd bought for her. That was definitely a romantic gesture. And now here they were walking together in the glow of a golden sunset. Part of her wanted to smile from the warm feelings she had just being with him, but she still felt bittersweet remembering the upset from the previous night.

'You're frowning,' he said softly. 'Are you okay?'

She shielded her eyes from the glow of the sun glinting off the water. 'Yes.'

Her reply didn't convince either of them, but Greg didn't pry. He couldn't expect her to forget about last night. He'd have to earn her trust again.

He paused. 'This is as far as the road goes here.'

'It's getting late. We should be heading back while there's still light.'

Retracing their route, they walked back to the picnic area. They were the only two people left.

'Everyone's gone home.' She looked over at Zack's cabin. Even Sylvie had packed up her artwork and left. She hugged her arms around herself, starting to feel a slight chill in the air.

Greg fought the urge to put a comforting arm around her, and instead lead the way back down to the main street.

Outside the cafe, she paused. 'I can walk safely to the lodge from here.'

'I don't mind going with you.' In the back of his mind he'd hoped their time together hadn't ended. Maybe she'd suggest they have dinner at the lodge. Or perhaps he should be the one to ask her.

Before he had a chance to do this, Lucie dashed his hopes. 'I had a nice time at the picnic. I'm going to relax and get some rest. I'll see you tomorrow night.'

He forced a smile to hide his disappointment. 'I'll pick you up as planned.'

She nodded, smiled and then walked away.

She'd never know how hard he fought the urge to run after her. In that moment, he was one step surer to knowing he was falling in love with Lucie.

Penny gave Lucie a welcoming smile as she walked into the lodge reception. 'Would you like to order dinner?'

'I'm not sure. I'd like to relax and freshen up in my room.'

Penny didn't pressure her. 'Ring through if you need anything. Oh and, housekeeping cleared out the flowers from the wedding. They've put the corsage and the bouquet aside rather than throw them away without confirming it's okay with you.'

'Thanks, Penny, I'm done with them.' She smiled and headed to her room.

Kicking off her shoes, she stretched out on top of her bed, wrapped the quilt around her and thought about Greg. Leaving him standing outside the cafe had made her heart ache. She'd wanted to run back to him, but resisted the temptation.

Lucie realized she must've fallen asleep. The next thing she knew, it was dark outside her room window and the lanterns in the garden were all aglow. A knock on her door had woken her up.

She threw the quilt aside and opened the door.

Kyle stood there smiling at her. He was wearing his chef whites. 'Dinner's ready. Would you like to join us in the dining room?'

Lucie blinked, still drowsy. 'Dinner?'

Kyle sounded enthusiastic. 'I've cooked something special. Spicy chicken with chocolate liqueur sauce and roast potatoes.'

All the fresh air and activity of a day at the cove had given her an appetite. 'I'll be through in a few minutes.'

Kyle smiled and hurried away.

Lucie freshened up, changed into the navy dress she'd brought with her, brushed her hair and headed through to dinner.

Kyle had set a place for her at a table for two near the window. She sat down. This suited her fine. The other guests were part of groups of family or friends.

She gazed out the window at the main street. The bridal banners had been taken down from the street lamps and replaced with springtime decorations. Even in the evening light they looked pretty.

There were only a few cars parked outside the lodge. Most of the wedding guests had left. It felt like the wedding really was over. So what now? Was she going to start looking at the possibility of settling down here, and where would she begin? She'd have to find work and accommodation. The cabins at the cove were lovely, but even if there ever was one for lease, would she be able to afford it? It would obviously depend on how successful she was with her baking in town, and whether she worked for someone else or struck out on her own with a little shop. In theory, her own shop sounded wonderful, but it would be a huge responsibility. Jessica and Virginia owned their own stores, however, their stock of quilts, dresses and fabric was different from fresh bakery products. Nate and Nancy's grocery store was sort of in between with fresh items and tinned and packaged goods that had a long shelf life. And they were a couple working together, backing each other up. She would have no support system except her own hard work. She didn't flinch at the thought of getting up early every day to bake cakes and bread. She was used to doing that in the city. But she'd have to rely on herself to order stock, keep the books, deal with banking, all sorts of things that didn't entirely appeal to her. When she locked up her shop at the end of each day, she wouldn't be finished work. She'd have to start on the admin side of it. It was the baking that she loved. Even Greg admitted he hated doing accounts and paperwork for the cafe and relied on his grandfather to do these. It was nice that this kept his grandfather part of the cafe he'd established so many years ago, but still...

The sharp and confident tone of Brielle's voice announced her arrival in the dining room. Lucie tensed seeing her walk in as if she was a star attraction. Those cold blue eyes flicked in Lucie's direction, and they both acknowledged that they'd seen each other. Thankfully, Brielle didn't come over. Instead she sat down to join a couple of friends, again fashionably late, and angled her chair so that she'd turned her back on Lucie.

Waiting staff began to serve the dinner orders to the guests. Lucie had yet to order from the menu, and as she reached for it, a hand stole it away. She looked up and saw Kyle smiling at her.

'I hope it's okay, but I've taken the liberty of preparing a plate of the spicy chicken for you.' He was holding a dinner plate with the chicken beautifully presented. He put it down on the table. 'If this is not to your liking, I'm happy to change it.'

The rich scent of the spices mixed with the chicken and roast potatoes set her appetite alight, and the chocolate sauce looked delicious.

'This is perfect, Kyle.'

He grinned, delighted that she was happy. 'I'll give you time to savor it,' he said, leaving her to enjoy her meal while he went back to the kitchen.

Brielle made a comment to Kyle as he walked past her table. He nodded, but didn't pause, having no inclination to listen to her. Brielle shifted uncomfortably in her seat and flicked her hair in annoyance that Kyle had made no time for her whatsoever.

Lucie tried to forget about Brielle and began enjoying the dinner Kyle had prepared for her. The subtle taste of the chocolate definitely brought out the flavor of the spicy chicken, and the roast potatoes were crisp and golden outside and fluffy perfection inside. She savored every morsel. Kyle was clearly an accomplished chef and had created a feast of flavors with his special chicken.

The waiting staff cleared away Lucie's plate and she opted for a slice of cream cake with fresh strawberries followed by coffee.

Kyle approached her table. 'I hope you enjoyed your meal.'

She sipped her coffee and nodded up at him. 'It was delicious.'

'The cake was a simple sponge that I baked and added cream and strawberries. As you know, baking is not my strong suit.'

'It was ideal, lovely and light after the main course. I wouldn't have wanted anything too rich. Besides, baking a basic cake and making it perfect is difficult. It's easier to create extra flavor and texture adding icing, buttercream, frosting and other things to a classic vanilla sponge to make it special.'

'From a cake baker like you, I'll take that as a compliment.' He smiled hesitantly. 'Would you mind if I sat down? There's something I'd like to talk to you about.'

She nodded, happy for Kyle to join her.

'This is cake related,' he said, sitting down opposite her.

She listened while he explained his plan.

'My uncle has been away at business conferences recently, and he's thinking of expanding the lodge dining room and creating a proper restaurant. The tourist trade in Snow Bells Haven has increased over the past three years, and the lodge could do with a restaurant to cater for non–guests as well as those booked in here. The function room caters to the town, as with Ana's party, but this would be a full–time restaurant. He's been phoning me and talking about this to Aunt Penny.'

'It's a busy small town, and the lodge is the main place to stay, so a restaurant would seem like a logical expansion.'

'We've got a lot of space out back in the garden to extend the function room and restructure it to create a restaurant. Zack drew up some plans a few months ago, and he says it's feasible to make more use of the space available. The kitchen is big enough, and all we'd need are extra ovens. They've asked me to advise them on the kitchen while I'm here.'

'It sounds exciting.'

Kyle nodded. 'It does, and now I'm wondering if I should give it a go, move back here and run the restaurant.'

'You'll know if this suits you.'

'Yes, but what do you think?'

'It's a great opportunity, especially for a skilled chef like you. Working with family, people you can trust, a town you're familiar with. But you have to make your own decisions.'

He agreed. 'You're right, but although I have a reputation for wanderlust, never settling down, I've always pictured that one day I would come home and feel content here. Maybe I've grown up a little since I've been away.' He gestured to Lucie. 'Look at you. You came here for a wedding and now you're practically living here.'

They laughed.

'That's so true. You've got an excuse having been raised here. I've rarely been outside of a city.'

He leaned forward. 'The thing is, cake baking really isn't my thing. I'll learn, get better at it, but if I create a restaurant menu I need to have beautiful cakes to balance the main courses I'll cook.' He leaned back in his chair. 'I could ask Penny to hire a local baker, or...'

He was looking right at Lucie.

She smiled. 'Or ask Greg to do it?'

He grinned and laughed. 'Very funny.'

'Sorry, I couldn't resist.'

'Seriously, would you be interested in joining forces with me? Even until you decide where your future lies?' He was giving her his best persuasive look.

'I'll definitely think it over.' In truth, the idea appealed to her immediately, but she didn't want to jump right in so easily. Being impulsive was one of the tags she'd add to herself along with troublemaker.

Kyle reached over and offered her his hand. 'Do we have a tentative deal? You'll think about it?'

Lucie shook hands with him. 'I'll consider it.'

One of the staff needed assistance in the kitchen, and beckoned Kyle. 'I'll catch you later, Lucie. And thanks.'

Kyle hurried away.

Brielle left the dining room without looking at Lucie.

Lucie sipped her coffee and sensed less tension in the air. Relaxing and gazing out the window, she mulled over Kyle's offer to work with him at the lodge. It would definitely solve half her problems. If she had her work sorted out, all she'd need to do was find suitable accommodation. Penny was adamant that she should stay at the lodge for the next two weeks. Surely she could find an apartment to lease in that time.

Greg was busy in the cafe cooking up savory flans and getting them ready for the following day. He sprinkled chopped chives over the bacon, egg and tomato flans and added a pinch of paprika.

There were no customers and he was closed for the night, but he hadn't locked the door, and Herb took him by surprise when he breezed in.

'Want a hand with the flans or the apple pies?' Herb offered.

'You're supposed to be enjoying a day off.'

'I did. I just walked my girl home and saw you working late. Thought I'd drop in and give you a hand to finish up.' Herb washed his hands and put his apron on without letting Greg refuse his help.

Greg grinned while he made the next flan. 'How did your second date go?'

'Great. Terrific in fact. We get along real well.' Herb's enthusiasm tailed off and he concentrated on putting the rolled pastry into the pie dishes.

Greg looked at him. 'What's wrong?'

Herb shrugged and continued making the pies, adding the prepared apples and then the top crusts.

'Are you going on a third date?' Greg asked tentatively.

'Yeah. I'm taking her to dinner a couple of nights from now. A meal at the diner.'

'So what's the problem?'

Herb sighed and popped the pies in the oven to bake. 'I'm not good enough for her.'

Greg frowned. 'Did she say that?'

'No.' Herb was quick to quell that idea. 'She seems to like me. We share the same interests. I've never met a woman who likes to discuss the best way to make cheesecake and the flavors of artisan bread.'

'So who said you weren't good enough for her?' Greg was ready to tell them to mind their own business for interfering with Herb's romance.

Herb shrugged. 'I guess it was me.' He sighed. 'You've seen her, you've met her. She's lovely. What's she doing with a dork like me?'

'Don't be putting yourself down.'

'Yes, but–'

'Nope. I don't want to hear it. Remember, women appreciate kind guys, and especially guys who have time to listen to them.'

'I'm a good listener. I love listening to her. She's smart.'

'Then don't spoil things,' Greg told him. 'If she thought you weren't good enough, she wouldn't be going on a third date with you.'

Herb bucked up. 'That's right. She wouldn't.'

'So quit talking like that.'

Herb nodded. 'Thanks, Greg.'

The pies were cooling on the trays when Brielle walked in, confident as ever. She smiled at Greg and ignored Herb. 'Working late, Greg?'

'We're just finishing up.' Greg sprinkled sugar on the apple pies.

Herb was used to being invisible to Brielle, and frankly it suited him. He continued to clear up while she targeted Greg.

She looked around the cafe. 'It's smaller in here than I remember.'

'I'm extending the cafe soon, adding extra tables for customers, patio doors and a cake counter.' Greg owed her no explanation, but he wanted to tell her about his plans.

'A cake counter?' She smiled sweetly, but all Greg sensed was bitterness. 'I trust you're not doing that because of Lucie. I wouldn't like to see your hopes dashed.' She left her comment dangling, inviting him to ask her what she was getting at.

Greg took the bait, but kept his guard up. 'What do you mean?'

'Well, I don't like to be the one to eavesdrop or spread gossip, but Lucie was having dinner with Kyle tonight at the lodge. He'd cooked something special for her, and served it up himself rather than let the waiting staff deal with it. Kyle was giving Lucie a very personal service.' She paused to gauge Greg's reaction. He didn't play into her games so she continued. 'I was there dining with friends. Kyle and Lucie were laughing and enjoying themselves so much they didn't realize that I could hear them. They were holding hands and Lucie agreed to accept Kyle's offer to work with him at the lodge, baking cakes. Kyle's staying in town and opening a restaurant in the lodge.'

Greg's guts were in turmoil, but he hid this from Brielle. 'Penny will be pleased. She's been wanting Kyle to settle down at home for a long time. A restaurant in the lodge will be great.'

Brielle's annoyance showed in her fake smile. She stared at him, analyzing every part of his expression, searching for the answer to whether he was telling the truth or hiding the intended hurt behind a facade of pleasantry.

She shrugged off her doubt and added a final stab to Greg's heart. 'I just thought you should know what Lucie's planning behind your back.'

Greg's response was genuine. 'I'm so glad you did.'

Flicking her hair, Brielle turned away from Greg and headed out of the cafe, casting a barbed comment in her wake. 'You never were lucky when it came to winning the girls of your dreams, were you, Greg? But good luck with your little cafe.' Her high heels sounded hollow on the cafe floor.

'Good–bye, Brie.' Greg closed and locked the door behind her as she left.

Greg didn't watch her strut away, annoyed that her plan to upset him hadn't worked. Instead he smiled at Herb and punched the air with a triumphant fist.

Herb gasped. 'Why are you so happy?'

'Because I'm finally over Brie,' Greg announced.

Herb cheered and they both did a little dance of celebration and finished with a high–five.

'What about Lucie working with Kyle?' Herb asked, bringing their victory celebration down a few notches.

Greg's tone was strong and determined. 'At least Lucie's going to stay in town. Now it's up to me to fight for her.'

Lucie was heading back to her room after dinner when Penny waylaid her.

'I'm so excited that Kyle is coming home.' Penny's face beamed with delight. 'He's creating a restaurant here at the lodge. It's a dream come true.'

Lucie gave her a hug. 'I'm happy for you, Penny.'

'I understand he's asked you to join him and take charge of the baking side, so that's double the excitement. Oh, and I know he can be a scoundrel at times, but his heart's in the right place. I'm glad you're going to consider working with him.'

'It's obviously a big commitment opening my own cake shop, but this would allow me to try settling into the town while having steady work.' She spread her arms. 'I love the lodge, but I do need to think things over.'

'Of course,' Penny assured her. 'I wouldn't want you to jump into something that wasn't right for you.' She lowered her voice. 'We both know that Kyle has a little crush on you, but I believe his offer is genuine, and it was clear to everyone at the picnic that it's Greg you're smitten with.'

Lucie blushed instantly. 'That noticeable, huh?'

Penny gestured and smiled. 'Like a banner across the sky.'

Lucie smiled. 'Everything's happening so fast. Every time I try to step back and relax to think things through properly, there's something else to consider.'

‘When I was a young single woman, I had this scenario in my mind where I pictured one day meeting a nice guy, he’d invite me out and we’d start dating and take things slow. I don’t like being rushed into anything.’

‘Is that what happened when you first met your husband?’

‘Nooo,’ Penny emphasized. ‘It was the fall, and I was outside in my garden picking chestnuts. I lived with my parents. There was a chestnut roast that night in town and I was helping out. Anyway, I was aware of this handsome young guy walking past, and you know what girls do, we pretend not to notice. So I kept on gathering the chestnuts, and then as he walked away I stepped up on to a log to sneak a peek at him. I was so busy looking at him, I stumbled and fell. I went flying and so did the chestnuts. They were scattered everywhere on the front lawn. Next thing I know, the guy is lifting me up in his big, strong arms and carrying me into my house.’

‘Were your parents there?’

‘Yes, and they appreciated his quick reaction. They liked him right away. He seemed to be a responsible young man.’

Lucie listened as Penny continued.

‘But my mother fussed so much wanting to put a quilt down on the couch, and he was left standing there holding me in his arms.’ She smiled at the recollection. ‘I still remember how I felt. There was this handsome stranger standing in our home, in front of the log fire, holding me safely as if it was easy, and I never wanted him to let me go. Thankfully, he never really did. My ankle was fine, just a sprain, and we all had coffee and supper together that first night. We started dating the following day and every day since then we’ve rarely been apart. The business conferences he goes to these days are the first time we’ve been separated since we got married.’

‘Did you know right away he was the guy for you?’

‘Definitely. I’ll be honest with you. I never thought I’d be that way. I planned to pick the right guy, keep my options open. But then I met him by chance and he was the one for me.’

‘Did you date long before you got married?’

Penny shook her head. ‘It was, as they say, a whirlwind romance. We got engaged pretty fast and married here in town. Now I’m not saying you should rush into a relationship with Greg. I’m just saying that when it comes to love and romance, be prepared to keep your plans open.’

'That's good advice.' Lucie paused and eased the tiredness of the day from her shoulders. 'If you hear someone in the lodge kitchen early in the morning, that will be me. I promised I'd bake for your guests.'

'You don't have to do that if you'd prefer to relax,' Penny assured her.

'I've been getting up early for years to start baking, and I'd like to do this in exchange for staying here.'

'We get a delivery of fresh milk, eggs and butter, that sort of thing in the morning, so use any eggs and other ingredients you need. We've got plenty.'

'I was planning to bake a selection of cakes and brownies.'

'The guests will enjoy those.'

Bidding Penny good–night, Lucie went to her room. Tuckered out from having had a full day, she got ready for bed.

As she snuggled under the quilts she thought about Greg and their time up at the cove. It was a day to remember. She would never forget how much she'd enjoyed being with him, especially walking together in the late afternoon sunlight. Tomorrow night she'd help him bake Sylvie's engagement cake at his house. She fell asleep, picturing what his house would be like, and looking forward to seeing the quilts he'd made.

Greg drove home feeling a bit tired but hopeful. It had been a long day. The picnic at the cove hadn't been on his agenda, but he was glad Zack had invited him to go. Spending time with Lucie had been wonderful.

Arriving back, he made a cup of coffee, relaxed in the lounge and worked on his quilting. He wanted to make something for Lucie and was determined to finish it that night.

Before going to bed, he made sure the house was tidy and looking its best. He kept a neat house, but he wanted everything in the kitchen to be ready for their cake baking.

Finally flicking the lights off, he went to bed.

In his mind, he went over the events of the day with Lucie, and tried to push aside the thought of her having had dinner with Kyle. That's if his ex was telling the truth, or slanting what really happened to upset him one last time before she left town.

Chapter Thirteen

The entire lodge was fast asleep as Lucie started work in the kitchen. The back door opened out on to the garden, and she enjoyed the early morning sunlight pouring in. The air had a crisp, clear, spring–like quality to it, and cooled the kitchen as she fired up the ovens ready to bake the cakes. She'd baked them so many times at work that she didn't need a recipe book.

Measuring out the ingredients, she soon felt at ease in the kitchen. The layout was practical and she thought it would work well for the restaurant, with a few tweaks of course, and extra ovens. When she'd baked the cupcakes here with Kyle, she'd been so intent on hurrying up to make them that she hadn't entirely taken in what a great kitchen it was.

She looked around while she made the cakes and smiled. Ana's wedding invitation had changed everything. For the better, she told herself firmly. Sometimes you just had to be bold to push yourself out of a familiar rut if you wanted more out of life than it was offering you. As she stood there, with her hair pinned up and wearing a chef's white jacket, she reckoned this was why she felt excited and anxious. Not in equal measures. The excitement far outweighed her anxiety. Perhaps some of that was due to her feelings for Greg.

With vanilla sponge cakes baking in one oven and chocolate and mocha cakes in another, she started to make the frosting and buttercream. She also made herself a quick cup of coffee and sipped it outside the kitchen in the sunshine. When she'd finished baking the cakes, she planned to have breakfast at the lodge and then head out to the main street stores. She'd only packed a few items of clothing to see her through the weekend. Although she'd used the lodge's laundry service, she intended buying herself more clothes to extend her basic wardrobe. It was a wonderful excuse for buying a new spring selection of clothes. The prices of items she'd seen in the windows were real bargains.

There was a vintage clothes shop that she'd walked past. In New York she loved browsing for vintage blouses and tops that could make a simple outfit special. She'd also seen a pretty handmade sweater in the window of the knitting shop near the road leading to the cove. As well as selling yarn, the shop sold knitted items, and the sweater was lovely shades of blue in a textured yarn.

And she intended buying a local newspaper to check out the ads for accommodation. Though maybe the lodge had a copy and she could read it at breakfast, and begin sussing out the viability of staying in town.

She took the cakes out of the oven and put them on a cooling rack. The smell of the baking was starting to give her a real appetite. She'd have breakfast as soon as the cakes were frosted. She planned not to have breakfast at Greg's cafe. She wanted to give him breathing space, and for herself. She'd see him later when he came to pick her up at the lodge. Until then, she wanted to stick to her plan of clothes shopping and find out more about the town.

After breakfast, Lucie headed along to the knitting shop which was on the same side of the main street as Virginia's dress shop and Jessica's quilt shop. A canopy shielded the front window from the bright sunlight. She saw the blue sweater on display and went inside to buy it. It looked as if it was her size.

The woman who owned the shop was busy knitting and smiled when Lucie walked in. She wore a hand–knitted lavender sweater.

She put her knitting aside. 'Can I help you, or would you like time to browse?'

Lucie wanted to browse immediately. The colors and textures of the yarn displayed neatly on the shelves made her yearn to take up knitting again. It had been so long since she'd knitted anything. The scarf she'd started and never finished was still tucked away in a bag in her apartment. Baking and a busy life pushed aside the ability to do all the things she loved. Somewhere along the line her knitting had been cast aside and not picked up again. Another thing she might have the time and inclination to do if she moved to Snow Bells Haven.

'I'm interested in the blue sweater in the window.'

'I'll get it for you.'

While the woman unhooked it from the display, Lucie fought the urge to touch the gorgeous skeins of yarn piled up on the counter.

'Those are a new range. You're welcome to pick them up.'

Lucie lifted one of them in shades of summery lemon and warm amber. Another was in sea tones of aquamarine and turquoise. 'The colors are beautiful.'

'It's hand dyed locally. The colorways are pretty. They blend so well.'

Lucie had no need to buy yarn, but she wanted all of these. She put them down as the woman handed her the sweater.

'Oh, it feels lovely and soft,' said Lucie.

'You can try it on if you want.'

Lucie held it against her, gauging the size. 'No, I'll take it. This will fit.' It had plenty of stretch in it. 'Did you knit it?'

'I did. I knit quite a few items. I love knitting and it lets me try out new patterns and the range of yarns.' She smiled as she folded the sweater and put it in a paper bag. 'Are you a knitter yourself?'

'I don't have time to knit these days, and I couldn't make anything as fancy as this sweater. I used to knit basic items, and started a scarf I never finished.'

'I've usually got two or three projects on the go, things I can pick and put down easily. I find knitting relaxing, and even though I work here all day, I love to unwind in the evenings with my knitting.'

'I quite like making small items, wrist warmers, things I can finish within a reasonable time.'

'You may like the sampler packs. They're fun and let you try out the different yarns.' These were on display — bags filled with samples from the stock available.

The packs were tied with ribbons and looked so enticing. Lucie picked one that she wanted. The colors ranged from candyfloss pink and fuchsia to sea blues. 'I'll take this too.' Knitting needles were on sale, so she bought a set of size 7.

Lucie paid for the items, happy with her purchases.

The woman popped everything in the bag with the sweater and handed it over.

'I won't pretend I don't know who you are, Lucie. I saw you at Ana and Caleb's wedding, but we weren't introduced. And it's a small town. People talk about visitors. I heard you're staying a bit longer in Snow Bells Haven.'

'Yes, I'm thinking about.'

She gave Lucie a leaflet. 'We have a knitting bee that you're welcome to join in with if you decide to stay.'

Lucie put the leaflet in her bag. 'Thank you.'

Leaving the knitting shop, Lucie browsed through other stores in the main street, picking up items of clothing, including a couple of tops and a blouse at the vintage clothes shop.

By lunchtime she'd bought a selection of clothes that she could mix and match to create different outfits, and picked up some real bargains.

As she headed back to the lodge she gazed across at Greg's cafe, being careful not to attract his attention. She didn't see him, but she supposed he was in there with Dwayne and Herb. The cafe was busy with customers wanting lunch, and she was starting to feel ready for something to eat herself.

She hung the clothes in her wardrobe and tried on the blue sweater. It fitted well, she loved the soft feel of it and planned to wear it later for her evening with Greg.

Sitting relaxing on the bed, she fell asleep and completely missed out on lunch and the entire afternoon. The events of the past few days had clearly caught up with her along with the early start that morning, and it was only when her phone alerted her it was almost 6:30 p.m. that she woke up. She'd set the alarm in the morning so that she wouldn't run late for her date with Greg. Now she had only a few minutes to get ready before he'd be there to pick her up.

Running around, freshening up, she tried to keep her excitement in check.

She put the new sweater on over a white top and black pants, brushed her hair, applied lipstick and picked up her purse. She viewed herself in the mirror. No blusher required. Her cheeks had a rosy glow from getting ready at speed.

A knock on her door make her jump.

'Lucie, it's Greg. Are you ready to go?'

She took a deep breath and tried to look calm as she opened the door and smiled at him. 'Yes, I'm ready.'

Greg was smartly dressed in a clean shirt that he'd changed into at the cafe. Her heart fluttered as he smiled at her, and she was looking forward to her evening with this handsome man.

'How was your day?' he asked as they walked outside to his car.

'I was up early baking cakes for the guests. Then I went shopping. I bought myself some new clothes, including this sweater.'

She didn't elaborate further. No telling him she'd missed lunch and had been sound asleep until a few minutes ago.

They got into the car and drove off.

The early evening light cast an amber glow over the town, and she enjoyed seeing the view of the countryside as they headed out towards his house.

He pointed towards it, and she saw the silhouette of the two–storey house against the landscape. The warm tones in the sky emphasized the traditional building and she noticed it had a front porch with a swing seat for two.

Trees were dotted around the house and different areas of the land grew a variety of plants that were starting to bloom in the springtime. She imagined how wonderful the garden areas would look in the summer, and in the fall it would be aglow with autumn colors.

'I grow the pumpkins over there, and the apple trees produce delicious fruit. I've got a herb garden outside the kitchen window, and a regular garden around the house that has a selection of flowers for most of the year.'

They drove up to the front of the house and parked outside.

Lucie stepped out of the car and looked around her. The air was filled with the scent of the plants and greenery. She breathed it in. 'What a great place to live.'

Greg started to unload items from the rear of the car. 'It is. It belonged to my grandfather. I spent a lot of time growing up here with him while my dad worked up north as a ranger.' He paused and gazed at the property. 'I've always loved this house.' He lifted two boxes that were packed with items from the cafe. 'When my grandfather retired to move to a town near here, to be with his closest friends without having to travel back and forth, I took over the cafe and the house.'

Lucie walked up to the front porch and sat down on the swing seat. 'This is perfect.' She had a view of the garden with the trees and flowers and the countryside stretching into the distance.

Realizing she'd left Greg to carry everything, she jumped up to help. 'Let me give you a hand.'

'No, you sit right there and relax. I brought a few things from the cafe we might need for dinner.'

She sat back down. 'If you insist.' She grinned at him and he smiled back.

There were quilted cushions on the seat and she sat there swinging gently. The tensions of the day melted away, and she pictured how great it would be to live like this.

'Did you make these cushions?' she called to him.

He dropped off the boxes in the kitchen and came back out to get the other two from the car. 'If it's a cushion and it's quilted, I stitched it.' He smiled at her. 'And be prepared for quilt overload inside the house.' He shrugged. 'Quilters quilt.'

'And bakers bake.'

Carrying the last two boxes he lead the way inside. 'Shall we get started baking?'

Lucie followed him into the lounge. The decor was warm with wood flooring covered with rugs. The couches had quilts folded over the back of them and were scattered with quilted cushions. The walls were soft cream, and lamps gave a welcoming glow to the lounge.

A log fire was all set ready to be lit, and extra logs were piled neatly at the side of the fireplace.

'Come on through to the kitchen,' he called to her.

The lounge led on to a large farmhouse style kitchen. He'd made the curtains for the windows from the same yellow and white gingham material he'd used for the cafe drapes. The kitchen was tidy, as she expected from a man like Greg, the owner of a cafe, and the cooker looked like it belonged to a chef.

'I thought we could bake the cake and get it in the oven on a low heat. It'll take a while to cook, but I'll give you a tour of the house and garden, and later I'll rustle up dinner. Is that okay with you?'

'Yes, I'll put my sweater in the lounge.' Moments later she was back, tying her hair into a ponytail and washing her hands at the sink. She peered out the window at the herb garden. He'd opened the back door and the fragrant scent of the herbs wafted in.

'I notice you've got a summerhouse out back. I've always wanted one of those.'

'You're welcome to come out any time and make the most of it here.'

He started to lay out the ingredients for Sylvie's engagement cake.

Lucie unhooked one of the clean aprons hanging up and tied it around her.

Greg looked at her, happy she was there with him.

She smiled, hoping he didn't hear the rumbling of her tummy. She wasn't sure it was entirely due to hunger. Being around Greg made her heart flutter and she was filled with nervous excitement to be here with him. His house was lovely, and she liked everything about it. If someone had asked her to describe her ideal home, this was close to the mark, probably even better than she could've imagined. She was standing in the type of kitchen she envisaged having when she was a little girl. A big, old–fashioned, family–sized kitchen with a table area to enjoy meals. The cooker was first–class, and he even had a herb garden right outside.

Gleaming utensils hung on the walls in an orderly fashion, and everything was a wonderful mix of traditional and modern with a few vintage items like the cookie jars.

'This is the recipe I use for the fruit cake.' He opened a folder packed with recipes.

Lucie read the ingredients and together they started making the cake.

His hand brushed against hers as they both reached for the cinnamon, and again she felt a surge of excitement shoot through her, setting her senses alight.

She could feel the fire burn in her cheeks and concentrated on adding the ingredients to the cake mix.

'Sorry,' he said.

'It's okay.' Her words didn't match how she really felt.

He blended in the glacé cherries. 'I intend keeping my promise that we'll start out again as friends, so there's no pressure tonight from me.'

Using a tiny grater, she added a touch of nutmeg. 'I know it seemed like things were heading in a closer direction, but it's better for both of us to make sure we don't make the wrong moves. Besides, I've lots of things to think about right now.'

He'd been waiting on an appropriate moment to bring up a touchy subject. 'Including Kyle's offer to work with him at the lodge?'

She wasn't entirely surprised. 'Did Nancy tell you?' She immediately assumed Penny would've told Nancy about Kyle's plans to stay.

'No, Brie told me.' He hadn't planned on mentioning her name, but he didn't want to put the blame on Nancy.

Lucie blinked. 'Brielle?'

'She came into the cafe. Herb was there.'

'What did she tell you?'

'She said you were having dinner with Kyle at the lodge, holding hands, insinuating the two of you were real cozy, and so busy laughing and chatting that she could hear your conversation.'

'That's slanting the truth.'

Greg held up his hands. 'You don't need to convince me.'

'No, but I want to explain.'

He tried to reassure her. 'Penny phoned me to let me know that Brie had checked out of the lodge and left town earlier today. She's gone. We don't need to argue in circles about this.'

'I'm not arguing. I want to set things straight. Brielle's left another dose of poison for us before she left, and that's just not right.'

Greg nodded. 'Okay. What really happened?'

'I had dinner on my own at the lodge. And yes, Kyle did fuss serving me the meal he'd cooked specially for the guests. He didn't sit down and join me until after I'd eaten, and even then it was for a few minutes before he had to hurry back to work in the kitchen.'

Greg accepted this as the truth. 'What about his offer? Did you make a deal with him?'

'No, I said I'd think about working with him. We shook hands on this. No promises made and none expected.'

'Sounds straightforward to me.'

'It was, and...' she hesitated. 'While I ate dinner, my mind was going over the options about staying in Snow Bells Haven. It boiled down to finding work or opening my own cake shop. I wasn't sure I wanted to take on such a huge responsibility — owning my own shop, and then Kyle made his offer and it seemed to have come at the right time. An offer to bake for the new restaurant.'

'It's a fine option. You really should think about it.'

She bit her lip.

'What's wrong?'

'I'm uneasy about accepting because, as Penny says, Kyle has a bit of a crush on me. That could be awkward. Kyle assures me it's just business, and although I'm inclined to believe him, I sort of feel disloyal to you.'

His heart filled with excitement at her compliment, showing how deeply she cared about him. 'I don't think of it like that. As long as we're both honest with each other, things should work out.'

She took a deep breath. 'Well, if we're being honest, Kyle's offer did appeal to me. The idea of baking for the restaurant felt like it would give me a solid start here in town. I could look for accommodation, knowing I had a steady income.'

'You could work at the lodge for a little while until...'

'Until what?'

'Other options become available.'

She frowned. 'I'm not sure I want to open a cake shop right away.'

'No, I wasn't meaning that. Once I've had the cafe expansion done, which should be soon...' His warm brown eyes gazed at her. 'You could come and work with me.'

Lucie's heart jumped as the surprise offer hit her.

He could tell from her expression that his idea had taken her aback, but she was smiling at him.

'Take your time, Lucie. Think about it.'

'Working with you and the guys at the cafe?' She sounded out the offer and liked the feeling it gave her.

'I fully intend to expand on the cake baking, and although Dwayne and Herb are great workers, they're not expert bakers like you. Think about it.' He drew an imaginary sign in the air. 'Lucie's cakes.'

'At Greg's cafe.'

'Teamwork.'

She nodded.

'There's also the hybrid option.'

'What's that?' she asked.

'Work mornings at the lodge with Kyle, and afternoons with me at the cafe.'

'The best of both worlds?'

'Until you decide what world's best for you. And maybe it would be both.' He shrugged and smiled, feeling like they'd spoken honestly and that their plans were feasible. 'But think things over. Take your time.'

Lucie smiled at him. 'I will. I'll do that. Thanks, Greg.'

They continued making the cake, but she seemed uneasy.

'Something else you want to discuss?'

'Yes.' She hesitated. 'Since we're being honest, I have a confession...

She told him about falling asleep and missing lunch.

He laughed as she got to the part of rushing to get ready to go out with him. 'You should've told me. I'd have waited until you were ready.'

'I was, sort of, but...when we finish baking the cake, before you give me a tour of the house, is there any chance we could have dinner first?'

'Sure.' He smiled happily. 'Why don't you finish making the cake and put it in the oven. I think we both know you can manage fine. I'll start cooking dinner.'

Lucie smiled at him.

She watched as Greg started to prepare their meal, and the strangest feelings of homeliness and excitement washed over her. Seeing him cooking dinner for them, and being there with him baking a cake, was like glimpsing the type of life she could have with Greg if they ever became more than just friends.

Lucie put the fruit cake in the oven, and soon the kitchen was filled with the scent of cinnamon, nutmeg, candied peel, orange and lemon.

Greg made a pasta dish for them, and the delicious aroma from the tomatoes, red onions and spices mingled with the baking. He also cooked up a medley of fresh vegetables including broccoli and mixed peppers.

After tidying away the cake ingredients, and swiftly finding her way around the kitchen, Lucie laid the table for dinner. She put quilted mats on the kitchen table and set the plates on them. 'These mats are so pretty.'

'They're quick and easy to make. It helps me use up scraps of fabric. I like sewing larger quilts, but often it's fun to sew something that I can finish in a night.'

She explained about the yarn she'd bought from the knitting shop. 'I went in to buy a sweater and ended up buying sampler packs and knitting needles.'

'What are you going to knit?'

'Squares probably, just to play around with the yarn. And maybe wrist warmers or a scarf knitted in simple stitches with different textures of yarn in various colors.'

'It's fun to make things. You'd enjoy an evening at the quilting bee. I'll show you my fabric stash after dinner and you can take whatever you want. And I have a surprise for you later. Something I hope you'll like.'

'What is it?'

'If I told you, it wouldn't be a surprise would it, Lucie?'

'Just a hint...'

He thought for a moment. 'It's a small gift from me. Something I made for you.'

'Now I'm even more intrigued.'

He smiled triumphantly. 'Great.'

Greg served up dinner and they sat opposite each other at the kitchen table enjoying their meal, chatting about baking and sewing.

'This is cozy,' she said.

He smiled across at her. 'It is. It's nice to have pleasant company for dinner.'

'Dinner is delicious, but that cake cooking in the oven is making me yearn for fruit cake. We may have to bake another cake for Sylvie if I give in to temptation.' She was joking and had no intention of eating Sylvie's cake.

'There's no need.' He pointed to a cake tin on a shelf. 'Remember I told you I'd baked you a fruit cake.'

Lucie's expression brightened.

'I'll clear these dishes and make the coffee if you want to cut us a couple of slices.' He lifted their plates and took them over to the sink and flicked the coffee pot on.

Lucie opened the cake tin. 'This smells gorgeous.'

'It's the same recipe, so you'll have a chance to taste what we're baking for Sylvie. I didn't ice it, but I decorated it with fruit and nuts.' He'd created a jewel effect by mixing dried fruit, glacé cherries, brazil nuts and almonds with syrup and topping the cake with it during the baking process.

She cut two slices for them and sat down at the table while Greg poured the coffee.

Greg was poised for her reaction as she bit into the cake.

She nodded and enjoyed the rich flavors. 'Perfect.'

'I'm pleased you like it.' He tucked into his slice.

Finishing their coffee and cake, Greg gave her a tour of the property.

'This is where I keep my sewing machines and fabric stash.' The room was on the ground floor with a view of the front garden. The decor was light and airy, and the shelves were neatly piled with pieces of cotton fabric, mainly fat quarter size bundles and bags of scraps that he used for quilting. 'Help yourself to any pieces you want.'

'That's a lot of fabric.'

He agreed. Then he handed her a beautiful quilted bag. 'I hope you like it. I was going to wrap it like a proper gift, but...' he shrugged.

Lucie was taken aback. 'I love it.'

'I thought you could use it to carry your fabric to the quilting bee, like a fancy sewing bag. I used Sylvie's floral fabric range.' The background colors were white and cream with all sorts of pretty flower prints from pink roses to snowdrops and bluebells.

Lucie unzipped the bag and saw that he'd lined it and added handy pockets. The handles were long enough to shrug the sizeable bag on to her shoulder.

'You made this for me?' It was so well stitched that it looked like something from a fashion boutique.

He nodded, happy that she liked his surprise gift.

She resisted hugging the breath from him, not wanting to give the wrong impression.

Still amazed by the gift, Lucie selected pieces of fabric from his stash, and by the time they'd finished, her new bag was kitted out for the quilting bee. He'd added gray, white, black and variegated colored thread to one of the pockets, a thimble, and a needle book he'd made from fabric and felt scraps.

Lucie opened the little book containing needles, pins, small scissors, and a measuring tape. 'This is so cute. Now I want to start sewing.'

'My plan worked.' He grinned at her. 'You'll also need these.' He picked up a selection of quilting clips, a set of patchwork templates and other little sewing accessories. Beside his sewing machines were boxes filled with all sorts of things. His hands were soon full of these extras, so he reached up to a shelf and brought down a couple of quilted zip pouches and put everything in these. He zipped them up and dropped them into her new bag. 'You are now fully equipped for the quilting bee.'

'I can't wait to go there and start quilting.' She smiled. 'I want to make a small quilt. I'm excited about having a go.'

'That's the beauty of quilting. I still get excited about making a new project. The enthusiasm never goes away. I only have to see one of those fabric bundles in Jessica's shop and I'm buying it and planning my next quilt. It could be a large quilt, or a mini, or a quilted bag, a pouch, whatever. I love baking and cooking, but I love quilting and the design work that goes into it. There's a skill to it, but an art to it as well. When you're quilting something and you blend the right fabrics with the right thread and details, maybe even appliqué, and it all works out, it feels good for the soul.'

Lucie understood. Often she felt like that with her cake baking, particularly if the cake was created for a celebration, an anniversary or wedding cake, there was a sense of having made something special. If she got hooked on the quilting, that was just fine by her. Except...

'With cake baking, quilting and knitting, there won't be enough hours in the day,' she grumbled jokingly.

Greg spread his arms wide. 'Welcome to my world.'

He continued to welcome her into his world by giving her a tour of his property.

'Come on, I'll show you the rest of the house and the garden.'

The lounge and his work room were downstairs, along with another spare room that he'd set up for dining, and the kitchen. He didn't take her upstairs because that's where his bedroom was and he felt it inappropriate to include this in the tour. He described that there were quilts on the bed, of course, and then invited her outside to see the garden.

He flicked on lanterns that illuminated the garden at the rear of the house, and she got to peek inside the summerhouse.

'It's best viewed in the sunlight.'

She peered inside. Light from the lanterns shone through the window and she saw it had a two–seater couch and table.

'I bought it a couple of years ago, but I haven't had time to use it much.'

'You should make time.'

He nodded.

They walked on and stood under the apple trees. The blossom glowed in the evening light. She felt like she was standing inside the pages of a fairytale story book. The moment was so wonderful.

Greg was telling her about using the apples to make apple crumble and pies, and was about to take her over to where he grew the pumpkins and then stopped.

He sighed heavily, hands on his hips, looked down and shook his head.

'What's wrong?' she asked.

'I shouldn't be doing this. It's like I'm giving you the grand tour, a sales pitch. Hey, look at me, look at my house and great garden.' He gazed at her, and the warm glow from the lanterns emphasized the hurt in his eyes. 'I'm no good at this... Guys like Kyle, they know how to talk to women, to impress them.'

'Kyle's back at the lodge. But I'm not there with him. I'm here with you, Greg.'

The straightforward truth hit him in a wave of emotion he wasn't ready for. He took a deep breath and tried to resist pulling Lucie into his arms and hugging her.

'You were going to show me where you grow the pumpkins,' she prompted him.

'Yeah... Yeah, I was. It's right over here.' He led the way.

They finally sat outside on the swing seat on the porch. 'You're fortunate to stay here, Greg.'

He pointed into the distance. 'You can see the lights of the town from here. My bedroom has a great view of the lights in the main street.' He stopped abruptly. 'I didn't mean...I wasn't hinting...'

'I know.'

'We should check on the cake.' He got up and hurried inside.

She followed him through to the kitchen.

'It's ready.' He took it out of the oven and put it aside to cool.

Lucie smiled. 'It looks good.'

‘I’ll ice it in the next couple of days, and if you’d like to help with that I’d welcome the company again.’

‘I’d like that too.’

It was getting late.

‘I should be going before it gets any later.’ Lucie started gathering her things.

In the hallway, she paused to admire her new bag, and accidentally clashed with Greg as he reached over to the hall table to pick up his car keys. Their closeness made her blush, something she’d been doing a lot recently.

They both pretended not to be affected.

Greg hoped Lucie couldn’t sense how hard his heart was pounding. He wanted to take her back safely to the lodge, and yet he yearned not to let her go.

Chapter Fourteen

Greg pulled up outside the lodge. Lamps gave a warm glow to the building, and lights from inside lit up the windows. The drive back had been filled with pleasant conversation about baking, and helped disguise the feelings Lucie had for Greg. The evening had given her a glimpse into his regular lifestyle, and she'd left with a better understanding of him, and of the effect he was having on her. It would've been easy to let herself fall in love with him, but the last thing she needed in the midst of leaving the city and moving to Snow Bells Haven was to risk getting her heart broken. He'd promised to give her time, to start again as friends, but what would she do if that's all they ended up as — just friends? What if Greg became so comfortable in her company that he could only look on her as his friend while she fell deeply in love with him? Greg was the type of guy women could be close friends with. Ana and Sylvie were prime examples.

'You're frowning,' he said, smiling at her.

She forced a yawn. 'I'm a little tired I guess.'

Greg reached over, and for a second she thought he was going to put his arm around her shoulders, but he was reaching into the back seat to lift her quilted bag over. In that moment, she felt a mix of relief and disappointment clash inside her. If he'd tried to kiss her goodnight, would she have let him? She couldn't say for sure that she wouldn't have. The urge to kiss him was strong. He had such a great smile, and she sensed an underlying passion in him the more she was around him.

'Don't forget this.' He handed her the bag. 'The quilting bee is on tomorrow night at the community hall.'

She lifted the bag, along with her purse, and got out of the car.

'I'll be there. Thanks again for the bag.' She closed the car door.

It was the strangest feeling waving him off. As if she'd been on a romantic date that had ended as friends.

She pushed these thoughts aside and went into the lodge. The reception was warmly lit and inviting, but there was no one around to welcome her, and she walked alone to her room, went inside and closed the door.

'I've been planning the new menu,' Kyle announced, practically bouncing into the lodge kitchen.

Lucie was busy baking cakes for the guests and had been up so early she barely remembered going to sleep. Life at the moment was one long rollercoaster ride and she was determined to hang on tight and go with the flow. This included continuing her early start work routine rather than relaxing in Snow Bells Haven, and reading Kyle's rough outline of the menu he was so excited to show her. He'd stuck the piece of paper under her nose so she could read it while mixing sponge cake ingredients.

She skimmed over the main courses. 'I like the idea of the seafood range and the pasta dishes sound wonderful.' She searched the items. 'Are you going to include traditional roast dinners?' These were a staple of the lodge's original menu and were something that she thought Kyle shouldn't exclude.

Kyle grabbed the list and scribbled this down. 'How could I have forgotten the roast dinners?' He smiled at her. 'See? We work well together bouncing ideas around. What do you think of the desserts? And I also want to make a big deal of the cakes.' Another piece of paper was stuck under her nose.

Lucie tried not to smile. His enthusiasm had wiped aside his manners, but she couldn't help but see the funny side of it.

Mistaking her smile for approval, he whipped the menus away and tucked them into the pocket of his chef's white jacket. 'Great. I knew you'd like them.' He rubbed his hands together. 'Okay, what can I do to help you? Want me to make the cupcakes?' He'd seen the paper cases lined up on the trays.

'Yes, I've prepared some of the ingredients for white chocolate cupcakes and vanilla cupcakes with traditional frosting.'

Kyle started right away, and she was glad of his assistance because she was busy icing a large chocolate layer cake and making a cream sponge cake.

'I know the restaurant hasn't even been established yet,' Kyle acknowledged. 'The building extension plans are out of my hands, but the menu is very much in our control. There's fun in the planning of it.'

'I've always liked planning menus,' Lucie admitted. 'Even if they were never accepted where I worked, I simply liked doing it.'

'I keep getting ideas and want to write them down. Some of them might not make the final cut of the menu, but many of them will.' He stopped, and took a breath. 'How did your date go with Greg last night?'

'We baked Sylvie's fruit cake. I'm going back again to help him make the fondant flowers and to decorate it.'

'Sounds like a fun date.' He grinned at her as if he doubted it.

She swiped him playfully. 'It was, but it wasn't a date type of date.'

Kyle smirked and continued making the cupcakes.

'What's that smirk for?'

'Nothing, just teasing you, Lucie.'

She held up a baking spatula. 'Well don't, especially when I'm armed and baking.'

Kyle guffawed. 'You're threatening me with a cake spatula?'

'Don't doubt it.' She jokingly wielded the spatula at him and he pretended to cower.

Unfortunately, that was the moment when the local delivery guy arrived to drop off the fresh milk, eggs and butter for the lodge. 'I'll put these down over here.' The man smiled tightly and couldn't wait to hurry away, as if he hadn't seen anything untoward.

Lucie and Kyle burst out laughing.

'His next delivery is to Nate and Nancy's grocery store.' There was an amused warning in his tone.

'Oh dear.' Then she shrugged. 'Maybe he won't mention it.'

Kyle gave her a disbelieving look.

'Okay, so he'll tell Nancy and she'll tell everyone that you're a wuss.'

Kyle laughed and started to chase her round the kitchen.

Lucie outran him, and both of them were carrying on like a couple of kids when Greg walked in.

'Sorry to interrupt.' Greg tried to smile. He really did.

Lucie had a smudge of buttercream on her nose where Kyle had managed to wipe it. She smiled at Greg. 'Hi, we're just baking cakes for the guests. Want a cup of coffee?'

Kyle motioned to Lucie, indicating she had buttercream on her face.

She quickly wiped it off, and pretended she wasn't squirming because she'd been caught looking like she was flirting with Kyle.

She wasn't flirting with him, she was being playful. It was just bad timing that Greg walked in on a situation that painted a completely different picture.

Greg's smile was forced. 'No, I eh...I have to open up the cafe.'

'Was there something you wanted?' she asked him.

He was already starting to look like he wanted to leave. 'I wondered if you'd like me to drop by later and we could walk together up to the community hall. But it's fine. I'll probably see you there.'

He smiled and went to walk away.

'No, I'd like to do that. What time will you drop by?' Lucie asked him.

'The quilting bee starts tonight around seven,' said Greg. 'I'll be here at six forty–five.'

'I'll be ready,' Lucie told him.

'Okay, see you later.' He nodded at Kyle and then walked out of the kitchen.

Lucie felt deflated.

'Cheer up, Lucie. Greg looked jealous. That's a good sign.'

Lucie stared at Kyle unconvinced.

'It is. And you've got another date with him.'

She sighed. 'I guess so.'

'Come on, let's get these cakes baked before the staff arrive to cook breakfast for the guests.'

Lucie picked up her mixing bowl and continued to make the cakes.

Greg looked forlorn as he walked to the cafe. Seeing Lucie so happy with Kyle felt like a kick in the guts. He wasn't usually the jealous type, and didn't like feeling that way, but when it came to Lucie his emotions were running high.

He was so lost in thought he didn't notice Sylvie wave to him. She hurried over, tucking her phone in her jacket pocket.

'Morning, Greg,' she said chirpily. It was another bright morning, but Greg looked like he had a storm cloud hanging over him.

He blinked out of his thoughts. 'Sylvie.' He was surprised to see her. Hardly anyone was around this early in the morning.

'I've been taking photographs of flowers for my new designs. Zack's garden has some nice snowdrops and daffodils, but I noticed yesterday that there were bluebells growing over there near the park. I popped out to take a few snaps before breakfast.'

'How is your design work going?' he asked her as she walked along with him to the cafe.

'I'm busy working on a new collection and wanted to include spring flowers.'

'Sounds lovely. I used your floral fabric to make a quilted bag for Lucie. She loves it. She's bringing it to the bee tonight, so if you're there you'll see it.'

She knew him well enough to sense an underlying tension. 'Is everything going okay between you and Lucie?' She'd noticed his car was parked outside the cafe and that he'd come from the direction of the lodge.

'Yeah,' he said unconvincingly. 'I was up at the lodge to invite her to go with me to the quilting bee tonight.'

By now they'd arrived at the cafe and he unlocked the door.

'So what's bugging you?' she asked him outright.

They went inside the cafe and he explained what had happened.

'It was probably one of those moments that gave the wrong impression,' said Sylvie.

'They were laughing, being playful and having so much fun — until I walked in.'

'I'm sure Lucie wasn't flirting with Kyle. She's smitten with you. She's not flighty. I don't think she's attracted to Kyle.'

'He's a good looking guy and a lot of fun. What if she hadn't walked into my cafe that first morning when she arrived in town? Kyle would've asked her out on a date, you know he would.'

'Okay, so maybe he would've, but she met you, and Kyle tried to sweet talk her and failed.'

'But what if I stopped Lucie being with the right guy? Maybe that's why things keep conspiring to keep us apart.'

'No, I don't buy that. Lucie likes you.'

'She likes me as a friend. Kyle's asked her to go into business with him.'

'I heard about that.' She paused. 'You should ask her to join you in the cafe.'

He gave her a sheepish look. 'I did. Last night. She was over at my house. We were baking your engagement cake. She's coming back to help me decorate it.'

'What did she say? Did you accept your offer?'

'I told her to take her time and think about it. I even gave her a hybrid option to work with Kyle and me.'

'So she hasn't decided yet?'

'Nope.' He sighed. 'I'm worried she'll end up with Kyle. I've just gotten over Brie and my heart felt clear of any feelings I had for her. Now if I let Lucie slip through my fingers I'll have another broken heart, wishing for a love that was never meant to be.'

'Lucie wouldn't have settled with Kyle. He's a handsome guy, but he's restless, never content. That's fine to begin with, however it becomes tiresome after a while.'

'Do you have time for a coffee?'

'Sure.' She sat down and continued to chat to him. 'Thanks for baking my cake by the way.'

He started to make the coffee. 'You're welcome. We'll have it finished in plenty of time for your engagement party. I'm looking forward to that.'

'Remember to invite Lucie as your date.'

Greg smiled at her. 'You really think I've got a chance with her?'

'Yes, but don't do anything foolish to mess things up,' she told him firmly.

'I always mess things up.'

She smiled at him, knowing this was true. 'At least you're taking Lucie to the bee tonight.'

He nodded and poured their coffee. He looked at the cake cabinet. 'Is it too early for a slice of lemon cake?'

'It's never too early for a slice of cake.'

He cut two pieces and they sat together at one of the tables.

'The bag you made for Lucie sounds lovely. When the women at the bee see it, you'll be inundated with orders to make them one. Including me.'

'You've just solved part of your engagement gift from me. Pretend to be totally surprised of course.'

She laughed and bit into her lemon cake.

'Remember when we were all making Ana's wedding quilt at the bee and Ana had to pretend she didn't know what we were doing?'

Sylvie nodded.

'You'll have to do the same. An engagement quilt is in the making. Jessica has started work on it so that it'll be ready in time for your party.'

'I don't want to cause you all to hurry up. I know the engagement was out of the blue. Zack even surprised me. Don't rush to finish the quilt.'

Greg shook his head. 'We're on it. You know nothing.'

Sylvie pressed her lips together and nodded. Then she gazed out the window and sighed. 'I love this town. I'm so happy I moved here.'

'I'm hoping Lucie will want to stay.'

'When is she going back to your house to finish the cake?'

'I was going to ask her over tomorrow night. When's Ana's housewarming?'

'Two nights from now. Everyone's looking forward to watching the wedding video.'

Lucie and Kyle had baked the cakes in time for the breakfasts to be made.

She helped herself to coffee and hot buttered toast and took it to her room to relax.

Kyle was still planning his menu and showing Penny his suggestions.

Lucie's room window was open and the scent of the flowers wafted in. It was lovely staying at the lodge, but she had to find accommodation. She wanted somewhere in the heart of the town so she could walk to the lodge or Greg's cafe, depending on where she ended up working. She could of course buy a car with some of her savings and live further out in the countryside. However, there had to be somewhere in the hub of the town or even up at the cove.

After breakfast she walked up to the cove to explore the area, enjoy the sunny morning, and check out the cabins. None were currently available, but it was fun to have a look. The air at the cove was so invigorating and the view made her long to stay there. Given the choice, she loved Greg's house the most, but the cabins were great.

There was no one about at this early hour and she meandered along the edge of the cove and breathed in the fresh air. The thought of leaving here and going back to live in the city jarred her. She was sure she was making the right decision to up sticks and settle in town.

No one at the bakery in New York had contacted her since she'd told them she was taking a vacation. Even the woman she shared her apartment with hadn't called or sent a text message. Nothing. Not a peep, like she hadn't existed, or was easily forgotten. If things were reversed and she went back to the city, she was sure she'd gets calls from Nancy, Penny, Jessica and the other girls, and Greg. They'd keep in touch. That's what was at the heart of Snow Bells Haven — not just the quaint small town — it was the people. The townsfolk gave her hope that people still had time for each other. Even when they were busy, they were still baking, sewing dresses and making quilts for their friends. And it was the best feeling in the world knowing she was now part of them.

'Lucie!'

She looked over at the sound of her voice and saw Sylvie standing outside Zack's cabin waving to her.

Lucie went over to the cabin.

'Come on in for a coffee,' said Sylvie, beckoning her inside.

Lucie went in. There was only Sylvie, no sign of Zack.

'Zack's at his house working on his architectural drawings.' She pointed over to her desk where she was painting watercolor flowers and sketching.

'I don't want to disturb you when you're busy working.'

'No, it's fine. I've made fresh coffee. I need a break and it'll be nice to have the company.'

Sylvie went over to the kitchen area and poured two cups of coffee.

Lucie studied the artwork on Sylvie's desk. 'I wish I could draw like this. These flowers are beautiful. I love the bluebells.'

Sylvie handed her a coffee. 'I'm working on a new collection and took photos of these flowers this morning to help me get the design right. I can draw from memory, and not everything is drawn to a botanical level, but I wanted the bluebells to add to this pattern. The bright blue color makes it pop.'

Lucie pulled up a chair and they sat together discussing the design work and then went on to chat about Greg.

'I saw Greg earlier. He said he made you a quilted bag.'

'He did. It's gorgeous.'

'I'll be at the quilting bee tonight, so be sure to bring it with you.'

'I will. He's kitted me out with lots of fabric and other accessories. The bag is brimming full.'

'You sound like I did. You're going to get the quilting bug.'

'Were you into quilting in New York?'

'I dabbled, but never had time to quilt a lot. Now that I live here, I'm busy with my design work, but I have time for hobbies too. The women at the quilting bee are so generous with sharing their skills and I've learned so many new techniques. I feel like I'm a real quilter now.' She pointed to a quilt folded along the back of a couch. 'I made that. Nancy gave me the pattern, and Jessica showed me a great way to stitch the binding on. I'm totally hooked on quilting, though not quite at Greg's level yet.'

'He does have plenty of quilts at home.'

Sylvie smiled and nodded. 'He said you'd been helping bake my cake, so thank you.'

'I had fun making it.'

'Greg's been so happy since you arrived in town.'

Lucie sipped her coffee.

'He's concerned that maybe you like Kyle, if you know what I mean.'

Lucie blinked. 'He told you about what happened this morning?'

Sylvie shrugged. 'He had to confide in someone. I happened to be nearby.'

'I can assure you there's nothing going on between Kyle and me.'

'Greg didn't think there was. He's just looking ahead. Guys like Kyle can wear a woman's defenses down even if he's not intentionally trying to break up a relationship.'

'I know Kyle is trouble. That type of guy isn't for me. He's fun to be around. Incorrigible is how Penny describes him.'

'That's pretty accurate.'

They both agreed.

'I'm not giving you advice, Lucie–'

Lucie cut–in. 'I'm open to advice.'

'You need to be careful not to let Kyle affect things between you and Greg. Hold strong to your feelings for the guy you really like, and don't let outside influences ruin your chance at happiness. I could've made that mistake myself, and I nearly did. Thank goodness I decided to stay here with Zack.'

Lucie finished her coffee. 'I appreciate the advice, Sylvie.'

'Drop by anytime.'

'See you tonight at the quilting bee.'

Sylvie waved her off.

Lucie walked back down to the main street. By now Jessica's quilt shop was open and she decided to pop in.

The sound of a sewing machine whirring in the back of the shop led her to where Jessica was busy making a quilt.

Jessica glanced up and smiled. 'Lucie.'

'Don't stop sewing.'

'I'm working on Sylvie's engagement quilt top. What do you think of the fabric? Nancy and Virginia helped me select it. We've used several floral designs from Sylvie's own collections. It didn't seem right to use someone else's fabric, and these are so pretty.'

'That's a lovely idea.'

'We know she loves patchwork quilts. We've incorporated lots of blues, pinks, lilac and yellow.'

'The colors and fabrics are beautiful.'

Jessica smiled. 'Are you in a hurry, or would you like to help me measure out the quilt batting and cut the backing fabric and the binding?'

'I've no plans for this morning and would love to help, but my quilting skills are basic. I was hoping to learn more at the quilting bee.'

Jessica got up and beckoned Lucie through to select what they needed for the quilt. 'Start learning now. This will let you see how a quilt is made from scratch.'

A surge of enthusiasm charged through Lucie and she happily started to learn what was needed to make the quilt.

Jessica showed her how to work out how much of the soft batting was needed. Lucie cut it. Then they selected the backing fabric.

'With it being a quilt with a floral theme,' Jessica explained, 'we want a pretty backing fabric that will work with it.' Jessica pointed to bolts of fabric that Sylvie had designed. 'One of these flower prints would be lovely.'

Lucie and Jessica lifted down a few rolls that were in the same color theme as the quilt top.

Together they whittled it down to two designs.

'This daisy print is nice,' said Lucie, comparing it to a ditsy floral design that had bluebells, snowdrops and lilac crocus. 'But I prefer the mix of colors in this one.'

'The ditsy print will be perfect.'

Jessica let Lucie measure and cut the fabric.

'I started work on the quilt so we can have it finished in time for Sylvie and Zack's engagement party this weekend. Virginia is due in soon to pick it up to sew some of it, then later this afternoon we're dropping it off to Nancy. She'll work on it and then bring it along to the quilting bee tonight.'

While Lucie put the bolts of fabric back up on the shelf, Virginia came in wearing a lovely cotton print tea dress.

'Lucie's been helping me,' Jessica explained to Virginia. She held up the ditsy print fabric. 'What do you think of this for the quilt backing.'

'It's ideal.'

'I'll fold up the quilt top and put it in a bag. It still needs finishing.' Jessica hurried through to the back of the shop.

Virginia smiled warmly at Lucie. 'How are things with you and Greg?'

Sylvie told her what happened with Kyle.

Virginia tried not to laugh.

'It's okay, I see the funny side of it too,' Lucie admitted.

'Romance is never straightforward, and definitely not in this town. But it keeps us busy.'

Jessica came through with the quilt in a bag and added the backing fabric and batting. Virginia picked up the bag.

'I love your dress,' Lucie commented to Virginia.

'I made it with one of the new fabrics I've got in. I used a vintage tea dress pattern and gave it a modern style update. I'm glad you like it.'

'It's so pretty and yet classy,' said Lucie, wondering if Virginia had others like it in her dress shop.

'And it's easy to wear.' Virginia gave a twirl. 'I like to feel comfortable in a dress. Tea dresses are one of my favorite designs.'

'Are you making any more? I've always wanted a tea dress.'

'Come with me and have a look at the new fabrics. I'll make one like this for you in whatever fabric you like.'

Jessica placed a restraining hand on Lucie's arm. 'Beware. The new fabrics are irresistible. I've already bought up several of the cottons that are part of Sylvie's new summer collection.'

Lucie laughed. 'Thanks for the warning. See you later at the bee, Jessica.' She left the quilt shop with Virginia.

Virginia unlocked the door of her dress shop. 'The new range of fabrics are on display over there.'

Lucie's eyes widened. 'This is going to be very difficult.' The rosebud prints caught her eye, and then Virginia pointed to another design.

'Sylvie's tea rose fabric is gorgeous. I was intending to make a tea dress with it because of the lovely soft rose, green and cream colors. It has a vintage feel to it.'

'Maybe this is going to be easier than I thought.' Lucie unrolled the fabric to picture how it would look as a dress. 'This has to be the perfect tea dress fabric for me. I love it.'

Virginia smiled at her. 'The pattern is for a wrap dress. I'll take your measurements, but it's easy to adjust to fit comfortably.'

Virginia measured Lucie and they decided on the length that she wanted the dress to be.

'I'll start on this soon and give you a call when it's ready, or drop by for a fitting anytime.'

Agreeing that they'd chat at the quilting bee later, Lucie left the dress shop and walked along the main street. The ice cream parlor had opened for the day, and as Lucie went by she noticed a postcard in the front window near the menu. She read it: Apartment available for short–term lease. Enquire here.

Wondering what type of apartment it was, Lucie went in and spoke to one of the ice cream parlor owners. It was owned by a couple and the woman greeted Lucie as she approached the counter.

'I saw the notice in the window about the apartment,' Lucie began.

'Yes, it's upstairs. A couple had planned to lease it for a long vacation, but they cancelled. Would you like to view it?'

'I would.'

'The entrance is outside.' The woman led the way.

Lucie had noticed a pale pink door at the side of the ice cream parlor but assumed it was part of the parlor premises. Instead it led upstairs to a quaint one bedroom apartment. The living room overlooked the main street. It had a bedroom at the back and a bathroom and small kitchen.

'This is a lovely little apartment,' Lucie said, looking around. The pastel colors reminded her of the vanilla, strawberry and pale green tones of the ice cream parlor.

'My husband and I have a house in town and we lease this out to tourists during the holidays, or to locals looking for temporary accommodation.' She smiled at Lucie. 'You're Greg's girlfriend, aren't you? I saw you dancing with him at Ana's wedding.'

The words Greg's girlfriend stirred a sense of excitement and confusion in her, causing her to hesitate before replying. 'We're friends.'

'Oh, right. Well, this is available on a monthly rental basis if you're interested. We only put the ad in the window this morning.' She explained the details and the monthly cost which was far less than Lucie had reckoned.

'I'll take it.' Lucie was never so sure of anything in a long time.

The woman popped downstairs to get the paperwork leaving Lucie to wander around the apartment.

Pale pink curtains on the living room windows gave a soft glow to the cream colored walls. The fact that it was furnished was so handy, and everything from the pretty decor to the fresh linen in the cupboards made her want to move in. She checked out the kitchen and pictured herself baking cakes. It was one of the sweetest apartments she'd ever seen. The rent was a lot less than she paid in the city.

The bathroom was clean, and soft, fluffy towels were provided. They'd thought of everything. She hadn't considered renting holiday accommodation, but this was perfect. A place to call home until she decided where her life was headed.

After signing the paperwork and paying a month's rent in advance, Lucie was free to move in whenever she wanted. The ice cream parlor was on the same side of the main street as Greg's cafe, a few businesses along from him, near the flower shop. It wasn't far to walk back to the lodge, and as she passed the cafe she caught a glimpse of Greg inside. He was busy serving customers and didn't see her, neither did Dwayne or Herb. She continued on to the lodge, almost stunned by the sheer luck of seeing the card in the parlor window. Now all she had to do was check out of the lodge and move into her new apartment.

Penny was pleased for Lucie and gave her a hug. 'That's wonderful. Of course I'd love for you stay at the lodge, but the apartment sounds ideal for you.'

'I can hardly believe I'm about to move in. I'll obviously continue to bake in the mornings for the guests.'

Penny frowned. 'You don't have to do that, Lucie.'

'I want to. To be honest, I'd be lost without early morning baking. Everything is happening so fast, it's the only thing at the moment that keeps me steady. I'm used to the early routine.'

'If you're sure...'

'I am. Besides, it's only a few minutes walk from the lodge.'

'I tell you what,' Penny suggested. 'Why don't you do as we agreed. You were going to stay here for two weeks, and do the baking in exchange for the room accommodation. So, come along and bake for the next two weeks, then we'll see what happens from there. You might be working with Kyle full–time at the restaurant, or at Greg's cafe.'

Penny's suggestion made sense. Lucie nodded and agreed.

'Now, can I get Kyle to help you carry your bags to the apartment?' Penny offered.

'No, I'll manage. I'll make a couple of trips if necessary.' She tried to think of the things she'd bought or accumulated since she'd arrived at the lodge. There was knitting, fabric, new dresses...

'What's all the excitement?' Kyle asked, overhearing their conversation.

'Lucie's moving into her new apartment above the ice cream parlor,' Penny announced.

A flicker of disappointment showed on his face, but he hid it with a smile. 'That's terrific. I'll give you a hand with your things.'

'No, there's no need. I have practically nothing to take with me.'

'Are you sure, because it's no bother,' said Kyle.

'I'm sure, but thanks.' Lucie smiled and then took a deep breath. 'Okay, I'd better get packed.' She headed to her room, leaving Penny happy for her and Kyle wishing she was staying at the lodge a bit longer.

Greg was in the back of the cafe while Dwayne and Herb were cooking pancakes and serving customers.

Dwayne folded blueberries into the pancakes and then blinked as he saw Lucie go past the front window. He nudged Herb, and they exchanged a surprised look.

'Hey, Greg,' Dwayne called through to him.

Greg came through carrying a bag of flour and sugar. 'Yeah?'

'We saw Lucie walk past the cafe. She was loaded down with luggage,' said Dwayne.

Herb frowned. 'She wouldn't leave town without saying good–bye to us, would she?'

The panic that gripped Greg was painful. He dumped the flour and sugar on the counter and ran outside. He looked up and down the street, but there was no sign of her, only a bus driving out of town heading for New York. He ran his hands through his hair, pushing it back from his troubled brow.

Fishing his car keys from his pocket, he hurried towards his car intending to chase after the bus. He brushed past Kyle who was walking down the street carrying a quilt.

'What's the rush, Greg?' Kyle called to him.

Greg paused. 'Have you seen Lucie?'

'Yes, she's just checked out of the lodge,' Kyle told him.

Greg sounded distraught. 'Did she say why she was leaving town?'

'Lucie hasn't left town.'

'Where is she?'

Kyle pointed a few doors along. 'She's rented an apartment above the ice cream parlor.'

The relief washed over Greg. He took a full, steadying breath.

Kyle held the folded quilt. 'She forgot her quilt. She left it on the bed. Penny found it. I was going to hand it to her.'

'I'll take it,' Greg insisted, relieving Kyle of the quilt.

Kyle didn't resist. He could see that Greg was anxious and didn't want to argue with him. 'Okay. Catch you later.'

Greg pressed the buzzer on the pink door. His heart was racing and he hadn't yet calmed down from the panic.

'Who is it?' Lucie said via the intercom.

'It's me, Greg.'

She buzzed him in and opened the apartment door. She was smiling, excited to show him around, until she saw his expression.

'Are you okay? You look stressed–out.'

He stepped inside. 'I thought you'd gone, left town without telling me. The guys saw you go past carrying your luggage, and I saw the bus drive off. I was going to drive after it, but Kyle told me you'd moved in here.' He handed her the quilt. 'You left this at the lodge.'

She took the quilt from him and put it on a chair. 'I would never have left without telling you.'

He gazed down, realizing how foolish he must appear. 'I...I'm so glad you're here.'

'I couldn't wait to move in. I saw the ad in the window and signed the lease. I could hardly believe I'd got such a nice apartment.' She smiled. 'I was about to go to the cafe to tell you. I thought you'd be pleased.'

'I am pleased.' His heart was still pounding. 'It's great.' He looked around and nodded. 'It's ideal for you.'

'I'd offer you a coffee but I haven't checked out the kitchen supplies yet.'

'That's fine,' he assured her. 'Anything you need, you can have from the cafe. Anything you want.'

She smiled at him. 'Thanks, Greg.'

He took a deep breath. 'Well, I'd better get back. The cafe's busy. I'll pick you up here instead of at the lodge.'

'Yes, I'm looking forward to the quilting bee.'

He smiled as she waved him off, and tried not to look like he'd been emotionally wrecked.

Despite the cafe being busy, Dwayne and Herb rushed over to Greg as he arrived back.

'Has she gone? Is she coming back?' Dwayne asked anxiously.

'Are you going after her?' Herb added.

'Everything's okay. She's moved into the apartment above the ice cream parlor.'

The guys were relieved.

'You look wrung out,' Herb told Greg.

'I feel like it,' Greg admitted.

Dwayne sat him down behind the counter near the back of the cafe. 'I'll make you a hot chocolate. That'll buck you up.'

Greg sat there and started to feel his heart rate notch down to normal.

Herb rustled up the customers orders while Dwayne hurried to make a hot chocolate.

Greg sighed heavily. 'When I thought Lucie had gone...' He shook his head. 'I didn't like how I felt.' His guts twisted as he relived it.

Dwayne handed him the hot chocolate. 'Get that down you, buddy.'

Greg took a sip. 'It's made me realize I need to stop messing around and let Lucie know how I really feel about her.' He sighed again. 'How easily she could've just been gone.'

Dwayne stopped him reliving it again. 'It didn't happen. She didn't leave. It was the complete opposite. She's moved into an apartment. That means she's serious about staying in town.'

Greg drank his hot chocolate. 'You're right. But I still think I need to figure out how to let her know I want to be more than friends with her, without pressurizing or hurrying her.'

Herb was listening. 'You're taking her to the quilting bee tonight, bud. You're in your element when it comes to sewing. That's where you shine.'

Greg smiled at them and planned to tell Lucie how he felt.

Chapter Fifteen

Lucie hurried to get ready for the quilting bee. Handily, her quilting bag was still filled with everything she needed. All she had to do was put on one of the vintage tops she'd bought and tidy her hair. She let her messy ponytail down, brushed her hair and applied some light makeup.

The day had passed in a blur of activity, getting things organized in her new apartment. She'd stocked up on food items from the grocery store and chatted to Nancy about what had happened. Nancy was delighted and would no doubt tell everyone in town, but she was fine with that.

Greg arrived on time. She opened the door and let him in. He was carrying two boxes of cupcakes and had a duffel bag slung over his shoulder. He smiled knowingly when he saw the rosy glow on her cheeks.

'Don't rush, I can wait.' He figured she'd lost track of time and had been running around getting ready.

'No, I'm ready,' she said chirpily. Then she sighed and smiled at him. 'I was busy sorting things here and didn't realize the time.' She held up the quilting bag. 'I assume I'm well kitted–out?'

'You are, and there are always items to share at the bee.'

She looked at the cupcakes.

'I never go empty–handed. I've made raspberry cupcakes with vanilla frosting and mocha cupcakes with chocolate sprinkles.'

'I haven't got any cakes to contribute.'

'You don't need to. Nancy and a few of the other women always bring some and we share them.'

He admired what she'd done with the apartment. She'd added vases of tulips and daffodils, and the quilt she'd bought was ready to snuggle under on the couch.

She showed him the kitchen. The cupboards were a pale pistachio green and matched the curtains on the window. She opened the cupboards to show him they were now stocked with grocery items.

'The kitchen is small but well–equipped.' She lifted up a set of baking bowls. 'I'll be able to bake whatever I need here. The cooker even has a double oven. I haven't used it yet, but everything's working.' She'd barely eaten anything all day and hoped her tummy wouldn't rumble.

Greg had aimed to talk to her before they left for the bee. In his mind he'd gone over all the things he wanted to say, and he'd been planning to tell her how he really felt about her.

Lucie continued to gush enthusiastically about her new apartment, and there wasn't the right moment to interrupt her. They left with Lucie still telling him about the things she'd been up to, and they walked to the community hall in a few minutes. It was only when they arrived that Lucie realized she'd been talking non–stop.

'Was there something you wanted to tell me?' she asked as they went inside the hall. It was busy with the women members. Long tables were set up, some with sewing machines, and there was an air of fun and chatter. Most of the women were working on quilts. A few were stitching appliqué and this was something Lucie had always wanted to learn. One woman was embroidering, and a couple of them were dressmaking.

Greg put the cupcakes down on a table and smiled at Lucie. 'We'll talk some other time. Let's grab a seat beside Nancy and Jessica.'

Lucie and Greg went over and sat down. Greg studied the engagement quilt they were working on. 'This is looking lovely. Sylvie will love it.'

Jessica flipped the edge of the quilt over to show Lucie. 'The ditsy print works so well as the backing fabric.' She went on to tell those around her how Lucie had helped select it. It seemed important to the members that several of them were involved in the making of Sylvie's quilt, even though Jessica and Virginia had stitched most of it.

'A quilt is filled with memories and special moments,' Jessica explained to Lucie. 'It belongs to the person it was made for, but every stitch retains the love put into it by the quilters that made it for them.'

Lucie smiled and nodded.

'We're hand stitching part of it and machine quilting the rest,' said Jessica. She gave Lucie the needle and thread she was using to sew part of the quilt. 'Now join in and add your stitches. Follow along the same lines as we've started. Shout if you get stuck.'

Lucie didn't want to waste the quilt, but straight stitching was something she could manage. They were using a lovely light turquoise thread that blended into the fabric design and yet subtly highlighted the neat stitches.

While Lucie worked on her part of the quilt, Jessica and Nancy stitched other parts, all while chatting about local news and gossip. Lucie's move to the new apartment was one of the prime topics, and she told them all about the things she'd done and how much she loved the kitchen.

'When I'm settled you'll have to come round for afternoon tea and cakes.' Lucie's invitation was met with enthusiasm by the women.

In all the chit–chat, Greg still hadn't had a moment to talk to Lucie. He supposed he could talk to her later when he walked her home, so he relaxed and started to fully enjoy the evening.

Greg dug out quilt patterns from his bag. 'I brought these so we can start planning Sylvie and Zack's wedding quilt. These are classic designs, but we can add a modern twist...'

The first part of the evening was productive and Lucie learned a couple of new quilting techniques including handy methods to tie off threads.

During the evening they took a break to enjoy coffee and cakes. Lucie helped Nancy and Virginia cut the larger cakes that members had contributed. These pieces were handed around along with Greg's cupcakes and chocolate cookies. No food or drinks were allowed near the quilts, and most of them stood near the serving tables.

The women were admiring the bag Greg had made for Lucie, and teasing him that he'd be inundated with orders to make similar bags for them, when Penny came hurrying in.

'Sorry I'm late,' said Penny, 'but Kyle had a slight accident and I had to deal with that.'

'Is he okay?' Lucie was the first to ask.

Penny nodded, but clearly she'd been distressed. 'Yes, he's sprained his ankle. I've left him relaxing at the lodge with his feet up. Staff are checking in on him, and I've told him to phone if he needs me.'

'How did he sprain his ankle?' Nancy asked Penny.

Penny sighed in exasperation. 'You know how Kyle likes to keep himself fit and has that restless streak in him?'

The women and Greg nodded.

'Well, I don't know what was wrong, but this afternoon he just couldn't settle. He said he was going up to the cove to burn off some energy. I thought that was fine, maybe it would shake off whatever was bugging him. Anyway, he was running along the edge of the cove and was making one of those jumps guys do up there.'

Nancy pursed her lips. 'Some guys have no sense. Those rocks can be dangerous. It's no place to leap around.'

The other ladies nodded, as did Greg. He'd tried it once and took a tumble, sustaining bruises. He never tried it again, and never told anyone. He kept his secret to himself as Penny continued.

'He said he made the jump fine, but went over on his ankle stepping across a gap.' Penny's tone indicated her disbelief. 'Thankfully, Zack saw what happened and drove Kyle back to the lodge. It's a minor sprain. He'll be fine in a couple of days. But of course, I went and gave two of our catering staff time off to visit their families in the city. I thought that with Kyle being around he could handle cooking for the guests, and he was happy to do this and try out some of the new menu dishes he's been planning.'

'So now you're short staffed?' said Nancy.

Penny nodded. 'We'll get by, but...' She shrugged. 'Kyle needs to calm down and deal with that restless streak in him.'

Lucie spoke up. 'I'd be glad to help out with the cooking at the lodge until Kyle's on his feet again.'

'No, you've just moved into your apartment. I don't want to impose on your time,' said Penny.

'I've almost finished doing what I need at the apartment. With it being a rental, there's little I can do or want to change. It's pretty much perfect.'

This was typical of Lucie, Greg thought, listening to her generously stepping in yet again to help the townsfolk. He could never imagine Brie doing something like this. Every time he thought how great Lucie was, she notched up the bar to another level.

Penny accepted Lucie's offer, but insisted she would be paid for it. Although Lucie wasn't seeking payment, they agreed to do this.

Lucie sipped her coffee and reached over to pick up one of Greg's cupcakes, and accidentally ended up closer to Greg than she'd intended. To prevent herself from spilling coffee on his shirt, she pressed her hand against his chest and felt the wall of muscle tense as she touched him. She looked up and their eyes met in a moment of the nearest to passion that she'd seen from him.

'Oops!' she stepped back, starting to blush.

Greg handed her a cupcake. She noticed how strong and yet artistic his hands were. Clean and smooth, and yet manly. For a second she thought about those hands of his touching her, holding her close, and the blush in her cheeks burned like fire.

Lucie tried to fan herself, but with a coffee in one hand and a cupcake in the other, she fumbled to put her cup down so she could waft her hand in front of her face.

Greg had no idea he was the cause of her flushed reaction. He blamed it on the heating. 'It's warm in here tonight.'

Lucie hid the truth behind his mistake. 'It is. But I'm enjoying the quilting bee. I've even learned new techniques.'

He smiled at her. 'Not bad for your first night as a member.'

Jessica joined them and lifted up one of the cupcakes. 'I believe Lucie has a hidden knack for quilting. I can always tell.' She smiled at Lucie. 'You're creative with your cake baking, and this will work with your quilting.'

'Thanks, Jessica,' said Lucie.

Penny hurried over to Lucie. 'I've just phoned Kyle and told him you're going to help with the cooking for the next couple of days, Lucie. He was planning to work sitting down in the kitchen to make the lunches and dinners.'

'That would be another accident waiting to happen,' said Nancy, overhearing them.

Penny nodded firmly. 'Exactly. So I've told him to relax.'

After the coffee and cake break, the sewing started up again, and they planned Sylvie's wedding quilt.

'I have a sample catalogue of all of Sylvie's fabric designs,' said Jessica. 'It was sent to me by the fabric company when I ordered more floral prints from her new summer collection. Some of the prints will eventually go out of production, so I thought I could do a bulk order of samples of every fabric she's designed and we could put them all into her wedding quilt.'

'That's a wonderful idea,' said Lucie. Everyone agreed.

'I'll order these tomorrow,' Jessica added. 'The company offered me a huge discount on fabric samples like this. It'll work out well.'

The members of the bee had a fund that they used to buy fabric for special projects and had more than enough money to afford to do this.

Penny came to join in their little circle as they worked on Sylvie's quilt and planned the wedding quilt design. They squeezed in an extra chair and this caused Greg to budge up closer to Lucie. He wanted to whisper to her how much he cared about her. His heart beat faster just being near her.

Penny brought an embroidery hoop from her sewing bag. A piece of white cotton fabric was stretched tight in the hoop. A floral and butterfly design was drawn on the fabric. Parts of it had been stitched with beautiful colors of embroidery thread. 'I didn't have time to bring the quilt I'm making, so I grabbed my embroidery.'

'I've always wanted to try embroidery,' said Lucie, leaning close to study the details. The wings of the butterfly were beautifully sewn and the smooth, neat stitches emphasized the silky cotton thread. 'What type of stitches are you using?'

'Satin stitch and some French knots. Would you like to try sewing the other part of the wing using satin stitches?'

Lucie nodded. 'I'd love to have a go.'

Penny showed her how to do this and then handed the embroidery hoop to Lucie.

Feeling nervous, but eager to learn, Lucie took the needle and started to embroider the wing. She kept her stitches neat, flat and close together and loved the vibrant colors of the thread Penny was using.

There was a little bumblebee design at the top of the embroidery. Penny encouraged Lucie to sew it using golden yellow, amber and chocolate brown thread. 'I prefer these tones rather than yellow and black. It creates a warmer look to the bee.'

Lucie surprised herself that she was managing to sew the satin stitches and finish the bee. She also learned how to create his eyes with French knots.

When it came to embroidering the leaves, Greg joined in. 'My favorite is the fishbone stitch for sewing leaves.' He showed Lucie how to sew this. Again, the touch of his hand brushing against hers sent her pulse racing.

Lucie tried this new stitch and then handed the embroidery hoop back to Penny, thanking her.

'Want to make a start on your small quilt?' Greg said to Lucie.

'Yes.' She dug out a selection of fabric pieces from her bag and he helped her cut the prints she wanted so that they were ready for sewing.

At the end of the evening the women packed their quilting away and headed home. Usually Nancy was picked up by Nate and they walked home together. However, Nancy and Penny were talking to Lucie. They were asking about her apartment, so she invited them to pop in on their way home to have a look. Virginia joined them.

Greg's plans to walk Lucie home were scuppered. He walked as far as the front of the ice cream parlor with them.

Lucie unlocked the pink door and the women went inside. She smiled at Greg. 'You're welcome to join us.'

'No, I'd better be heading home. It's quite late and I have an early start in the morning.' He tried to sound cheerful despite being disappointed.

The excited chatter of the women drifted out from the doorway.

Greg went to walk away and then paused. 'Are we still on for tomorrow night at my house, decorating Sylvie's cake?'

'Yes, sure. Oh wait, why don't we finish icing it here at my apartment? That would save you having to drive me back and forth to your house.' Lucie's suggestion seemed sensible, and she was obviously keen to try out her new kitchen.

'Okay. Great idea. I'll bring the cake with me.'

'See you then,' Lucie said, smiling at him.

Greg nodded, waved and walked away to his car.

The weight of the night pressed heavily on his shoulders as he drove home. He was happy for Lucie. She'd found an apartment and enjoyed the quilting bee, but now she wasn't going to finish decorating the cake at his house. It felt like she was drifting away from him, and he'd have to fight even harder not to let that happen.

Lucie was tucked up in bed. The first night in her new apartment was a mix of excitement and hoping she wouldn't sleep in. She'd promised Penny she would be at the lodge early to bake the cakes and then help cook the breakfasts. She set two alarms on her phone and snuggled under the covers and her comforting quilt.

She'd had fun showing Nancy, Penny and Virginia the apartment, and sharing her excitement with them. Although the women lived in town, they hadn't seen inside the ice cream parlor's apartment, so their interest was genuine and she enjoyed their company.

Drifting off to sleep, she thought about Greg and wondered how to deal with the telltale blushes his closeness caused in her. She also wished she hadn't cancelled her visit to his house. Yes, she loved the apartment, and the cabins at the cove, but that house of his was perfect.

Still thinking of Greg, she fell asleep and woke up on her first alarm.

Kyle could be so stubborn. Lucie couldn't work with him directing every move she made in the kitchen from the chair he was sitting on. His injured ankle was rested up on a footstool.

'Make sure to keep the scrambled eggs warm on the hot plates,' Kyle instructed her. 'And fry the bacon before making the toast.'

At one point Lucie burst out laughing.

'What's so funny?' he asked.

'How close to the wind you're sailing.' She held up a cooking spatula.

He pretended to feel threatened, and then smiled.

This sort of eased the tension, and it probably occurred to him that he was being bossy, because he quit telling her what to do.

Penny darted in and out of the kitchen.

'Calm down, Aunt Penny,' Kyle told her. 'Lucie's got everything in hand.'

And Lucie had. The breakfasts were served to the guests without a hitch, even with Kyle hopping about the kitchen insisting he should decorate the eggs with sprigs of parsley.

Lucie let him hop around, and then made a bolt back to her apartment when the happy chaos was over.

The rest of her day was a whirlwind of phone calls to New York to organize her belongings to be packed up and sent to the town, and picking up other essentials for her new apartment. She also helped cook the lunches at the lodge. Kyle said the staff had the dinner schedule covered.

In the late afternoon she flopped down on the couch, threw her quilt over herself and unintentionally fell asleep. The buzzer woke her with a start.

The evening light shining in the living room window gave her no reason to check the time. She'd done it again! Greg was here and she wasn't ready. Nothing was prepared in the kitchen, and her hair was a ruffled mess.

Taking a steadying breath, she buzzed him in and decided to jump off into the deep end.

Her messy ponytail told him everything he needed to know.

He tried not to laugh and failed.

'I'm glad you're amused, Greg.'

'I can wait or come back later.' He'd brought the fruit cake with him. He also had icing sugar, fondant icing and several other items. Greg was prepared and she was the complete opposite.

'No, let's get this cake finished.'

He headed into the kitchen and started to sort out the baking bowls.

'I don't ever sleep in,' Lucie objected.

He gave her a look.

'Except when it comes to dates with you,' she said.

'Well, you can have another crack at it tomorrow night.'

She frowned. 'What's on our agenda then?'

'Ana and Caleb's housewarming party.'

'Ah, I definitely don't want to miss that.'

'You mean you can't wait to laugh at my dancing,' Greg corrected her.

'Our dancing. Remember, I was part of the fiasco.'

He conceded the point. 'It should be entertaining.'

'Oh, yeah!'

He moved around her in the tight confines of the kitchen, expertly measuring out the ingredients.

She looked at him. The kitchen felt smaller having Greg standing there. His broad shoulders and height seemed to fill it. He paused to roll up his sleeves, revealing the whipcord lean muscles in his forearms. She'd seen his fit physique when he was swimming at the cove, and even the thought of this sent her emotions haywire.

He glanced at her. Had he sensed the effect he had on her? Was it that obvious? Her heart thundered as he stepped closer like he was about to confide in her.

But his phone rang and he stepped back to take the call, recognizing the caller ID. 'Hi. Right. No, I'm still in town. I'm near the ice cream parlor. Okay. Yeah. I'll be right there.' He clicked the call off.

Lucie's eyes were anxious. 'Something wrong?'

'That was the diner. They're having a birthday party there right now, but two car loads of tourists have dropped by. They're short staffed. They haven't found a suitable replacement for Ana. They saw me lock up the cafe and wondered if I could help tonight. We always help each other out.'

'You should go.'

He nodded and walked out of the kitchen.

'I could go with you if you want,' she offered.

'No, but if you could finish icing the cake, that would be great.'

'I'll do that, Greg.'

He smiled tightly, clearly willing to help the diner, but disappointed that he had to leave Lucie. 'Pick you up here tomorrow night? Around seven?'

'I promise I'll be ready.'

'Just promise to go with me to the housewarming party.'

'I promise.'

He smiled again and hurried away.

She ran to the living room window and peered out, watching him walk away towards the diner, and her heart ached a little seeing him go.

Lucie was glad to have the cake decorating to keep her occupied, but that didn't stop her thinking about Greg. She thought about him being there in her kitchen, and now she had another glimpse into what her life would be like if Greg was in it full–time.

She made lots of fondant flowers, including daffodils, bluebells, snowdrops and other spring flowers — signifying Sylvie and Zack's springtime engagement. If they got married in the summer, Greg would probably bake their wedding cake, and this would allow for an array of summertime flowers. She finished by icing the couple's name on the top of the cake and entwining it with pink hearts.

This was the type of cake she thought Sylvie would like as it reminded Lucie of some of her fabric designs. It was also the kind of cake Lucie would want if someone ever asked her to marry him and she'd found the man she wanted to accept.

It was late when Lucie finally put the cake in the white cardboard box Greg had brought, and sat it safely in the kitchen.

She gazed out the living room window before getting ready for bed. The chaos at the diner would be finished by now. She couldn't see the diner from here, but she noticed that the glow on the sidewalk from the diner lights had dimmed, suggesting it was closed for the night.

Greg would be home now too, in bed, asleep.

Lucie flicked the lights off in the living room and padded through to the bedroom. A bright moon shone in the night sky and she watched it for a few moments before closing her eyes. Another day would be dawning soon, and another date with Greg.

'You're not going to be fit to go to Ana's housewarming if you don't sit down,' Lucie scolded Kyle.

He limped around the lodge kitchen the next morning. 'My ankle is a lot better.'

'Yes, but you've got all day to rest it and make sure it's okay for the party,' she reasoned with him. 'Stop bouncing around like a bunny rabbit.'

He sat down on a chair, shoulders slumped, and sighed. 'I'm no good at sitting around doing nothing,' he complained.

Lucie handed him a bowl of frosting. 'You can ice the vanilla cupcakes while I make the eggs and the toast.'

He whipped up the frosting in the mixing bowl and started to swirl it on to the cupcakes. 'Extra guests arrived for an overnight stay, so we need plenty of scrambled eggs for breakfast.'

Lucie figured it was the tourists from the diner. She told Kyle what had happened with Greg.

'Is Greg taking you to the housewarming tonight?'

'Yes, he is.'

Kyle smiled. 'I'll try not to laugh when we watch Greg's dancing in the wedding video.' He concentrated on the bowl of frosting, but his shoulders couldn't hide his snickering.

'No you won't, Kyle,' she said, and then smiled.

'It should be a fun party. Caleb and the guys have set up a temporary dance floor in the garden. Ana wants guests to enjoy dancing.'

Lucie cooked the scrambled eggs and bacon. 'This town seems to be one continuous list of parties and fun events.' She wouldn't be able to relax any time soon with everything like this going on.

Kyle frowned. 'I fail to see the downside of that.'
Lucie reconsidered. 'Neither do I.'

Lucie was determined to be ready for her date with Greg. She'd helped cook the lunches and prepared the dinner menu for the lodge. Between all the cooking, she'd gone shopping and bought a dress that was in the window of the vintage clothes shop. It was different from the tea dress Virginia was making for her. The vintage dress had a pretty butterfly print and could be dressed up for a party or worn during the day. She'd laid it out on her bed ready to wear to the housewarming, along with the shoes she'd worn to the wedding.

She showered and washed her hair, drying it smooth and silky, applied her makeup and then sat down on the couch to relax. She had her quilting bag beside her and passed the time sorting through the pieces of fabric Greg had helped her cut for her small quilt, imagining what it would look like when she started sewing it. He'd said she could use his machines whenever she wanted.

Despite the best of intentions, Lucie became so engrossed in the quilting, laying out the different prints, matching them with the thread, that she forgot the time. It was only when her phone alarm alerted her it was five minutes to seven that she jumped up and ran through to the bedroom.

Five minutes to throw her dress on. She could do this.

She'd just stepped into her shoes when Greg pressed the buzzer.

Checking her hair in the mirror, she decided she didn't look like she'd been running around late again.

Smiling brightly she let him in.

He'd gone home to shower and change into smart casuals. He was looking handsome and her heart squeezed when he smiled at her.

'Pretty dress,' he said.

'I bought it from the vintage shop. All these party events have forced me to rethink my wardrobe.' She shrugged. 'Not that I need an excuse for buying new things. The bargains in this town are great.'

He stepped inside and looked around while she fetched her purse and jacket. There was no sign of her having slept in, but he sensed she'd been dashing around again. She had that look to her. He was beginning to know every little expression on that lovely face of hers.

She saw him glance at her, and sighed. ‘Okay, I was so engrossed in the quilting fabrics that I—’

He cut–in. ‘Relax. It’s fine.’

She smiled, and they headed out, got in his car and drove to Ana and Caleb’s house.

Greg pulled up outside the house. Quite a few cars were there already.

As she stepped out of the car she jolted. ‘I forgot to buy a housewarming gift.’

Greg reached into the back seat and lifted out a gift wrapped parcel. ‘It’s a set of quilted cushions. We’re not arriving empty handed.’

Lucie smiled at him.

Music sounded from inside the house and the windows were aglow with lights.

Ana and Caleb welcomed them in, and soon they were in the hub of the party.

Nate and Nancy were there, along with Jessica and the sheriff, and others that Lucie had met at the wedding. The house was busy, and she thought the dance floor outside in the garden was a great idea to handle the overspill and give couples a chance to dance.

‘I’d invite you to dance but...’ Greg winced.

Instead, they took a look around the house, admiring the decor.

‘This is a nice house,’ Lucie said to Greg.

‘Do you ever picture yourself having something like this?’ Greg looked right at her.

Her heart started to pound, wondering how to reply without encouraging him too much or too little.

Before she could respond, Nate and Nancy joined them. ‘Isn’t this a great house for a newly wed couple?’ said Nancy.

‘I was just saying something like that to Lucie,’ Greg replied.

Nate smiled at Lucie. ‘I hear you’re living above the ice cream parlor. We’re so glad you’re moving to Snow Bells Haven.’

‘Thank you, Nate.’

Nearby, the wedding quilt was on display.

Lucie smiled at Nancy. ‘There’s so much work that’s gone into it.’

'The members of the quilting bee all contributed to it. Several of us, including Greg, stitched it. We used one of Greg's design suggestions.'

Penny joined them. 'Now we've Sylvie and Zack's wedding quilt to start on. I do love when we've got a project like this.'

Nancy gave a knowing look to Lucie and Greg. 'Perhaps we'll be making plans for another engagement quilt soon.'

Before Lucie or Greg could respond, Kyle cut–in on the conversation. 'I'm not planning to get engaged yet.' He grinned at Nancy.

Nancy smiled at him. 'How is your ankle?'

'It's fine,' said Kyle. 'I should be able to manage a dance later.'

Ana's voice sounded over everything. 'We're showing the wedding video folks. Come and join us.'

The guests gathered in the living room, and Caleb played the video on their large screen television. The lights were dimmed and everyone was eager to see the events of the wedding day.

Greg stood close to Lucie. They were standing together behind Nancy, Nate, Jessica and the sheriff who were seated on a couch. Penny sat on a chair with Kyle balanced on the arm of it. Everyone was quiet as the music began, introducing the couple, and then showed the bride arriving in the horse–drawn carriage, followed by the bridesmaids. A close–up of Brielle jarred Lucie. She knew Greg didn't love his ex, but it still upset her slightly especially as Brielle had tried to ruin her chances with Greg.

Moving on from the arrival of the wedding party, the video continued with the events of the day, leading on to the dancing in the evening.

Lucie sensed Greg's tension. She glanced at him, giving him a look of assurance.

The video highlighted more of Greg's dancing than he'd hoped for, but he found himself happy to see Lucie there, in his arms, smiling at him, no matter how out of step his waltzing was. They looked like a couple, a real couple, happy to be together dancing at the wedding.

Lucie didn't know Greg's reaction as he hid it well.

She smiled at him and squeezed his hand. He smiled back at her, and as she went to let go of his hand, he kept a hold of it, keeping her close.

The guests were laughing at Greg's antics, enjoying the fun of it, seeing that he didn't care and was happy to be dancing with Lucie.

Greg started to laugh at a particularly ridiculous bit when he'd attempted to keep up with everyone in a circle dance.

'I thought my waltz was bad,' said Greg.

Everyone laughed that he was prepared to laugh at himself.

Lucie joined in, but every time the video showed Greg she couldn't help but feel that he looked so handsome. Kyle was a good looking guy, but didn't come across as handsome on screen as her Greg. She jolted. She'd just called him *her* Greg.

In that moment her uncertain thoughts came flooding back. Greg obviously liked her as a friend, but was that all they'd ever be?

The tension showed on her face. Greg squeezed her hand and whispered to her. 'Everything okay?'

'Yes,' she lied, and continued to watch the video conclude with Ana and Caleb leaving in the horse–drawn carriage.

A cheer and round of applause filled the living room as the video ended. Caleb flicked the lights on again. 'If anyone wants a copy let me know.'

Greg raised his hand. 'I do.'

Caleb nodded. 'I'll make sure you get one, Greg.'

Others then started to want copies.

'The dancing is about to start again now,' Ana announced.

People began heading outside for the dancing.

The dance floor was lit with garden lanterns. Ana and Caleb took to the floor along with other couples. Dwayne and Herb were there with their ladies.

'Shall we?' Greg held his hand out to Lucie.

She accepted, and as he held her in his arms, she forgot about the music, and danced to the rhythm that Greg set. As they waltzed around the floor she didn't care that they were out of time with the others, because they were almost in step with each other and that's all that mattered to Lucie.

Kyle's injury had more or less healed and he danced a couple of times with Penny, Ana and Virginia. He smiled at Lucie but didn't cut–in on Greg. It was pretty clear that they only had eyes for each other. As did Sylvie and Zack. Kyle hadn't found the woman for him, but maybe one day she'd arrive in town.

As the housewarming party drew to a close and guests started to leave, people agreed that it had been a joyful time.

Lucie rewound Greg's question from earlier. Did she ever picture herself having something like this? A settled life with a man she loved dearly? Her reply now was a heartfelt yes.

After the party Greg drove Lucie to her apartment. He pulled up outside the door.

'I had a nice time, Greg.'

He wanted to tell her how he felt, to take her in his arms and never let her go. However, the evening had gone so well he didn't want to jeopardize it, and so he kept his feelings to himself and waved her off as she stepped out of the car.

'Good–night, Lucie.' He smiled and waited until she was safely inside.

She glanced back at him. 'Good–night, Greg.' Then she closed the door.

It felt like it slammed against his heart.

Trying to shoulder the pressure of his feelings, he drove off home.

When he arrived back he noticed that his house didn't provide the comfort it used to. Something had changed. He'd changed. He was in love with Lucie, and anywhere without her would always be a little bit empty no matter how warm and welcoming.

Later that night, Lucie hung her butterfly dress in the closet and went to bed. For some reason she wasn't tired. If the night had been later, closer to the early hours of the morning, she'd have headed along to the lodge to start baking. To do this right now would signal that something wasn't settled in her world, so she lay in bed and rewound the evening with Greg. The way he'd said good–night was friendly, no more, no less. She'd have to find a way to speak up and tell him that she wanted his friendship, but also his love. To do this would require the courage to risk rejection and she wasn't confident she could do this. However, to stay quiet was the surest way to let the love of her life slip through her fingers. When he'd held her in his arms while they were dancing, it was the closest to happiness she could imagine. She'd have to find the right moment to tell him how she really felt about him, no matter what the consequences.

Greg couldn't sleep a wink. He got up and went outside, hoping to clear his thoughts in the night air.

He sat on the porch gazing out at the vast night sky. The dawn hadn't even hinted of its arrival yet. He was deep in the middle of the night, alone with his thoughts, wondering if he should do something drastic and out of character. He had to believe that Lucie cared about him. He'd seen how she blushed when they were close. She wasn't a particularly shy young woman, in fact, she was capable and confident. Only a woman with a strong nature would pack up her life in the city and take the most amazing chance at a new life here in Snow Bells Haven. No matter what happened, he'd admire her forever for having the strength to do that.

The air bore the scent of the trees and flowers, and the house was quietly watching his back. This was a house he'd always felt at home in, and it bothered him deeply when this ceased to be the case. It felt like a betrayal of his home, of his heritage, of the roof over his head that had sheltered him from when he was a young boy to the man he was today. He shook his head in a futile attempt to realign his feelings to how they used to be. But loving Lucie...now there was no going back. The only way was forward. This house would only feel like home again when he had the true love of his life here with him to share it.

He looked at his car, and it took all his strength to stop himself from getting in it and driving into town to tell her how he felt. In a short time he'd fallen in love more intensely and decidedly than in all the years he'd foolishly spent wanting Brie.

Gazing at the sky that was scattered with stars, he wanted to shout Lucie's name out into the vast landscape where no one would hear him. He stood up and looked at the expanse of the dark sky and took a long, steadying breath. In his heart he called her name, hearing it burn through every part of his being. His breathing was tense, and again he fought against the urge to jump in the car and drive off. He considered his options...

Start work early, work off his feelings... Make himself a strong cup of coffee and study the plans for the cafe's renovation... Throw himself in bed like any sensible man and get some sleep...

But none of these options felt right, and so, despite everything, he went inside, got dressed, picked up his car keys and drove into town to get Lucie.

Lucie couldn't get back to sleep. It was like someone had shouted her name in her dreams and woken her up. The feeling disturbed her. She put it down to sleeping in a new apartment. It was obviously going to take time for her to settle.

She got up and made a cup of warm milk. She sipped it curled up on the couch and gazed out the window at the night sky.

She kept thinking about Greg. The more she was in his company the deeper in love she was falling.

She remembered her first impression of the town, waking up in the bus and seeing it full of tree blossom and spring flowers. It had offered her more potential for happiness in a short time than in all her years in the city.

If she hadn't met Greg she would still have wanted to move here. But no man she'd ever met affected her the way he did.

Restless, she got up from the couch and went over to the window, opening it to breath in the night air. The town was so quiet. She listened. Not a peep from anything. Then in the distance the sound of a car approaching disturbed the quietude. She sighed. Even here some people never slept. She smiled at her own silliness. She was the one watching out the window instead of being tucked up in bed.

The sound of the car drew nearer. The driver seemed to be in a hurry.

Curious to see who it was, she peered out the window as the headlights shone further along the main street. Then she saw the car pull up outside her apartment, and realized it was Greg.

She watched him get out quickly, the urgency in him was clear.

He glanced up at her and she nodded, buzzing him in.

Her heart was racing as she opened the door. He stood there looking the most handsome she'd ever seen him. She wanted to ask what was wrong, but all her instincts told her nothing was wrong. Nothing that two stubborn people who loved each other couldn't mend in a heartbeat.

Greg stepped close and gazed at her. 'I couldn't sleep. I had to see you, to tell you how I feel.'

She felt the tears of happiness well up as she realized they both wanted the same thing — each other.

He pulled her close and she melted into him.

'I love you, Lucie,' he said, his voice deep and true.

'I love you too,' she murmured, and then let herself feel everything she'd held back from him.

She kissed him with love, with passion, and yes with friendship, for they were indeed friends, but more than that, they were meant for each other. She'd found the man she believed she would be happy with.

'Will you go with me to Sylvie and Zack's engagement party this weekend?' he asked her.

'Yes, I will.'

'As my date, a real date, Lucie?'

She nodded and smiled at him. 'A real date.'

He wrapped her in a warm embrace like he'd never let her go. 'I want to date you the way we were supposed to have been. Not just friends.'

'I want that too,' she said.

He hugged the breath from her, and then he kissed her again. Finally, they were both sure they could begin planning a happy future together in Snow Bells Haven.

At Sylvie and Zack's engagement party, Greg and Lucie arrived together holding hands. The clearest signal to everyone that they were now together. Lucie wore the tea dress that Virginia had made for her.

The cake they'd baked for the party was set up on the buffet table and greatly appreciated, as was the engagement quilt the members of the quilting bee had made.

Greg and Lucie celebrated their friends' engagement, dancing at the community hall, showing the townsfolk that they were another well–matched couple.

Nancy was the first to comment to Lucie and Greg. 'Snow Bells Haven certainly has a reputation for creating love and romance. I'm so happy for both of you.'

Greg smiled at Nancy.

'Thank you, Nancy,' said Lucie.

Greg danced a slow waltz with Lucie. 'I guess everyone will know we're together now.'

Lucie smiled. 'I wonder what type of quilt they'll sew for us?'

'It'll have flowers galore and cupcakes for sure,' he said.

'It sounds perfect.'

As the lights in the hall dimmed for a romantic slow dance, Greg pulled Lucie close to him. He gazed down at her and smiled warmly. 'I love you with all my heart, Lucie.'

She kissed him, and for the first time ever he danced in perfect step with her.

End

About the Author:

De-ann Black is a bestselling author, scriptwriter and former newspaper journalist. She has over 70 books published. Romance, crime thrillers, espionage novels, action adventure. And children's books (non-fiction rocket science books and children's fiction). She became an Amazon All-Star author in 2014 and 2015.

She previously worked as a full-time newspaper journalist for several years. She had her own weekly columns in the press. This included being a motoring correspondent where she got to test drive cars every week for the press for three years.

Before being asked to work for the press, De-ann worked in magazine editorial writing everything from fashion features to social news. She was the marketing editor of a glossy magazine. She is also a professional artist and illustrator. Fabric design, dressmaking, sewing, knitting and fashion are part of her work.

Additionally, De-ann has always been interested in fitness, and was a fitness and bodybuilding champion, 100 metre runner and mountaineer. As a former N.A.B.B.A. Miss Scotland, she had a weekly fitness show on the radio that ran for over three years.

De-ann trained in Shukokai karate, boxing, kickboxing, Dayan Qigong and Jiu Jitsu. She is currently based in Scotland.

Her colouring books and embroidery design books are available in paperback. Find out more at: www.de-annblack.com

Printed in Great Britain
by Amazon

50595095R00119